Roxy
C
S
XY

BOOTH

Dear Reader,

Summers were a special time while I was growing up. My father owned a beach house and my sister, brother, and I spent our vacation days frolicking in the Pacific, having barbecues, building sand castles, hunting shells, and sitting around the fire pit in the evenings. My dad would also take us to fun places around Southern California, including Los Angeles Dodgers games. I cherish the memories of sitting by my father in the stands, surrounded by the smells of popcorn and hot dogs, the images of the players on the colorful field under the bright lights, and the sounds of the bat slamming into the ball and the roar of the crowd. While writing *Disappearing Acts*, I was able to relive nostalgic summer moments with Mary and Betty as they participated in summer events and attended baseball games.

The baseball league in Ivy Bay is loosely based on the real Cape Cod Baseball League, which is a collegiate league that attracts players from all over the country. Many of these players go on to play professional ball as Brent and Tyler want to do. I also became quite intrigued with the history of baseball and the enthusiastic hobby of collecting sports memorabilia. The worth of some of these items is astonishing, as Mary learns as she seeks to find her missing baseball.

I hope you enjoy reading about Mary's baseball mystery amidst the splendor of Cape Cod, and may it bring back special summer memories for you too.

Best wishes,
Kelly Ann Riley

Secrets of Mary's Bookshop

SECRETS *of* MARY'S
BOOKSHOP

Disappearing Acts
Kelly Ann Riley

Guideposts
New York

Acknowledgments

Every attempt has been made to credit the sources of copyrighted material used in this book. If any such acknowledgment has been inadvertently omitted or miscredited, receipt of such information would be appreciated.

"From the Guideposts Archives" originally appeared in *Daily Guideposts 2011*. Copyright © 2010 by Guideposts. All rights reserved.

Cover and interior design by Müllerhaus
Cover illustration by Ross Jones, represented by Deborah Wolfe, Ltd.
Typeset by Aptara, Inc.

Printed and bound in the United States of America
10 9 8 7 6 5 4 3 2 1

Disappearing Acts

ONE

❖

Mary Fisher stepped out of her Ivy Bay home into the blazing summer sun, and as she walked down the street, she caught glimpses of the waves of Cape Cod Bay tipped white by the wind. She breathed in the briny air as seagulls called to one another overhead, swooping over the dunes looking for breakfast. She adjusted the strap holding the carrier containing her faithful feline companion Gus, who accompanied her to work each day. She crossed a small stone footbridge passing over the cranberry bog and turned onto Main Street toward the town hall, hoping she wasn't late in meeting with sports memorabilia collector Charles Rigsby.

Baseball season was in full swing in Ivy Bay, and everyone seemed to have caught the fever. Not only were youngsters involved in T-ball, Little League, and softball games, but Cape Cod hosted a summer amateur-baseball league, which attracted collegiate players and local talent from all over New England.

Ivy Bay boasted its own team, the Blue Jays, which played in a small stadium outside of town in Bayside Park. Because the league did not sell tickets for the games, keeping them family-friendly, it held fund-raisers such as the fish fry that evening and the baseball exhibit in the town hall.

With the play-offs looming, even Mary had been caught up in the excitement as the Blue Jays battled to second place in their division. She'd ordered mysteries with baseball themes, and her sister Betty had decorated the bookstore window in honor of the sport.

Her late husband's love of the game had prompted Mary to volunteer to be on the new Ivy Bay Sports Artifacts Committee led by Bea Winslow, who ran the county clerk's office, and Tess Bailey, owner of Bailey's Ice Cream Shop. They had organized a New England baseball display to help solicit donations for the Blue Jays and the local recreation fund, which provided sports equipment to underprivileged children. Local citizens and summer visitors had provided memorabilia for the display. In honor of John's memory, Mary had made a special loan of her own.

Not only was this week her turn to check on the artifacts and keep them dusted and organized, but Bea had called Mary last evening to let her know that baseball collector Charles Rigsby, who owned a memorabilia store in Hyannis, wanted to loan them additional artifacts. He'd seen one of their posters advertising the display and stopped by the town hall when Bea had been there. Bea couldn't get to the town hall that morning to meet Charles and asked if Mary could help him get set up. Tess's sons would be there too, to put up more tables and help organize.

As Mary walked by Jimmy's Hardware Store, she saw people dressed in bright summer clothing already strolling along the wide boulevard. Across the street, beyond Bailey's Ice Cream Shop, happy chatter spilled out from the Black & White Diner's door. The smell of bacon and coffee from the diner mingled with the enticing homey smell of baking bread as she approached Sweet Susan's Bakery.

Susan Crosby waved as she placed a lovely triple-layer coconut cake in the window display, which reminded Mary that Betty's birthday was next week and she still hadn't decided on a gift. Mary thanked God frequently that He'd provided her with such a wonderful sister to live with after John's passing. Happy childhood memories were centered in Ivy Bay, and reaching her goal of opening a mystery bookshop made her feel young and excited about life again. She wanted to do something extraordinary to celebrate her sister and this special time in their lives.

She hurried on past her own store, Mary's Mystery Bookshop, and went farther up Main Street and crossed Meeting House Road and Water Street to the town hall, a Federal-style building with majestic columns lining the front. Built in 1874, the gray-blue two-story building with crisp white trim contained an assembly hall where the town could hold local meetings and where the committee had decided to put the baseball exhibit. Recently, the building had been undergoing storm repair. Scaffolding hugged the back half of the structure, where plastic sheets protected the exposed walls and workers milled about, but the sound of hammering and the busy hum of machinery didn't deter visitors from stopping by.

A banner advertising Baseball Exhibit was staked on the small square of lawn by the cracked sidewalk that led to white stone steps. The committee had also put up posters around town and advertised in the *Ivy Bay Bugle*.

Mary opened one side of the massive double doors, and the smell of fresh wax and aged wood greeted her. The night janitor must have polished the hardwood floors of the large assembly room, for they gleamed under the large chandelier hanging beneath the beautiful ceiling with its tan, brown, and gold-leaf stenciling.

An antique wooden desk, placed between the front door and the display, held a computer and a donation box. The chair behind it was empty, and Mary wondered where Stephanie Doyle, the new political intern, had disappeared. Perhaps she'd gone down the hall that housed several offices.

Mary set Gus's carrier down by the door. The grand opening of the display had been three weeks ago, and the room had been filled with townsfolk and tourists for a fun-filled evening. Since then, the visitation ebbed and flowed with the tide of tourists and fans attending baseball games. Right now, the room was empty because the display didn't open until ten and Charles Rigsby hadn't arrived yet. Mary breathed out a relieved sigh and crossed the floor, the sound of her footsteps echoing off the walls.

She ducked under the velvet ropes that sectioned off the tables by a couple of feet to discourage handling of the artifacts. She grabbed the feather duster from under the long blue tablecloths and walked down the length of the five tables covered with a couple dozen autographed baseballs, worn brown mitts, bats, decades of brightly colored programs, and several collections of baseball cards. Posters featuring famous New England players leaned against the wall, but Mary's favorite section on the far end of the display contained framed amateur photographs taken at the Ivy Bay stadium over the years. They brought back happy memories of her childhood summers with her grandparents on the Cape.

She swiped the duster over the mitts and rows of baseballs and noted that the information placard in front of her contribution had fallen over. Most of the donated items had a little information card beside them containing the loaner's name and brief history.

Tess Bailey's sons Brent and Joe, along with a young man Mary didn't recognize, came in the door, each carrying a wooden table. Through conversations with Tess, Mary knew that Joe and Brent, both in their midtwenties, lived in Boston. Brent had recently come home to try out for the minors with the Blue Jays and landed a starting pitching position. Joe was on vacation for a couple of weeks to visit and watch the play-offs. Tess had told Mary on several occasions how ecstatic she was to have her whole family together.

Brent turned and caught sight of Mary. "Hey, Mrs. Fisher. Mom told us to help you get Mr. Rigsby set up. Do you think three tables will be enough?"

Mary set down her duster and hurried forward to move the rope partition out of the way. "I think so," she said, walking toward them. "I don't know how much he's bringing, but it'd be great if we could space everything out more."

"Hey, watch out," Joe said as Brent swung his table around and brushed some baseball cards to the floor.

"Oops." Brent set the table by the wall and bent over to scoop up the fallen cards. "Someday, I'm going to be on one of these."

Joe grinned. "Dream on, big brother."

"Tyler knows it's true, don't you, Ty?" Brent set the cards on the display.

"Of course," Tyler said, helping Joe unfold the table legs and set it up. A sun-kissed blond with gray-blue eyes, Tyler's fair features stood out in sharp contrast to the Bailey boys, who'd inherited their father's dark features.

Mary smiled at the lanky young man. "Hi, Tyler. I'm Mary Fisher."

"Oh, sorry. I should've introduced you. Mom says the older I get, the fewer manners I have," Brent said.

"I didn't think you had any to start with," Joe teased.

Brent opened his mouth as if to retort but then gave a little shrug. "Anyway, this is Tyler Matthews. He's playing third base for the Blue Jays and is one of our best players. He's going to the pros someday, right, Ty?"

Ty's face flushed slightly. "Well, yes, I want to."

"Bill Halliday is even interested in him."

"Is he a recruiter?" Mary asked politely. There were scores of agents and recruiters following the young talent to the prestigious summer leagues on Cape Cod.

"Sports agent," Brent answered. "He's a legend in the biz. Negotiates contracts for some of the top players. You've probably seen him at the games. He always sits behind the catcher. Wears a Red Sox cap and cowboy boots. We're hoping for a chance at the Red Sox someday. My dream job."

"Los Angeles Dodgers for me," Tyler added. "And actually, Halliday is more interested in Brent than me." Tyler returned Mary's smile, and Mary was charmed by the two friends showing such pride in each other. "It's nice to meet you, Mrs. Fisher."

"Nice to meet you too, Tyler. How are you enjoying your stay in Ivy Bay?"

"It's awesome. I've always wanted to play for the Cape League, and I think the Blue Jays are the best," Tyler said, helping Joe put up the last table.

"And we're going to prove it." Brent turned back to the collection. "So, any idea of what we should do with all this?"

"The table with the baseballs and mitts is pretty crowded. Maybe we can spread those out and then see what Mr. Rigsby brings."

"Good idea." Brent picked up Mary's Red Sox baseball from its little wooden stand and read the placard. He did a double take at the information on the card. "I didn't realize this ball was yours. Wow. You got the whole team to sign it. I want to have one of these for my collection. Right now, I have a couple of single-signed balls that I'm hoping are going to be worth a lot someday." He cast a wistful glance over the baseball. "Where'd you get this one?"

Mary smiled at Brent's enthusiasm. "My husband caught it in 1970, and I got it signed for him as a wedding gift." She was about to point out John's favorite feature on the ball, a smudged fingerprint under Sparky Lyle's signature, when a female voice called out.

"Excuse me."

Mary turned to see Stephanie Doyle hurrying across the room from the hallway. Stephanie had arrived last week to finish out some small-town government projects for her summer internship. She started out helping Bea Winslow in the county clerk's office but then moved to the town hall to work on reports and perform miscellaneous jobs with Mrs. Leary, the town hall manager. One of Stephanie's tasks was keeping paperwork on the display and greeting guests.

The petite young woman with black iron-straight long hair and pale delicate features was dressed professionally in navy slacks and a jacket. She had an armload of blue cloths. Her focus was on Brent, who was moving the table closer to the wall. "Mrs. Leary wanted to be sure you didn't scratch the floors."

Brent's gaze swept over the new arrival, and he self-consciously smoothed his shirt as he straightened. "Oh, hi, you must be Stephanie. My mom said you'd know where the tablecloths were. And don't worry, we're being careful. But if you *are* worried, you can boss us around all you want."

Stephanie's green eyes softened slightly behind her dark-rimmed glasses at the light teasing in his voice. "Look, I just don't want to get in trouble with my boss. She was already on my case about jamming the copy machine or I would've been at my desk."

Stephanie shifted her feet and still looked tense, so Mary stepped forward. "Thanks for the tablecloths. Have you met these guys yet?"

Stephanie shook her head. "I've just seen them around." Mary introduced her to the men and added, "Stephanie's been a big help with the display. We'll be sorry to see her go when she finishes her college project."

Tyler offered to take the tablecloths and asked, "Where do you go to school?"

"BU," Stephanie said, referring to Boston University.

"Douglas University, here. You must be a political science major," Tyler said.

"Actually, I'm doing a double major," Stephanie said with a smile that revealed a tiny dimple in her right cheek. "Political science and business."

"Awesome." Tyler handed a tablecloth to Joe and Brent. "I'm business too, but I plan to play pro ball, which is why I'm down here. Lots of agents and recruiters check out the up-and-coming players."

"And I'm just a boring person who works for a living," Joe said playfully with an exaggerated roll of his eyes. "I'm here to watch these two play." Joe slung his cloth over one of the new tables.

"Ty is third baseman. You've probably seen us play," Brent added, moving slightly in front of Ty. He was obviously interested in the girl because he hadn't taken his eyes off of her since she came in. Stephanie seemed oblivious.

"Oh, um, I don't go to the games. Sports kind of seem like a waste of time and...a little boring," Stephanie said with a little shrug. "Sorry."

Joe glanced at Tyler and then elbowed his brother, who seemed speechless at her proclamation. Tyler just grinned.

The door opened and a round, middle-aged man with graying hair, wire-rimmed glasses, and a brown suit squeezed through, carrying a plastic tub.

"That must be Mr. Rigsby," Stephanie said in a low voice as she and Mary crossed the room to meet him.

"Hi, I'm Mary Fisher."

"Charles Rigsby. It's a pleasure to meet you." He set his tub down on one of the tables, and Mary introduced him to the others. He fished a ring of keys out of his pocket. "Can any of you strapping young men bring in the bins from the back of my car?"

"No problem," Brent said, grabbing the keys. Tyler and Joe followed him to the door.

"Thank you so much for contributing to our display, and especially for coming from Hyannis," Mary said, recalling the little information that Bea had provided.

"No trouble at all, especially for a worthy cause." Charles looked over the tables. "I travel around a bit during the summer, trying to get to most of the games. You've done a great job with this."

He walked down the length of the tables, pausing to read some of the information placards, and then asked, "You're the Mary Fisher who owns the 1970s baseball here, right?"

"Why, yes," Mary said, startled. "It was my husband's."

"I noticed the ball last week when Bea invited me in for a private viewing. I've been looking for one similar to round out my 1970s collection. May I examine it more closely?"

"Please do."

He turned the ball over in his hands, studying the signatures. "Very nice. Signed by the team. Would you be interested in selling it? Say, $150?"

Mary blinked with surprise. She had no idea the ball was worth that much. John had been so thrilled to get the baseball signed by the team. The memory caused her a twinge of momentary pain. She missed him so much and wished he were here to make new memories with her. She looked at John's baseball, picturing the surprised pleasure on his face when he'd opened her gift. He had jumped up and given her a big kiss.

"I appreciate the offer, but I can't part with it," Mary said with a smile. "Sentimental reasons."

"Ah yes, I understand. Sentimentality drives a lot of my sales."

A clatter at the door heralded the guys' return. Tyler and Joe lugged two large blue rubber tubs between them, and Brent carried a smaller one.

After carefully setting down the tubs, Tyler lifted his cap and wiped his forehead. "I gotta get going down to the stadium and help the coach get set up for tonight. Coming, Brent?"

"Is there a game?" Mary asked.

"Not tonight. The Blue Jays have a booth at the fish fry to promote the team and we gotta transport everything over to school and set up before practice this afternoon," Brent explained. "It'll be cool. People can stop by and get autographs and photos."

"The girls always want photos with Brent, although I can't figure out why," Joe teased and earned a punch in the arm from his brother.

"I'll be over soon," Brent said to Tyler.

"Nice meeting you, Mrs. Fisher and Mr. Rigsby." Tyler gave a little wave and ambled toward the exit.

Charles yanked off the lid of one of his storage tubs. "Anyone care to help me unpack?"

"Sure." Brent eagerly moved forward, and Charles handed packages to Brent and Joe.

As they unwound the bubble wrap, Mary could see why the tubs had seemed so heavy. Most of Mr. Rigsby's baseball items were encased in glass boxes.

Charles picked up the smaller tub and set it on the table. It contained cleaning supplies, brushes, and markers. He pulled out a soft towel and smiled at Mary. "Tools of the trade."

Brent unwrapped another package. "Wow! Dom DiMaggio's cap." Brent held up a case with the Red Sox cap.

"*Dom* DiMaggio?" Joe asked, reaching for another package.

"Joe DiMaggio's brother," Brent said in a tone that indicated his brother should know that. "And I've seen these caps for sale. They go for something like three grand."

"I didn't realize either," Mary said with a wink at Joe. She took charge of arranging the new items, very pleased at how generous Charles had been. His contributions certainly added more pizzazz to the display.

"Dom was a good player." Charles meticulously wiped finger marks and dust off each case. He rattled off some statistics, and the boys launched into a discussion about historic players and who was the best.

Mary glanced over at the sound of a drawer being yanked open. Stephanie, who sat at her desk, popped some earbuds in and attached the cord to her computer. "Online class," she mouthed. Mary smiled, finding the stats being rattled off by the men a little tedious too, but everyone seemed to be having a good time as they emptied the tubs.

Mary looked at her watch and was surprised to see that it was already ten and time to open the bookshop. She grabbed her phone and texted her assistant Rebecca that she'd be a little late. As she clicked the phone off, she heard a noise behind her.

She turned as bats shifted and started to fall toward the line of Mr. Rigsby's glass cases.

"Get 'em!" Joe yelled.

Mary dropped her phone as she and Brent grabbed the bats, inches before they hit the cases.

"Whew! Great catch," Charles said, hurrying toward them.

"Sorry about that." Brent set the bats back in place and moved them farther down the table.

"No harm done," Charles said. "You've both been a great help. And you too, Mary."

"My pleasure." Mary stepped back and gave a nod of approval at their work. "I'm afraid I have to head back to my shop."

Joe looked up from where he was straightening the baseball-card display. "We'll finish up here, Mrs. Fisher."

"Thanks, guys," Mary said, picking up her purse.

"Before you go, let me try one more time. I'd still like to buy your baseball. I'll even up my offer to $250."

Joe looked up from a row of photos, and Brent let out a low whistle.

"That's very generous... but, no, thank you. It means too much to me."

"Well, you can't fault a fan for trying," Charles said with a smile. He pulled out his wallet and extracted a business card. "Here's my number, if you change your mind."

Mary dropped the card in her purse, although she was positive she would never be interested in selling. After saying good-bye to the men and Stephanie, she picked up the cat carrier and went out the door. She hurried down Main Street, trying not to jostle Gus, and pondered Charles's offer. John would've gotten a kick out of knowing how much he could have sold his ball for, although she doubted he ever would.

She opened the door to her pride and joy, Mary's Mystery Bookshop, and took a deep breath. Rebecca stood behind the counter by the cash register. They exchanged warm smiles as Rebecca finished bagging a book for a customer.

Rebecca's seven-year-old daughter Ashley sat cross-legged in the small pedestal bathtub in the children's nook. The bathtub, a gift from Betty, was lined on the inside with padded, powder-blue carpeting, which made it a favorite spot for children to read. A baseball cap covered Ashley's blonde hair. She looked up from her book as Mary set Gus's carrier on the floor and opened the door. The cat bounded into the room.

"Hi, Gus! Come here," Ashley said and wiggled her fingers on the side of the tub. Gus's eyes widened. He crouched and then pounced. Ashley laughed and scooped him up in her arms. "Good kitty."

"Hi, sweetie." Mary gave Ashley a little wave before carrying the cat carrier into the back room. She so enjoyed having Ashley and her mother working in the shop.

"Thanks for opening," Mary said as she returned to the counter and tucked her purse in the cubby.

"No problem. We were already close by." Rebecca tapped open a roll of quarters and added them to the cash register. "It was such a gorgeous morning Ashley and I got out early and went for a walk on the beach."

"I found some pretty shells." Ashley stood, climbed out of the tub, and reached into her pocket as she walked over to Mary. "Do you want to see?"

"I sure do," Mary said as Ashley set her finds on the counter. After inspecting Ashley's shells and exclaiming over how pretty they were, Mary got to work, and the morning flew by. Summer brought in tourists looking for beach reads, anxious to wring the most relaxation out of their vacation days.

Mary's son Jack had brought his family from Chicago for the Fourth of July parade, and she was hoping her daughter Lizzie and grandchildren Emma and Luke could make it down before school started. She reached in her purse for her cell phone to give Lizzie a call, but the phone wasn't there. After a moment of confusion, she remembered she'd dropped it on the display table when she grabbed the bats.

Mary sighed. "I have to run back to the town hall. I left my phone there."

Rebecca looked up with a worried expression. "Oh dear, I hope no one took it."

"Me too." Mary grabbed her purse and hurried up the street.

A group of noisy teen boys came out of the town hall door, and she stepped aside to let them pass her on the steps. Once inside, the closed door shut out their laughter. Mary waved at Stephanie, who was chatting with an elderly couple, as she headed across the room and ducked under the ropes. With relief, she found her cell phone behind one of Charles's glass cases.

She blew out a deep breath and returned to the other side of the ropes. The boys had done a great job straightening everything up after she'd left. Items had been grouped by type, which made it very interesting to compare the subtle changes in the equipment and other artifacts over the years. She reached the end of the display and paused by the Ivy Bay baseball photographs from past decades.

Mary smiled as she spied Betty and herself sitting in the bleachers at one of the league games; a towhead and a sun-kissed brunette, carefree and enjoying life at the beach when summers seemed long and each day an exciting adventure. Who would've guessed they'd end up back here, living together? Which reminded her, she still needed to figure out what to do for Betty's birthday. Something special and memorable, like the gift of the signed baseball had been for John.

She picked up the ball and marveled at the attention it had drawn from Brent and Charles. She had never thought of it being extraordinary beyond John's love of her gift. She stroked the leather, worn and showing fine cracks with age under the black signatures, and traced the fine red stitching, remembering how John had inspected the ball the day he'd caught it. Like it was a fine jewel.

She closed her fingers around it, cradling it in her hands the way he had, feeling closer to the man she'd loved so much. With a sigh, she set it back on the stand, turning it the way John had displayed it in his office. There was Sparky Lyle's signature as always, but—but something wasn't right. She picked up the ball again. Could it be?

The smudged fingerprint under Sparky Lyle's signature that had made the ball so special to John was gone.

TWO

———◆◆———

Mary picked up the baseball, her mind reeling with confusion. Was she imagining things? No, the small smudged fingerprint that had been under Sparky Lyle's signature for the last four decades was definitely gone.

The elderly couple had meandered over to the photograph section of the display, and Stephanie strode across the room to Mary. "Mrs. Fisher, you're back. Is something wrong?"

"No...Yes." Mary was so dumbstruck she didn't know what to say. She ducked under the rope to where Stephanie stood and glanced over the display again, her attention landing on Mr. Rigsby's glass cases. He'd been so meticulous, and he had that tub of cleaning and restoration supplies. "Tools of the trade," he'd called them. Maybe he thought he was doing her a favor by removing the smudge.

"Stephanie, do you know if anyone cleaned any of the pieces in the display since I left? Like this ball?"

Stephanie raised her eyebrows. "I don't think so. At least I didn't notice. Joe left soon after you did, and Brent hung around a little while and helped Mr. Rigsby. But they just straightened things and left." Stephanie looked at the baseball in Mary's hand. "Why would it matter if someone cleaned it?"

"My late husband caught this baseball at a Red Sox game in 1970. We'd just gotten engaged, and I wanted to do something special for him as a wedding present. I borrowed it without him knowing and arranged for the players to sign it."

"You got him that for his wedding gift?" Stephanie said with a small smile. "He must've loved baseball."

"He was a big Red Sox fan," Mary said, remembering John's excitement every year as the baseball season opened. "He used to tease me that he'd been so worried about his missing baseball that he didn't have time to get cold feet before the wedding."

"Aw, that's sweet, but…" Stephanie let out a little sigh.

Mary waited patiently for her to continue.

"Why do people get so crazy over sports?" Stephanie asked. "I mean, baseball is just a game."

"You were never on a sports team in school?"

"When they made me. I'd rather read a book." She gave a little laugh, but there was no humor in it. "It's just…"

"Everyone's different?" Mary inserted when Stephanie didn't finish her thought.

Stephanie nodded. "From what my mom says, my dad was a ballplayer and fanatical about the sport. I never knew him. He left before I was born, and I guess I don't take after him." She glanced at the door as it opened, and two girls walked in, giggling. "Sorry, I didn't mean to change the subject. What were you saying about the ball being cleaned?"

Mary was intrigued by Stephanie opening up about her family. She hoped to get to know the girl better as the month went on, but she didn't want to press now. "There used to be a smudge on it under Sparky Lyle's name. Like a partial fingerprint. My husband liked to think it was Sparky's thumbprint. Right here."

Stephanie leaned over and examined where Mary pointed. "It's a little gray, but it looks like dirt. Could the fingerprint just have been rubbed off?"

"That's what I'm wondering." Mary rubbed her finger over it, and the ball lightened some where the smudge had been. "John, my late husband, handled the ball many, many times over the years, and the smudge never rubbed off."

"This is just weird," Stephanie said as her desk phone rang. She glanced at Mary apologetically. "Duty calls."

But Stephanie was right. It was weird that the smudge had disappeared after all these years. If someone had used a chemical to take off the smudge, wouldn't they have taken some of Sparky's signature with it? Unless, Mary realized, it was someone skillful at restoring items. Someone like Charles Rigsby. But why would he clean it, especially after she refused to sell it to him? Perhaps it was just a kind gesture. He clearly was impressed by the ball, so maybe he just wanted to help Mary keep it in tip-top shape.

She followed Stephanie to the desk, holding the ball a little more tightly. Maybe she should have been more careful with it, displaying it under lock and key.

Now she was just being paranoid. Surely, the wiped-off smudge was nothing more than a kind gesture. Although . . . was it just her imagination or did the ball feel different? Was that possible? Baseballs were pretty much all the same, weren't they? She looked at the ball again, which was slightly yellow with age. The signatures contrasted sharply. She looked closer. Maybe too sharply. How could that be? She rubbed Sparky

Lyle's signature with her thumb. The ink, of course, didn't smear. But other than the missing fingerprint, why did the ball feel different?

The thought she'd been trying to avoid finally came to the surface. Was this even John's ball? He'd know for sure, but Mary never really paid close attention. She felt a twinge of longing. Oh, how she wished he were here.

If this wasn't John's ball, whose was it? And why would they replace John's ball with what Mary could only presume was a copy?

Unless they wanted the original. But why? Charles Rigsby had offered $250 for it. That was a nice chunk of change, but not necessarily enough money for someone to go to the effort of carefully replicating and then stealing someone's beloved souvenir.

The elderly man cleared his throat, and Mary blinked, realizing she'd been staring blankly at the display. She gave them a smile and then motioned to Stephanie that she was going to take the ball with her. Stephanie nodded that she understood, and Mary tucked the ball and her phone in her purse and headed back to her store.

The brisk walk and fresh air helped her focus on her whirling questions. As far as she could tell, there were only two possibilities of what happened. Either someone had innocently removed the smudge or this wasn't John's ball.

She turned on Meeting House Road toward the county clerk's office. Bea had arranged for Charles Rigsby's donation, and maybe she knew more about him. A note on the door indicated the office was already closed for lunch, although it was ten minutes to noon, according to Mary's watch. The office would be reopened at one.

Maybe she could catch Bea at lunch. She called Bea's cell, and it went straight to voice mail. Mary left a message for Bea to call her when she had a free moment. Mary retraced her steps back to Main Street and her shop.

Rebecca smiled at her from behind the counter. Two tourists leisurely browsed the front table. Gus was lying upside down against Ashley's feet as Mary shut the door behind her. He opened his eyes and twitched his tail at the sight of Mary, then sighed back into his peaceful slumber.

Ashley looked up from her book. "Did you find your phone? I said a prayer that'd you find it."

"It must've worked because I did find it just where I left it," Mary said with a smile. Although Ashley appeared engrossed in her books, she was very aware of what was happening around her. Mary felt a distinct sense of grandmotherly pride in the precocious girl.

Ashley's face lit up. "That's good." She gave a little contented sigh and went back to reading.

Mary stood for a moment, still a bit discombobulated, and not sure what to do. First, she decided, she'd do what she'd originally wanted to do when she realized she'd left her phone. She would call her daughter. A phone call with Lizzie was always comforting.

The two customers were checking out with Rebecca, and the rest of the store was quiet, so Mary headed to the back room to make her call.

As the phone rang, Mary's thoughts remained on the ball. Lizzie knew how special the baseball had been to her father. What would Lizzie think about Mary's suspicions? Maybe she could offer some logical solution to what had happened that

Mary hadn't considered, but to Mary's disappointment, the answering machine kicked on. She took a breath and left a cheerful message, adding a half-serious, half-playful hint that her and Betty's home was always open to guests, especially family members, *ahem*, and especially during the next couple of weeks when Ivy Bay baseball season was the most exciting.

After she hung up, she headed back to the front of the store. A new customer entered and began browsing. Mary was about to give Ashley a nod, signaling the girl to greet the new guest, but Ashley was already on top of the task.

"Welcome to Mary's Mystery Bookshop," the girl said to the customer, who gave her a surprised look. "May I help you find anything?"

The amused look on the customer's face was one of many Mary had seen since Rebecca and her daughter first began working at the bookshop, and it always delighted Mary to watch how Ashley charmed one customer after another.

"And another one bites the dust," Mary said to Rebecca with a wink.

"Russell and I are in big trouble, aren't we?" Rebecca replied.

"Oh yeah," Mary said, and they both chuckled.

After Ashley told the customer that she was there if he needed her but that he should feel free to browse, Mary moved to her computer. She opened Google and started a search for baseball memorabilia. She was astounded at all the links that appeared. She scanned a long list of them, narrowing her search until she found an article about the appraisal of Babe Ruth's cap that interested her. She clicked on the link, began to read the article, and gasped.

"What's the matter?" Rebecca asked before Mary realized she'd reacted out loud.

"I just read that a cap worn by Babe Ruth is worth over $325,000, one of his bats is going for $200,000, and a game-worn jersey is worth as much as $2 million."

Rebecca stepped closer to look over Mary's shoulder. "You're kidding."

"It's amazing to me how much money people will pay for a simple article of clothing," Mary said. At Rebecca's questioning look, Mary added, "I'm trying to find out how much my husband's old Red Sox ball is worth." She went on to explain to Rebecca how Charles Rigsby had offered to buy her ball, and how, when she'd returned to the display, it appeared that the ball had been either cleaned or replaced.

"Well, $250 hardly seems like a high enough dollar amount for what would have to be a fairly elaborate forgery process," Rebecca said. She scooted next to Mary at the computer and began scanning the article. "Wow, look at this. It says that a ball signed by Babe Ruth is going for $45,000," she said, clearly as amazed as Mary.

"Wow is right." Mary thought for a moment. "But then again, Babe Ruth is incredibly famous. No one like that signed John's ball. Even Sparky Lyle's signature wouldn't add that much to the ball's value." She clicked another link that listed other signed baseballs, and they seemed to range anywhere between a few dollars to tens of thousands, depending on a number of variables, such as how old the ball was, the condition, if it was signed after a winning game, who and how many players signed the ball, or if it was in the play-offs or the World Series. Basically, the price was set by how badly the fans wanted it.

Mary wondered about her ball and Charles Rigsby's offer. She couldn't be sure, but it seemed to her that after doing this research, the ball could be worth more than $250.

Mary continued her search on the Web and found a site that narrowed her search down to Red Sox team-signed balls. She found Red Sox team-signed balls ranging from $140 to $4,000 depending on the particular ball. She speculated on how much John's ball was really worth. Would a smudge decrease the value of a ball? Or if it was Sparky's fingerprint, as John liked to think, would that make it more valuable? With a sigh, she closed the browser. What she really needed was someone used to dealing in the antique world to give her an opinion. And she knew just who to ask.

When Mary entered Gems and Antiques across the street, she took a deep breath, just as she always seemed to do upon walking into the store. Jayne Tucker and her husband, Rich, had opened the shop more than twenty years ago, which added to the room's truly antique feeling. The place smelled like aged oak and was filled with New England treasures. Antique quilts, desks and dressers handcrafted in the 1800s, Paul Revere silver, wooden rocking horses, and old cradles packed the shelves and crowded the floorboards. A European section featured silver, exquisite china, broaches, and jewelry chock-full of gemstones.

Jayne sat behind the counter. Her head, with its vibrant auburn hair, had been bent over a newspaper when Mary walked in. Jayne looked up and smiled warmly. "Hi, Mary. Have a seat. How goes it?" She pulled out a stool for her.

Mary scooted up beside Jayne. "It's been really busy, but I love it."

Jayne nodded. "Me too. With all these baseball fans in town, there are more customers for everyone."

Mary smiled. She knew how much Jayne and Rich enjoyed their business and the travel involved. Every winter, they closed up shop for up to a month and traveled abroad in search of gems and antiques they could bring back to sell. During the rest of the year, they would slip away to estate sales all over the Northeast.

"I was wondering how familiar you are with sports memorabilia," Mary said.

"Not too much. I mean, we deal with some, if it's special. We come across some sports antiques from time to time when we are at estate sales, but it's a very subjective side of the business with a narrow market." Jayne smiled. "Well, all antiques are, to some degree. Why? Is there something you're looking for?"

"Actually, I just got interested in autographed baseballs. I had an offer for John's, and I'm not sure if it's in line with what it's worth or not." She pulled the ball out of her purse and told the story of how John caught the ball and she had it signed by the team. Jayne giggled over John's comment about cold feet.

"How much was the offer?" Rich said, coming out from the back room, his blue eyes inquisitive. "I was eavesdropping, as usual. Sorry."

Jayne let out a playful snort. "If you were really sorry, you'd stop doing it."

"Then I wouldn't learn anything I wasn't supposed to," Rich said with a grin.

Mary grinned too. "I don't mind. Saves me having to tell my story twice." She handed the ball to Rich. "I was offered $250. What do you think?"

Rich rubbed the top of his bald head as he examined the ball. "*Hmm.* I see it's dated 1970."

"Yep, it was the next to the last game of the season."

Rich turned it over, studying all sides. "Hard to say how much it's worth without a little research. Usually, these go for a couple hundred bucks, but you never know. I'd hold off selling until you get a couple of estimates of its value. You have to be really careful. There are a lot of crooks out there."

"That's what I'm afraid of," Mary said, wondering if the crook category included Charles Rigsby, and worse, if it meant Charles was a ball thief. Another thought came to mind. "Suppose the baseball has a unique feature, like a player's fingerprint on it. How would that affect its value?"

"Depends on who it was, but generally, anything that makes the ball unique would add value." Add value? Mary had assumed the opposite when she first saw the mar on the ball. John had loved it, though. Although they couldn't prove it, he assumed Sparky Lyle had left his fingerprint.

Rich turned the ball over. "Is there a fingerprint on this one?"

"No, not on this one. I'm just curious," Mary said. "Say, someone like Sparky Lyle's."

Rich looked at her with narrowed eyes. "Mary Fisher, are you looking into another one of your mysteries?"

Mary smiled and winked. "I'll never tell."

Jayne chuckled as Rich examined the ball.

"Well, I'm not an expert, but I can check with some of my sources today and see if I can give you a more specific idea of its value. If they aren't helpful, we're going up to Boston this weekend for some estate sales, and sometimes we meet dealers there that do business with sports memorabilia. I can take some pictures of the ball and then make some inquiries for you."

"That would be wonderful, Rich."

Rich set the baseball on the counter. Jayne opened a drawer and got out a fancy camera. Rich shot the ball from all sides. "That should do it. I'll let you know if we find anything."

"Thank you so much, but please don't go to too much trouble."

"No trouble at all." Jayne smiled at her husband. "We enjoy the research part of our job."

As Mary walked to the door, Rich called after her. "One last thing. Do you happen to have a copy of the ball's certification?"

"I don't think so. What is that?"

"It's a form that certifies that the ball is an original and that the signatures are real," Jayne said.

Mary thought back to when the package arrived at their home in Boston. "I know I got a letter from the manager who had the ball signed, but I don't recall a certificate. John kept his letter."

"That might be all you need, but if it becomes an issue, you can get the ball appraised. An expert will give a letter of authenticity, but there is a charge and it could take several weeks, maybe more, depending on where you send it," Rich said.

"It just ensures the ball is genuine and signatures aren't forged," Jayne added.

Mary thanked them again and stepped out onto the street, thinking about how very helpful an expert could be in her case. She thought again about her feeling that the ball just seemed different. Could it really be a counterfeit? She still wasn't sure someone would have stolen John's ball and gone to the trouble to replace it. Then again, the answer was right in front of her face: If the ball was worth more than Charles Rigsby offered—a lot more—then the potential thief's motive became crystal clear.

She waited for a car to pass before crossing the street and decided that there was only one logical plan of action at this point. She needed to determine if the ball in her purse was John's true ball or not. Rich had mentioned considering an appraisal of the ball to check for forgeries, and he was right. Finding out whether these signatures were authentic could make this an open-and-shut case. Lucky for her, she already knew a handwriting and forgeries expert whom she'd come to care for since she'd moved to Ivy Bay.

She pulled out her phone and looked up Lincoln King's phone number on her contact list. Lincoln lived on the outskirts of Ivy Bay, and Mary had worked with him before.

His phone rang several times, and Mary was preparing to leave a voice message when his deep voice answered. "Good afternoon. How may I be of assistance?"

"Good afternoon, Lincoln. This is Mary Fisher."

Mary could nearly hear the man's smile. "Good to hear from you, Mary. How are you?"

"I'm well, thanks, Lincoln. Betty and I love the summer, and especially baseball season this year. And speaking of, I have a problem I think you might be able to help me with. It's about signatures on a baseball."

"A baseball? How interesting."

"Would it be all right if I came over to see you? It'd be easier to explain this in person."

"Oh, Mary, I'm sorry to say that I'm leaving on a trip this afternoon and won't be back until next week. Is this urgent?"

Mary considered the question. It was urgent to her but certainly not enough to cause Lincoln to delay his trip. If her ball had been stolen, the more time that passed, the less chance she had in finding the culprit and recovering the ball. If Lincoln couldn't do it, then maybe she could find another expert in the area.

"It's not an emergency," Mary answered, "but I really don't want to wait too long. I'm trying to figure out if the signatures on the ball are authentic."

"*Hmm*. Well, I suppose . . . I was going to stop at the Tea Shoppe for lunch on my way out of town," he said. "Could you possibly meet me there at one o'clock?"

Mary smiled at Lincoln's friendly offer. This was not the first time he'd gone above and beyond for her. "That would work out great."

When Mary arrived at the Tea Shoppe, Lincoln King was already seated at one of the few mission-style tables in the café area. His black trench coat hung on the back of the metal chair, and his matching black rain hat perched on an old-fashioned briefcase beside his feet. Mary gave Lincoln a little wave and walked across the wide-planked floor to the refrigerated cooler that offered an array of delectable premade salads and sandwiches. She breathed in the fragrant air, richly scented from the many jars of spiced teas and baked goods as she tried to choose between a Cobb salad and tuna sandwich.

She chose the sandwich, and as she waited behind a gentleman in line for the cash register, Mary glanced around the quaint shop. Lace curtains hung over the windows. An antique china cabinet on the wall opposite the door featured a colorful array of teapots and matching cups.

Sophie Mershon, the store owner, swept back a strand of blonde hair that had escaped the long braid, which hung almost to her waist. Tall and lithe, she moved behind the counter with graceful ease, reminding Mary that Sophie had danced with a Boston ballet company before moving to Ivy Bay to open the Tea Shoppe.

"Hi, Sophie. How are you?" Mary asked when it was her turn.

"Doing fabulous. Thanks." Sophie gave Mary a brilliant smile and looked over at the door as it opened again and a family of four entered. The two small children, holding on to their parents' hands, had the pink glow of having spent time outside.

Sophie rang up Mary's sandwich. "Would you like anything to drink? I have a fresh pitcher of raspberry iced tea. Really yummy."

"That sounds perfect," Mary said, digging in her purse for her wallet.

"One of my faves." Sophie poured the colorful tea into a tall glass and passed it over to Mary.

Lincoln rose as Mary approached the table, his shoulders slightly hunched. "Mary, so nice to see you again."

"Likewise, Lincoln." Mary sat in the metal chair he'd pulled out for her. "I hope you weren't waiting long."

"Not at all. I got here a little early." Lincoln settled back in his chair. "I wanted to get a head start on my lunch so I had more time to hear about this baseball of yours." He finished his salad as Mary explained the situation and her growing uneasiness. "I really appreciate your taking the time to look at it."

"Well, as always, you've piqued my curiosity." Lincoln took the baseball from Mary. He peered at the ball through his very thick glasses. He reached into his coat pocket and pulled out his magnifying glass. Mary waited, her chest squeezing as moments passed. He set the magnifying glass down. "Interesting. You never had the signatures authenticated?"

"Unfortunately, it never occurred to me. The ball served its purpose as is. It made John happy. I never planned to sell it, although I did have an offer today. Do the signatures look authentic to you?"

"I'd have to have the original signatures to compare, but if you look closely at a couple of these, you notice minute similarities." He lifted his butter knife and pointed to the Tony Conigliaro and Sparky Lyle signatures. "Notice the curve in the *a* between these two and the way the lines curve after the *y* and *g*."

Mary was confused. "So you're suggesting it's possible that one person signed all the names?"

"Possibly. Because I don't have the original signatures, it's difficult for me to confirm. But, yes, my guess is that at least some of the signatures have been copied by the same person. Were you there when this ball was signed?"

Mary sighed. "No, I sent it in to the manager, and we never had it appraised. I just assumed he had passed it around to all the players for their signatures." Mary realized it was possible that someone back in the seventies may have forged some signatures.

She mulled that over as she nibbled at her sandwich. As always, Sophie's tuna salad on multigrain bread was delicious. "So the signatures could have been forged when the ball was originally signed, but even if that were so, what could have happened to the smudge under Sparky Lyle's name? It'd been on the ball forty-three years. You'd think it would've been permanent like the signatures."

"You'd think so," Lincoln agreed and studied the ball with his magnifying glass again. "If you examine the ball closely, you'll note minor defects that most likely indicate normal wear and tear during a game, which are visible here. But you'd also expect some uneven fading of the ink over time and from possible handling, yet these signatures are pretty uniform. Was the ball handled much?"

"Quite a bit, yes. My husband had it out on his desk for years, and people often were drawn to it."

"I see." He continued to peer closely at the ball. "And here, there's also a bit of dark residue ingrained in the leather under Sparky's signature."

Mary took a guess. "Ink?"

"Difficult to say. Whatever was there was removed or worn off." Lincoln set the ball down on the table and leaned forward. "It's only an educated guess, but I believe that at least some of these signatures are forged. And considering the question of the smudge, and the lack of fading of the ink, I'd say the probability is high that this is not your husband's ball."

THREE

Mary spent the rest of that afternoon arranging a large shipment of new books on the front table. She loved the rote job of stamping each book with the Mary's Mystery Bookshop stamp. And the creative work of arranging the books so they'd be most enticing to customers was especially satisfying. It was usually a slower job than it needed to be because she couldn't resist opening many of the books and reading several of the first pages before moving on to a new title.

She placed the last copy of the most recent James Patterson mystery on a stack and then paused over a *Murder, She Wrote* novel that had just come in that she'd been eyeing. She scanned the back cover, wishing she could just settle in her grandmother's rocker by the window and read. Hot summer afternoons were perfect for frolicking in Cape Cod Bay or reading a good mystery on the beach, or both, which she assumed her customers were doing right now because the shop had been empty for the last hour and a half.

Rebecca sat behind the counter, leafing through the current issue of *Mystery Scene* magazine, while Ashley lay on the floor in the children's nook, reading softly to Gus, who was curled up on her stomach.

Mary thought back over her lunch with Lincoln as she continued to arrange the books. After they'd left the Tea Shoppe, Lincoln told Mary that he'd do more research on the signatures if he had some spare time while out of town. Mary hadn't wanted to send the ball with him, and remembering what she had done with Rich, she suggested she could e-mail him photos of the signatures.

She set a book down on the display table and moved behind the front counter, where she took the baseball and her cell phone out of her purse.

Ashley set Gus in the rocking chair and moseyed over. "What are you doing?"

"I'm taking photos of this baseball. I want to send them to someone."

Ashley took a closer look. "Oh no. Someone scribbled all over your ball," she said with a touch of alarm.

"It's okay, sweetie. It's a good thing. Those are signatures," Mary assured her. "The Red Sox team signed it a long, long time ago." *Supposedly* signed by the team anyway. When she got home tonight, she'd hunt down the letter from the Red Sox manager, whom she believed had stated that the ball had been passed around the players.

"Are people supposed to put their names on them? My softball doesn't have any on it." Ashley pulled a pristine new ball out of her backpack.

"It depends," Mary said. "Sometimes, when a person catches a ball at a major-league game, he or she asks a player or the team to sign it to make it special."

Rebecca looked up and smiled. "You can put your name on your ball, Ashley, if you want to. That way, if you lose it, whoever finds it will know it's yours."

"Can I use a pink marker? That would be prettier."

"You can use any color you'd like," Rebecca said, and Ashley dug through her backpack to find her markers.

Mary lined up the ball on top of the counter where the sunlight streamed in and took several close-up pictures of the signatures. She tried with the camera's flash on, and that seemed to work better. She'd e-mail the photos to Lincoln tonight to use as a comparison with other signed memorabilia.

Meanwhile, she should get the ball back to the display. If indeed someone had switched her ball with a counterfeit, she didn't want to tip the culprit off that she suspected something was wrong, assuming he or she hadn't already noticed it was gone.

"I know that I've been running in and out all day, but I need to head out again," she told Rebecca. "Would you mind closing up if I don't get back in time?"

"Sure thing," Rebecca said cheerfully.

Mary checked on Gus, who was in the rocker and taking a bath. He seemed content hanging with Ashley, who now had gone beyond signing her softball to decorating it with little blue flowers.

Mary stepped out into Main Street and turned left. The sun was lower in the western horizon, but there were still several hours before sunset on these long summer days. When she reached the intersection of Main and Water streets and saw the white concrete modern building of the Ivy Bay Police Station, she had a strong urge to talk to Chief

McArthur, but what could she say? That she suspected that John's baseball was stolen, but she didn't know how or why? She needed more evidence before she went to the police.

As she strode toward the town hall steps, the screeching sound of a saw filled the air. Men wearing yellow construction hats milled around the far end of the building where plastic flapped in the breeze. It appeared they were putting up the siding.

Stephanie was standing by her desk when Mary walked in the building. "You're back again? That makes three times today, not that I'm not glad to see you," she said with a little laugh as she dangled a ring of keys. "I was just going to lock up as soon as this group leaves."

Mary smiled. "I'm sure getting my exercise today, walking back and forth. I won't keep you. I'm just returning the baseball to the display." Mary walked over to the display, placed the ball on the little wooden stand, and set the information placard against it.

Her gaze wandered to the other autographed balls and memorabilia. Had any of them been tampered with? She really didn't know a whole lot about the sport. She'd enjoyed going to the games with John and the kids, but other than knowing the major players, she hadn't paid much attention. Tomorrow, she'd try to get over to the library and see what books they had on the subject.

As she was turning to leave, she spied a magazine on the edge of the table, looking like it could fall off any second. She began to set it properly on the table with the other baseball programs and then realized that the magazine featured cars, not sports. What was it doing back here? She hadn't noticed it when she'd retrieved her phone.

"Do you know whose magazine this is?" Mary asked, walking over to where Stephanie was shutting down her computer.

"Oh, I think it belongs to Brent or Ty. This afternoon, they were showing a man something in the display. I figured it was okay for them to be back there since Brent and Ty were helping out earlier."

"Who was the man? Another ballplayer?"

Stephanie shook her head. "He wears a baseball cap, but he's too old to be a ballplayer. He's been in here a lot, doing some sort of research. He usually drops a donation in the box too."

"Was he interested in any particular part of the display?" *Like John's baseball?*

"Not that I noticed. Today, I think they were hanging near Mr. Rigsby's things and talking. I wasn't paying much attention. We had lots of visitors this afternoon, and they kept me busy. Then Bea came in, and she was back there by the display tables doing something too. She sure liked Mr. Rigsby's contributions."

"That's good, especially since she was the one who encouraged him to loan us his memorabilia," Mary said.

Stephanie unlocked the donation box and put the money in a brown envelope and sealed it. "She invited me to go to the fish fry tonight. She said there'd be music. I thought, why not?"

"I'm glad you are both going. I'll be there too," Mary said, happy that Bea had taken the girl under her wing. She hoped she'd be able to talk to her friend tonight and see if she knew anything about John's baseball or Charles Rigsby.

"What about Mrs. Leary? Does she come out here a lot?" Mary asked, wondering if the manager might've noticed anything suspicious.

"No. Hardly at all." Stephanie let out a snort. "She's so busy trying to organize the offices and go through back paperwork that she hardly ever comes out here except to boss me around. I don't know why she took a job here. She's so tense all the time and doesn't seem to like people."

"Maybe things will change, and she can relax once things are set up and the construction is over."

Stephanie opened a drawer and extracted a black purse trimmed with silver studs. "I sure hope so." She glanced at the magazine in Mary's hand. "You can leave the magazine on the desk, if you want, and I'll give it to them when they come in again."

"Or I can just drop by the ice-cream shop on my way home and see if it's Brent's," Mary offered, thinking it might give her a chance to talk to Brent if he were there. Who was this man Brent and Tyler had been associating with? Could he be involved in the theft of John's ball?

Stephanie smiled, revealing her dimple again. "That works too."

Mary waited for Stephanie to take the cash to the back room and then followed her outside. Men still scurried in the construction zone. One of the men was directing a lumber truck as it backed up. The sign on the truck indicated it belonged to Baxter Construction. Mary vaguely recalled Betty saying they'd brought in a Boston company who specialized in restoration to work on the town hall. The company had given them a special deal.

As they went down the steps, a thought occurred to Mary. "Hey, Stephanie, can you do me a favor? Let's keep my concern about the baseball confidential for a little while."

Stephanie shot her a curious look. "Sure, whatever you say."

"Thanks. I'll explain later." Assuming she ever figured out what was going on with John's ball. "And maybe you could let me know if anyone seems off or acts suspiciously around the display?"

"No problem," Stephanie said, now a bit conspiratorially.

"See you tonight," Mary said with a wave as Stephanie headed up the sidewalk.

Mary turned in the opposite direction toward the downtown area. She still clutched the magazine she'd found on the table. It was earmarked, and she flipped the page open to reveal a new Corvette Stingray. Whoever owned the magazine had expensive taste. She'd drop by the Bailey's shop and see if it belonged to Brent or Joe. Again, she wondered when it had been left by the display.

It was almost six when Mary entered the ice-cream parlor. She loved the vintage decor with its bubblegum-pink-and-white-striped wallpaper and the matching pink padded stools lining the counter at the front of the store. Almost every one of the small, round white wrought-iron tables scattered throughout the shop was filled with happy customers. The Bailey daughters, Paige and Jamie, worked behind the counter.

"Mary!" Tess Bailey, her pleasantly plump friend, waved her to the far end of the counter where it seemed quieter. "Are you bringing me a new recipe?"

As an ice-cream hobbyist, Mary brought Tess a new flavor of ice cream every month. "Not yet, but I think I've got one of your sons' magazines."

Tess glanced at the cover page and rolled her eyes. "Most likely Brent's."

Brent breezed out from the back wearing a Blue Jays uniform and eating an ice-cream cone. "I heard my name."

"Is that your magazine? Mrs. Fisher brought it over."

"I wondered what I did with it. Thanks, Mrs. Fisher." He rolled the magazine and stuck it in his back pocket.

"Thanks for all your help this morning."

"No problem. I like hanging around all that baseball stuff."

And Mary imagined the pretty girl in the building might be an incentive too. "I was just wondering if you or Mr. Rigsby cleaned any of the artifacts."

"Nope. Did you want us to?"

"No, no. I was just wondering because it looked like someone might have," Mary said, trying not to stumble over her words.

Brent glanced at the wall clock and did a double take. "Yikes. Look at the time. I gotta get down to the field." He turned to Tess. "Can I borrow twenty bucks?"

Tess sighed. "I suppose. Get it out of my purse."

Brent leaned over, pecked Tess on the cheek, and darted back into the kitchen.

A couple vacated a table by the wall. "Have a seat, if you have a few minutes," Tess urged Mary. "Want to try a limeade? We mixed up a couple of gallons this morning using fresh limes."

"Oh yes, that would hit the spot."

"Be right back." Tess scooted behind the counter and returned with two pretty green drinks. She settled in the chair with a sigh. "This feels good. I've been on my feet all day."

Brent rushed out the kitchen and headed toward the door. "I'm late. See ya!"

"Of course you are," Tess muttered ruefully and then smiled at Mary. "Sorry, that's my problem child. Or rather, adult. Seems adulthood by age doesn't necessarily mean adulthood by maturity."

Mary laughed, although Tess had never opened up to her about Brent like this before, so she was all ears.

"Don't get me wrong; I'm thrilled he's here for the summer, but it can be exhausting. No buffer zone for worrying."

Mary took a long swallow of the tart lime drink. It was just what she needed. "He's doing well on the team, right?"

"Oh, he is. I just hope..." Her voice trailed away as something behind the counter caught her attention. "Paige, the freezer door got left open."

Paige spun and pushed the door, the air ruffling her dark pixie cut.

Mary could see the worry in Tess's eyes and tried to lighten the mood. "Joe and Brent were a big help this morning." She told Tess about Charles Rigsby and his collection. "While we were working on the display, I learned that a sports agent is interested in Brent."

"Yes, and I think a recruiter for one of the minor leagues is too."

"That's terrific. He mentioned he wanted to play pro ball."

"Well, if he hadn't gotten sidetracked and dropped out of college, he might be by now." Tess swished her glass, and the slush swirled against the sides. "Even in the best of circumstances, it's a long shot. And I just don't know what he's going to do if he doesn't make it. He has nothing in Boston now."

"Oh dear. What happened?" Mary asked.

"Got downsized. And he loved that job."

"That's rough. What did he do?"

"Sports merchandising. He was a buyer for a chain of stores."

"That sounds perfect for him. I'm so sorry it didn't work out."

"Yeah. It was a blow. He's always lived and breathed sports since he was a little kid. Being a buyer wasn't his dream job, but at least it was in a field he was interested in. Anyway, he hasn't found anything else, and he had to give up his apartment and trade in his car. Now he's putting all his hopes into getting picked up by a team."

"Do you think he has a good chance?" Mary asked. Brent had almost vibrated with enthusiasm for the game when they were in the town hall.

"I hope so! You know how it is. You try to steer your kids down the most sensible route, but they have minds of their own. Now, Joe, on the other hand, finished college, got a decent job at a bank. Now if only he'd find a sweet girl to marry."

"Mom, can you come here?" Jamie called. "I'm having trouble with the shake machine again."

"Just a sec, honey," Tess replied and turned back to Mary. "And here I wanted to discuss ice-cream flavors and all I did was talk about my kids."

"Oh, that's perfectly okay. I know how it is. I guess we never stop being mothers no matter how old our kids get."

Tess smiled as they got up. "That's for sure."

"We can talk ice cream next time. I still haven't decided what I want to make yet, but I'll try to get something to you this week."

"Sounds good. I'm sure it will be brilliant, as always." Tess hurried behind the counter to assist her daughter.

Mary waved at Tess and the Bailey girls as she went back outside under the large elm tree. The air had cooled some as the day slid into evening. She waited for a car to pass so she could cross the street, and wondered again why someone would take the baseball. It wasn't worth that much compared to some other memorabilia, but if someone was broke, then it might be a temptation.

She thought about the three young men who had helped with the display that morning. Joe Bailey hadn't seemed interested in any of the memorabilia and, according to his mother, he was doing well. Mary didn't know much about Tyler, but he didn't seem very interested in the display either and was an LA Dodgers fan. He, like Brent, wanted to play pro ball, but Brent Bailey with his recent job loss was the one with the greatest motivation to succeed.

According to Tess, life hadn't been easy for Brent lately. How badly did he need money? Enough to steal? Or perhaps he just wanted it for his collection as he'd mentioned. But did he have the skills to counterfeit signatures or the inclination to risk his future over a ball that as far as Mary could tell had a fairly low resale value?

Mary's thoughts naturally moved on to Charles Rigsby. He'd made her an offer on the ball. How badly did he want it? She'd gotten a glimpse of his equipment in one of his tubs. Certainly he had the knowledge to know what was valuable and possibly how to get something forged quickly. He'd been in the building after she'd left this morning. Maybe nobody noticed if he put the ball in his pocket. Stephanie admitted there were times she had to leave her desk. Bea had shown him the display the week before. That gave him time to make a copy of John's ball. But why? The ball wasn't worth enough for either Brent or Charles to take such a risk. Unless, of course, they knew something about the ball that she didn't.

She continued to mull this over as she reached her shop. Rebecca had locked up, and as Mary used her key, something caught her attention in the display window. Betty had designed the window for that month with a baseball theme. She had cleaned up an old bat and ball and put them in the window surrounded by mysteries related to baseball or ballplayers.

In the center of the display was an old nonfiction book that Mary had found years ago in a consignment shop. She had never read it. *Obscure Facts of New England Baseball.* When she got inside, she plucked the book out from the display and rearranged the other books to fill the gap.

"Come on, Gus. Supper time." Mary scooped up the cat and put him in his carrier. She glanced around the store, pleased at how neat Rebecca had left it.

She locked up and started down Main Street toward home. As she was passing the hardware store, her cell phone rang. "Gems and Antiques" popped up on the screen.

"Mary? Rich Tucker here. Are you sitting down? Man, do I have some news for you."

FOUR

◆◆◆

When Mary reached home, the tantalizing smell of Boston baked beans filled the house. She set Gus's carrier down and freed the cat.

"Betty," she called, anxious to share the events of the day and what she'd learned from Rich's phone call. She moved through the rooms to the kitchen. A basket with towels wrapped around something sat on the counter. Mary assumed it was the baked beans ready to take to the fish fry. She checked Betty's bedroom. The door stood open. Maybe her sister had gone out on an errand. She glanced at the clock. They were supposed to leave in half an hour.

She hurried upstairs and changed into a pretty pale-blue dress with flowing skirt that stopped just below her knees. She grabbed a white sweater and slipped her feet into white sandals. She glanced in the mirror and fluffed up her curly, short gray hair.

She and Betty had planned on wearing the dresses they'd bought earlier in the month to the picnic for old times' sake. When their grandmother was alive, she'd insisted they change out of their play clothes and dress up a bit for some of the summer events. After all, as she said, if you are going to attend the festivities, you should feel and look festive.

Mary smiled at the memory. Her usual wardrobe consisted of sensible khakis and blouses or knit sweaters. But now that she had her new dress on, she did indeed feel more festive. She had been looking forward to the evening. If only the mystery of John's baseball didn't swirl around her like a fog.

"Bets?" she called downstairs. When Betty didn't answer, she moved over to the closet. Rich had said it was important to see if she could find anything that authenticated the ball. She'd saved some of John's treasured items in moving boxes in her closet. That was where she kept the ball.

She opened the closet, and the faint scent of John's cologne washed over her. She took a deeper breath and stroked his old black cashmere coat that she couldn't bear to part with. She closed her eyes and got a vision of John shrugging into the coat on a cold Boston morning and then sweeping her into his arms and giving her a good-bye kiss before going off to work. It was little sweet moments like that that Mary was coming to miss the most.

She found the box that contained the small wooden chest that John had kept in his dresser and opened the lid. Inside was an assortment of things John had found special. Among them were cuff links from their wedding, a small worn Bible he'd kept in his backpack during law school, a tie clasp Lizzie had gotten him for Christmas, his Swiss Army knife, and a framed family photo taken when the kids were small. Each object held a special memory. Tears pricked her eyes as she set the photo aside. At the bottom was an assortment of envelopes. She thumbed through them until she found the letter from the Red Sox management that arrived with the signed ball.

She scanned the print until she found the sentence where the manager said that the ball had been passed to and signed by all the players for that game.

As she replaced the letter, she realized another envelope was stuck to the back of the Red Sox one. She pulled it off and opened it. Inside was a letter from a charity called Loving Hearts.

Dear John Fisher,

We just wanted to let you know how much we appreciate your donation of the Red Sox baseball for our fund-raiser for Maria Bontvello. We will send you a receipt once we receive your donation.

God Bless you in helping each of these little ones have a life.

Sincerely,
Laura MacAfee

Mary glanced at the date of the letter and sat back on the bed, her breathing painful. The letter had been mailed the week before John passed away. Why hadn't he told her about this? Maybe he hadn't had a chance. Oh, John. He was willing to give his beloved baseball to help a child he most likely didn't know. A tear rolled down her cheek, and she wiped it away.

Oh, dear Lord. Help me make this right.

She searched through the envelopes and found nothing else related to the charity. She put everything back in the chest except the Loving Hearts letter and walked downstairs to the kitchen. The back door opened, and Betty hobbled in. She collapsed in a chair with her soiled gardening gloves resting in her lap.

Mary swallowed hard, tamping down her feelings to concentrate on her sister. "Oh, Bets, what happened?"

"I'm afraid I overdid it. I should've known better." Her sister shook her head and then grabbed the back of her neck. "I just felt like I needed to trim the roses, but then once I got going, I decided to do the bushes. Then I noticed some weeds creeping in the planter."

Mary's lips twitched despite her concern. This was so like the Betty she grew up with. Whatever Betty did, she threw all her effort into it. It was one of the things Mary loved about her.

"You should know better when to quit," Mary scolded gently. "Can I get you something?"

"My pain pills. The ones I keep in the cupboard."

Mary found the prescription bottle and a glass of water. "We'll stay home. I'll make us dinner, and we can just relax."

"I'm not going to have you miss the fish fry just because of my foolishness."

"I don't mind at all. There are some things I can catch up on too." Mary didn't like how pale Betty's face appeared and the way her lips pinched together whenever she moved. Her sister rarely complained, even when her rheumatoid arthritis was really hurting her.

"If you went, you could take some photos of Allison playing softball for me. I know Evan will be videoing, but I'd like some photos to put in the album."

"I'd be happy to take some pictures for you, but at least let me fix you something before I go." Mary moved to the refrigerator. "There's a little bit of leftover chicken. How about a chicken-salad sandwich and a cup of soup?"

"Just the sandwich will be fine. I'm not very hungry, but I had better eat something with this medication." Betty leaned back in her chair. "How was your day?"

"Interesting," Mary said with her head in the refrigerator. She pulled out the small plate of chicken, celery, half an onion, fresh lemon, and the mayonnaise.

"Interesting? As in good or bad?"

"Well, I'm leaning toward bad. I'm a little upset." Mary got out the cutting board, and after rinsing the celery, she began finely chopping it. "I'm not sure where to even start. I think someone stole John's ball."

"Oh my! When?"

"This is where it gets interesting." She found the photos she'd taken of the ball on her phone and handed it to Betty. "I don't think that's John's ball. I think it's a copy. Counterfeit." She shredded the chicken and put it in the bowl.

Betty clicked through the photos. "Really? How can you tell? It looks the same to me."

"Remember there used to be a smudge under Sparky Lyle's name? It's gone."

"I remember you showed it to me years ago, but..." Betty nibbled on her lower lip, her gaze fixed on the photo showing Sparky's autograph. "I don't recall seeing it when you got it out a couple of weeks ago. Could maybe it have worn off after all these years?"

"That's a possibility, but I'm sure the smudge was there when I took the ball over to the display. It had faded over the years so it was barely visible, but it was there." Mary squirted a lemon wedge over the chicken and then mixed the bowl's contents together with mayonnaise. She added salt and pepper and popped some whole-grain bread in the toaster. "John liked to think it was Sparky's fingerprint. It made the ball extraspecial to him."

The longing for the man she knew so well threatened to choke her, and her voice cracked a little. "That's why it's still so special to me too." Mary sprinkled some dill seeds over the chicken salad for a finishing touch. "I even thought someone might've cleaned the ball, but there is something about it that just seems different from the one I put in that display. The way it feels. Maybe it's the weight. I know it's weird. I even showed it to Lincoln King over lunch."

"Good idea."

"Here is the interesting part," Mary said as she assembled the sandwich. "He says that at least several of the signatures appear to have been written by the same person. But of course the question is *when* that was done. When I got it signed originally, or did it recently happen?"

Mary added some strawberries to the plate and placed it and a glass of iced tea in front of Betty.

"I'm so sorry, Mar." Betty nibbled on her sandwich. "What a mystery. Why would anyone steal the baseball? Or go to the trouble to make a copy." She took a sip of the iced tea.

"That's what's troubling me too. A collector came in earlier today and offered me $250 for it."

"Wow, $250 for a baseball?" Betty said, forgetting to put her drink down for a moment.

"It may be worth even more than that," Mary said, feeling a little breathless, as she had after Rich called her. "Rich Tucker made some phone calls to some experts on sports autographs and found out something very interesting. The ball may be worth between $2,000 and $4,000, assuming it's authentic."

Betty's mouth dropped open. "You're kidding!"

Mary shook her head. "I have trouble believing it too. Seems there's a signature from a player on it named Bucky Swarnson. The ball was from his last game before he joined the war effort. He became a hero. I'm going to look up the story later because Rich wasn't able to give me many details, but Bucky passed away recently, and this sparked interest in his legacy."

"So, Mr. Rigsby could have known this and wanted it badly enough to steal it?"

"That's sort of what I'm thinking. But surely, he of all people would know how to make a convincing forgery, or know someone who could. After all, he is a sports memorabilia expert. I guess it seems logical to try to copy the ball because if it just disappeared, then it would raise an alarm. This way, a smidgen of doubt remains."

"I guess that makes sense, but how could he do it so quickly? You said he was in there this morning and then you noticed the smudge was gone later today."

"That's been bothering me too. Problem is, I didn't notice that the fingerprint was gone until this morning, so it could've happened anytime during the last week. Mr. Rigsby mentioned he'd seen the ball the week before. Maybe he switched balls earlier and then offered to buy mine as a diversion. If he had both, then no one would ever know this was a counterfeit."

"I guess that makes sense. Do you have other suspects?"

Mary nodded. "There are some other possibilities. Stephanie, the summer intern, is keeping an eye on things. Only certain people are allowed behind the ropes around the display. That doesn't mean someone else didn't get back there

unnoticed, but maybe it will narrow the number of suspects."
At least she hoped so. She explained briefly about Tyler, Brent,
and Joe being around the display along with another man and
how she'd learned that Brent needed money. "But I hate to
think that one of Tess's boys would be involved."

"I remember when Brent and Joe were younger," Betty
said. "What a pair of rascals. Always getting into mischief but
nothing too serious. Things like toilet papering the principal's
house or supergluing glasses to a table. They were too cute to
stay angry with for long. Of course, when they got older, it
wasn't so funny. Brent and several other boys got suspended
for some prank they pulled. Tess was beside herself, as you
can imagine. Luckily, they allowed him to graduate, especially
since he'd gotten offered several athletic scholarships."

"But then he dropped out of college anyway, according to
Tess. She said he missed his chance at the big leagues."

"Maybe it'll work out now. Because of the way the league
is set up, he's got a shot at being noticed by the major leagues
again."

"As long as he doesn't blow it," Mary said, wondering
again if Brent would risk his future by stealing. "There's one
other thing that happened today." Mary's throat threatened
to close up.

"I can't imagine anything else." Betty glanced at her face.
"Oh, Mar, what is it?"

Mary got out John's letter and gave it to Betty to read.

When she finished, Betty reached across the table and
squeezed Mary's hand. "Oh my. He never told you?"

Mary shook her head and swallowed hard. "The letter
was stuck to the back of another envelope. I've never seen it

until now. He was so sick at the end he must've just assumed I'd see the letter and follow through."

Mary wiped her eyes and then glanced at the clock. "I had better get going. Allison's game starts in twenty minutes, and I need to deliver the baked beans."

"I know you're feeling sad, but it's better that you get out and have a good time. John would have wanted that," Betty said gently. "And please tell the kids I'm sorry I couldn't make it to today's game, but I'm planning on all the rest."

Mary picked up the basket holding the crock of beans. "I won't be back too late."

"Don't worry about me. I'm thinking of a long, hot bath."

Mary opened the kitchen door.

"And, Mar, try to have fun and relax," Betty said. "I'm really sorry about John's baseball and everything. I'll pray that you get it back."

Mary closed the door, thinking she wasn't ever going to be able to relax again until she solved the mystery of John's baseball and his wishes were carried out.

FIVE

◆◆◆

The sun hung low on the horizon as Mary walked behind the elementary school. Festive colored lights had been strewn along the fence around the athletic field. Red-checkered tablecloths adorned tables loaded with dishes. Smoke rose from the big black barbecue grills in the back.

"I brought baked beans," she said to Sherry Walinski, who supervised the side-dishes table. "It's Betty's recipe."

"Oh, they smell so good. I love Betty's beans." Sherry and her teens lived next door to Betty and Mary and attended Mary's church. Mary helped extract the hot crock from the basket and set it on one of the hot plates. Then, Betty's eight-year-old granddaughter ran up to Mary dressed in a green-and-white uniform.

"My team plays next!" Allison said with a little hop. "Are you coming, Aunt Mary?"

"Can't wait." Mary smiled. "I'll be over to watch in few minutes." Allison ran back to the cluster of little girls around the pitcher's mound.

Evan, Betty's son, and his wife, Mindy, and their other daughter Betsy hurried across the field to the bleachers. Evan set down some blankets and then approached the food tables, carrying a covered square dish.

"Aunt Mary. Hi!" He looked around at the chairs spread out across the lawn. "I'm starving. Where's Mom?"

"She's home. Her arthritis is acting up. She sends her apologies and asked me to take lots of pictures."

Evan frowned with a concerned expression. "She just told me yesterday how much she was looking forward to this. I hope she's better in time for her big birthday celebration."

"I think she will be. I'll keep reminding her to take it extra easy until this flare-up subsides." Mary glanced at the covered dish in Evan's hands. "What did you bring?"

"Green-bean casserole with extra onions on top."

"Sounds good. I brought baked beans. Your mom's recipe."

"Yum." Evan grinned and glanced over at the tables laden with food. "Which dish is hers?"

"The blue crock on the end of the table."

"That's where I'm headed after I get my fish. Mindy told me to get a plate, and then she'll be over. We're on the bleachers closest to the batting cage, bottom row."

Mary dropped money in the donation jar and got her hand stamped, meaning she could visit the tables as much as she liked. She picked up a portion of fish and added coleslaw, potato chips, red Jell-O salad, and, of course, the baked beans.

She was headed over to the field when she crossed paths with Bob Hiller, the town mailman, and his granddaughter Isabella, who wore the same green-striped uniform as Allison.

"Hello, Mary," Bob said, slightly out of breath. He was dressed in khaki slacks and a white polo shirt, one of the rare occasions he wasn't dressed in his postal uniform. "Isn't it a great evening?"

"Sure is. Perfect weather. We're going to get a crowd." Mary smiled at Bob's granddaughter. "And how nice to see you, Isabella. I like your uniform. Are you having fun playing baseball?"

"Oh yeah! I caught a fly ball last time, and we won," Isabella said, bouncing on her toes.

"Oh, that's terrific!" Mary said, happy for the little girl. Poor Isabella had been plagued with some health problems over the years but was a real trouper.

Isabella looked up at Bob and smiled. "My grandpa's been practicing with me."

Bob rested a hand on Isabella's shoulder. "She's doing so well she doesn't need my help, but we're having lots of fun playing catch."

A whistle blew, and a coach standing on the pitcher's mound waved her arm.

"Gotta go!" Isabella said, breaking into a run.

"I'll be cheering for you and Allison," Mary called after her and walked with Bob over to the field where she joined Evan and Mindy. Allison's older sister Betsy sat nearby on a blanket with her friends. They cheered for Allison and Isabella during the game, which went fairly quickly because the girls were inexperienced. But what they lacked in skill, they made up for in enthusiasm and lots of squeals and giggling.

Mary snapped photos while Evan manned a video camera. Between the two of them, they sufficiently covered almost every move that Allison made. Both Allison and Isabella were able to get on base and reach home. Isabella played center field and caught a fly ball again, and Allison did a great job as second baseman.

A team of boys set up to play, and Mary walked back to the picnic festivities. There were games for the kids, including egg tosses, water-balloon fights, and relays.

"There you are!" Mary's friend Bea Winslow—a tiny woman with short, closely trimmed silver hair—rushed up to Mary. She had Stephanie in tow, who appeared to be having trouble keeping up. "We've been looking all over for you."

"Oh, I was over watching Allison's game." Mary smiled at Stephanie. "Having a good time?"

Stephanie nodded as she tucked a strand of dark hair behind her ear. She glanced at the band, which consisted of veterans and their horns and woodwinds. The band kicked into a tune that blended perfectly with the balmy evening.

Stephanie raised her voice above the song. "I expected different music, but it's okay, I guess."

Bea leaned closer. "I've been introducing Stephanie around to some of the young people. She stays cooped up in the town hall too much. Young women need to get out, make friends, and have some summer fun."

"I have fun!"

"I mean, besides reading." Bea winked at Mary.

Stephanie rolled her eyes, but the hint of a smile indicated she was enjoying Bea's attention.

"Now go over there and get an autograph." Bea gave her a gentle push in the direction of the ballplayers. "And smile."

"I wanted to ask you something," Mary said, but a trumpet blast drowned out her words. Mary motioned for Bea to follow her away from the band's brass section.

When they'd gone enough distance for the music to fade to a pleasant background volume, she asked, "What do you know about Charles Rigsby?"

"Charles? Isn't he great?" Bea said, tapping her foot to the music. "The display looks wonderful with his contribution."

"It does, but—"

Bea held up a finger. "Hold on a sec." Bea reached into her pocket and pulled out her cell phone. She turned away for a few moments and then tucked her phone away. "Sorry about that. I've got to go. If you see Stephanie, can you tell her I had to run?" Bea said, her voice cracking a little.

"Is everything okay?"

"Oh, sure, sure. Nothing I can't deal with." Bea turned to go and then hesitated. "Did you need to talk to me about something?"

Mary was confused about events at the town hall, but this was clearly not the time to talk about it with Bea. "It's okay. We can talk tomorrow."

Mary watched Bea disappear into the crowd, wondering what had caused the pinched look on Bea's face after she got that phone call.

Mary ambled back over to the dessert table but still felt too satisfied from the scrumptious dinner. She found a vacant lawn chair and let the music wash over her.

"Hey, there, stranger." Henry Woodrow stood beside her.

"Stranger?" Mary smiled at her longtime friend, and her heart gave a little flutter. "Has it been that long?"

"At least a week." Henry grinned. "Anyone sitting there?" He indicated the chair beside Mary.

Mary shook her head. "You're welcome to it. I'd love the company."

Henry settled on the chair and balanced his full plate on his knee.

"I heard you donated a lot of the fish for the fry tonight." Henry owned Woodrow Fishery and delivered fish to local merchants and restaurants.

"Yep. Some of the guys volunteered to help, and we went out this morning. Got lucky."

"The fund-raisers must be really grateful," Mary said, watching the line grow longer by the donation table.

Henry forked up some coleslaw and glanced over at Mary. "You had that faraway look again. Everything okay?"

Mary debated whether to share with Henry about John's baseball. It was such a lovely evening to just relax, but the loss kept bothering her. Maybe, if she talked about it with Henry, she'd get some peace. Plus, he often came up with good ideas.

"It wasn't a great day. I don't even know where to begin."

"The beginning's as good a place as any."

"I think I told you before that I volunteered to help out with the baseball display at the town hall."

Henry nodded. "Yep. You all did a good job. I like the photos. Do you know there's one of you and Betty at a game? I didn't realize it at that time, but you two were pretty cute."

Mary's cheeks warmed. "So were you. There's one of you playing ball."

"Yep. Fun times," Henry said. "So continue, what happened?"

"I loaned John's baseball to the exhibit, and well, it sort of disappeared." She went on to tell him the whole story from giving the ball to John as a wedding present to suspecting the current one as a counterfeit and finding the Loving Hearts letter to John. Henry listened intently, sometimes forgetting to eat when she covered some intriguing details.

"I had no plans to sell the ball, so the monetary value doesn't matter to me. But now that I know what John wanted to do with it, I feel even more obligated to find the ball and make sure it gets sent to the charity."

Henry set his fork down. "Finding that ball is important because of what it meant to someone you loved. If you say it isn't the original ball, I believe you. Now what's the next step?"

A rush of thankfulness filled Mary. She was so blessed to have a friend like Henry who believed in her.

"I need to find out more about Charles Rigsby, the memorabilia collector, tomorrow. He really wanted to purchase the ball and offered me a shamefully low price for it. Then there's Brent Bailey. I hate to think he'd be involved in something like this, but he has a motive," Mary said. "I also asked Stephanie to keep an eye out for people who visit the display frequently."

"Sounds like a good place to start. Does the town hall keep any record of the visitors?"

"No. We'd thought of putting out a guest book, but it never materialized." She smiled at Henry. "Thanks for the reminder. It might be too late to help find John's ball, but it can't hurt to track who is going in there. What if this person strikes again? Thanks, Henry."

"Anytime." Henry scraped his paper plate clean with his fork. "I really want to sample that dessert table, but I'm stuffed. Want to take a little walk?"

The sound of a bat cracking and the crowd cheering indicated a new game had started. Close to the stands, a table had been set up where several adult ballplayers lingered chatting with people.

As they drew closer, Mary could see a tall vertical banner advertising the Cape League and a poster offering photo opportunities with players. A line had formed by the table. There were a few starstruck-looking young boys, but the line consisted mostly of teen girls waiting their turn for a photograph. Mary couldn't blame them. Most of the players looked dashing in their uniforms.

Tyler and Brent stood in the group of ballplayers, taking turns smiling at the camera and signing autographs. Stephanie lingered off to the side.

"Did you want a photo or an autograph?" Henry asked in a teasing voice. "I remember one summer you and Betty had a competition going to see how many autographs you could collect."

Mary stopped short. "That's right. I'd forgotten. My aunt gave us each an autograph book, and we ran all over the place being little pests trying to get the players' autographs." Mary laughed. The competition had been mostly Betty's idea. The novelty of the game had worn off after a couple of weeks for Mary, especially since Betty was beating her. She wondered what had become of those books. She didn't remember taking them home at the summer's end. She'd have to ask Betty if she remembered.

"Wasn't that the summer you worked at the stadium selling popcorn after helping your dad in the mornings?" Mary asked.

Henry grinned. "Yeah, and I gained five pounds from getting to eat the leftovers."

Mary laughed. "Not that anyone could tell. You must have shot up half a foot that next year."

"Seven inches, and it was about time, if you ask me. Thought I'd never grow."

Mary laughed. "And then you eventually ended up being taller than your dad," she said. Mr. Woodrow had been an inch and one-half shy of Henry's six feet, but he'd been thinner than Henry, who carried more bulk in the muscle department. Even now, after all these years, the work on his boat had kept him lean and strong.

They were passing the crowd of baseball fans when a burly man with a scruffy beard approached them. Mary recognized him as one of the fishermen for hire who worked various boats. "Hey, Henry. Got a minute?"

When Henry looked at her, Mary said, "Go ahead. I'm in no hurry."

Mary stepped discreetly away as they discussed business. She watched the still-growing crowd, searching for familiar faces. There were several people from her church. As she lifted her hand to wave, a familiar male voice behind her said, "It's not fair."

"Son, life isn't supposed to be fair."

Mary looked over her shoulder. Brent stood facing someone hidden behind the Blue Jays' banner.

A flush had brightened Brent's face. "I earned this chance."

"Look, I don't know what to tell you. Timing is everything. If you listen to me, maybe, just maybe, I can make things happen for you. You do for me; I do for you. Got it?"

"Whatever." Brent stormed off.

A wiry, middle-aged man with a timeworn Red Sox cap tucked over gray hair and cowboy boots on his feet stepped out from behind the banner. He caught Mary's eye and tipped his cap at her before walking back to the ballplayers. He fit Brent's earlier description of Bill Halliday, and maybe he was the one Stephanie had seen visit the display frequently.

Mary wondered what the man wanted Brent to do for him. She sidled over to Stephanie while Henry continued talking to the fisherman. "Bea said to let you know she had to leave."

"It's cool. I was getting ready to go home anyway. I appreciate her trying so hard to get me involved with the community, but baseball is just not my thing."

"Not everyone is fascinated by baseball," Mary said as two girls squealed when Tyler put his arms over their shoulders for a photo. "She just wants you to have friends here in town."

"Oh, I know. I just don't mind being alone," she said, but the look in Stephanie's eyes belied her words. Bea probably spotted that hint of loneliness or perhaps insecurity and taken the young woman under her wing.

Mary nodded to the cowboy. "Is that the man who comes in to see the display a lot?"

"Oh yeah. That's him," Stephanie said. "He seems like a nice guy when he stops to talk to me."

"Hi, Mrs. Fisher," Tyler called, jogging up to them. "Are you having fun, Stephanie?"

"Sure," Stephanie said with another shrug.

"Want to hang with us?"

"Uh." She glanced over at the rambunctious crowd huddled around the Blue Jays' table. "Thanks, but I gotta go. Excuse me." She stepped around Tyler and melted into the crowd.

Tyler stared after her with a puzzled expression, and Mary wondered whether Stephanie was avoiding them because she just didn't have anything in common with the kids who loved sports, or if she was just shy.

"It's been a really nice evening," Mary said. "The turnout looks great. I hope this will give a big boost to the team."

"Me too." Tyler dragged his focus back to Mary. "This summer has been a great experience."

Mary spotted the man in the boots again. "Is that Bill Halliday that you and Brent were talking about?"

Tyler looked over his shoulder. "Yep. The great man himself." He gave her a rueful grin. "I got to talk to him this afternoon."

"Do you think he might take you guys on as clients?"

"Who knows? Like I said before, he seems more interested in Brent."

Henry joined them and gave Tyler a smile. "Sorry that took so long."

"Have you met Tyler Matthews yet?" Mary asked.

"Don't think so, but I've seen your photo in the Blue Jays summer program." He shook Tyler's hand. "Matthews. There was a yacht in the marina by the name *Meandering Matthews*."

Tyler nodded. "My parents'."

"Nice boat. I've been admiring it for weeks and then noticed it left yesterday."

Tyler smiled. "Yeah, they had to get back to Boston, but hopefully they can get down later." He looked over at the booth. "I should probably get back. Nice meeting you, Henry."

Mary and Henry resumed their walk. Mary fell into rhythm with Henry's stride, and they walked in the comfortable silence of old friends until they reached the path to the beach.

"How are Karen and Kimberly doing?" she asked, referring to Henry's grown twin daughters.

"Doing okay. I'm hoping I can visit my grandsons before school starts," Henry said as they arrived at the beach.

Mary took a deep breath of the salty breeze. The tide was rising, and small waves rolled in with churning white foam, bright in the moonlight against the sand. If it'd been the old days, Mary would've kicked off her sandals and frolicked in the gentle bay waves. But this was nice too, talking with Henry, enjoying the summer evening. They turned back toward the school, and by the time they arrived, Mary was feeling ready for dessert.

Strings of lights, hung on the fences surrounding the field and on the bandstand, cast a festive glow under the starry sky. Flickering lanterns had been set on the tables adorned with a wide variety of desserts with plenty left for the choosing, despite the crowd. Layered cakes ranging from chocolate to lemon supreme. Platters of cookies. A peach trifle. Brownies loaded with walnuts.

"Blueberry pie! One of my favorites," Henry said.

"Oh, mine too. It always reminds me of summers on the shore."

Henry scooped up a slice of the blueberry and another of peach pie. "Your grandmother used to make the best pies, remember that? You had to be near the front of the line at the church potluck to get a piece."

Mary reached for the blueberry pie too. "She used to get up at 5:00 AM and make two to four pies before breakfast. Sometimes more, depending on the occasion. She'd save one for us and give the rest away to people. I remember that Betty used to get up and help Gram, but I always preferred playing outside."

"Can I have everyone's attention?" The band had stopped playing, and Mr. Owen Cooper, president of Ivy Bay Bank & Trust, stood on the small platform, holding a jar in his hand. "We're going to draw for our door prizes. I need a young volunteer. Yes, you, young lady."

Isabella ran up to the front, reached into the jar and pulled out a folded paper.

"This one is for four free ice-cream sundaes at Bailey's Ice Cream Shop." Mr. Owens unfolded the paper and called out, "Tara Monroe."

A young woman answered with a squeal and waved her hand.

"Okay, another young volunteer."

Mary leaned back on her chair and enjoyed watching the people. Mr. Cooper gave away tickets to the local theater, a coupon for a free car wash, and other prizes.

"The last drawing is for four front-row reserved seats to a ball game tomorrow night. Blue Jays against the Mariners." The little boy volunteer handed Mr. Cooper the paper. "Henry Woodrow."

"You won!" Mary said with a clap of delight as Henry went up front to collect his prize.

When he returned, he was smiling. "I was just thinking before I came here that I really needed to make time to get over to watch a game before the season ended. Now, I have a really good excuse with front-row seats. Would you and Betty like to go? We'll pretend we're ten years old without a care in the world, eat gallons of popcorn and peanuts, and just have fun."

"That sounds perfect," Mary said with a laugh.

"Good. For now, I'd better get on home and get some things done for tomorrow so I can go with a clear conscience. How about I pick you ladies up around six?"

"Sounds wonderful. See you tomorrow." Mary watched him walk away and sat for a little while enjoying the balmy air and the band music until a yawn snuck up on her. Time to head home.

She picked up her purse and stopped by the food table to get Betty's dish. She passed the empty dessert tables. Piecrust crumbs littered the white tablecloths. She smiled, thinking of those bygone summer days, and then she had an idea. She knew just what she wanted to give Betty for her birthday.

———

Mary hummed one of her favorite hymns, "Blest Be the Tie That Binds," as she stepped around the cat sitting in the middle of the kitchen floor. "What do you think, Gus? Won't this make a nice surprise for Betty?"

Gus yawned and flopped over in a furry lump. Mary grinned and shrugged. She didn't need her lazy cat's approval.

Mary had awakened to a quiet house and a cheerful note on the kitchen counter. Betty had gone to a breakfast meeting with a church committee at the Black & White Diner. Mary took it as a good sign her sister must be feeling better, and staying home last night had been a wise choice.

Despite missing Betty, Mary had enjoyed her evening with family and Henry. And the best thing of all was that she'd decided what to do for Betty's birthday. After talking about her grandmother's pies with Henry, Mary thought a homemade pie in celebration of their life together now and in memory of those special summer days with Gram and Gramps was the perfect gift.

The only problem was that Mary's baking skills were a bit rusty. Sure, she'd made cookies and cakes for John and the children, but pie had always seemed on the more difficult side. It was easier to just purchase a frozen one to bake or pick up a fresh one from the bakery.

She wondered if Betty had Gram's old recipes. But she couldn't ask her without Betty asking why. Maybe she kept them somewhere in the kitchen. Mary opened the cupboard containing cookbooks. Nothing personal in there. She searched the cupboard and finally found a recipe box.

Mary thumbed through the cards and discovered Gram's recipes for Italian meat loaf and beef stew. There were other cards labeled as Ida Nelson's recipes, including several cake recipes, all done in Betty's neat handwriting, but no pies. How strange. Maybe Betty kept the remainder somewhere else. No matter. She'd use a cookbook.

She grabbed an old Betty Crocker cookbook from the pantry shelf and with dismay found the entire pie section missing. What was going on? Where had Betty put the pie recipes?

Mary finally resorted to getting a simple apple-pie recipe off the Internet. She hadn't decided what kind of pie to make for Betty's birthday, but since they had apples in the refrigerator, she figured they were good to practice with. She got out the other ingredients to make a pie.

Mary measured out the flour into a large ceramic mixing bowl, added salt, and then dropped in pieces of cold butter. The recipe instructed her to cut in the butter with two knives until the dough was crumbly. Mary worked at cutting the butter, but it just didn't seem to cooperate. Finally, she mixed the dough together with her hands and put it on wax paper on the counter to roll out.

She'd seen her grandmother roll out dough hundreds of times, and it looked simple enough. But as Mary rolled, she couldn't seem to get the pie dough evenly spread. She gathered it up and mashed it into a ball and then tried rolling again.

After three tries, she decided it was good enough and put the dough into a pie plate. It settled in nicely, and she turned to the apples she'd peeled, cored, and sliced. She sprinkled brown sugar and cinnamon on them and placed the apples in the crust. She went through the piecrust-rolling business again, and placed the top crust over the apples.

She cocked her head and studied her efforts. A verse from Luke 6 came to mind. *Give, and it will be given to you. A good measure, pressed down, and shaken together and running over...*

Well, she'd certainly measured and pressed down and given her best effort. She just hoped she'd produced something edible. Maybe it would look better once baked. She'd take it to the shop today to share with Rebecca and Ashley.

Gus twitched his tail, his blue eyes unblinking as he studied her, no doubt trying to figure out what was going on. This wasn't their normal routine.

She slid her creation into the oven and set the timer. After cleaning the kitchen mess, she ran upstairs to take a shower. She tucked her flour-coated clothes in the hamper. It looked like another hot day, so she topped her usual khakis with a sleeveless tan-and-white blouse.

She picked up the book, *Obscure Facts of New England Baseball*, that she'd gotten from her shop. She'd meant to read it last night, but after getting home, she'd uploaded the photos she'd taken of the baseball and e-mailed them to Lincoln. She barely made it through her devotions before falling asleep.

She glanced at the time as she went downstairs to the kitchen. It was after nine. Maybe Loving Hearts would be open now. She took out John's letter and dialed the number.

"Loving Hearts," a female voice answered. "This is Laura MacAfee."

"Hello, I'm Mary Fisher. My husband, John, received a letter from Loving Hearts thanking him for a Red Sox baseball he was going to donate for a fund-raising auction last year, but he passed away, and I didn't find out about this until recently."

"Oh, I'm sorry to hear about your husband. My condolences to you and your family."

"Thank you. I appreciate it," Mary said. "Now if only I can make sure John's wishes are carried out."

"Hold on a minute. Let me check my records," Laura said in a kind voice.

Mary could hear the sound of a filing drawer being opened. Laura returned a moment later. "Ah yes. John Fisher. I have a note that we made a follow-up call to his firm and a note that someone would get back to us."

"May I ask what the donation was for?"

"Certainly. Loving Hearts is a charity that helps children with congenital heart defects. We hold various fund-raisers, including auctions, and the need is growing."

"Oh, that sounds like such a worthy cause," Mary said.

"It is. I wish you could meet these precious children that need help. We have another charity auction coming up in three weeks for a sweet three-year-old who desperately needs surgery next month. We find that auctions are particularly successful because people get competitive with their bids and don't mind donating more for a good cause. Perhaps you can still send in the baseball."

"Oh dear, I'm not sure I'll be able to do that. There are extenuating circumstances, but I'll see what I can do. I will contribute something," Mary said with a lump in her throat. "Can I get back with you?"

"Of course," Laura said, her appreciation evident. "Again, I'm sorry about your husband. He must've been very special."

He was.

Mary turned off the phone and carefully folded the letter and put it back into its envelope. She told herself she wasn't going to cry, even though a tear slipped down her cheek. If she never recovered the ball, she would make sure Loving Hearts received a donation from her of some kind. But she was going to do her best to find John's baseball and follow his wishes.

She poured herself a cup of coffee and settled at the kitchen table. She turned to the index in the baseball book and found Bucky Swarnson's name. She flipped to the page with his story. Apparently, he'd been a rising young rookie but wanted to serve his country. He enlisted and was deployed to Vietnam in 1970 as a medic. He managed to help save more than 120 soldiers before being injured himself. He received a Purple Heart and never returned to baseball. Was that why the baseball was worth so much now, as Rich suggested? John must've known this, and that was why he'd donated the ball.

She got out her laptop and searched for Bucky Swarnson. She verified the information that was in the book. Bucky Swarnson had gone on to form charities and spent the rest of his life helping others. He'd died last year, and a park in New York City was being named after him. That also might explain why Bucky's signature was so special now.

Before shutting down the laptop, she checked her e-mail. To her surprise, Lincoln had already replied.

Mrs. Fisher,

I was able to compare some of the signatures to the Red Sox signatures on other memorabilia on the Web, and it's still my conclusion that a single person was responsible for most, if not all, the signatures. The autographs are almost identical to the authentic signatures, but appear to be forgeries nonetheless. Further testing of the ball would provide more definitive results.

Sincerely,
Lincoln

Mary leaned back in her chair and let out a deep breath. She'd sensed the ball wasn't the original since handling it yesterday, but it still knocked the wind out of her to think someone went to all that trouble to steal John's ball.

The oven timer buzzed, startling her. The pie must be done. If it tasted half as good as it smelled, she'd be very pleased. She got the pie out of the oven, glad she'd put a cookie sheet under it since the juices had bubbled over. The baked piecrust did look better, even though it was still a bit lopsided and hadn't browned evenly.

She let the pie cool while she fed Gus and then decided to have a taste of the pie. She cut out a slice and frowned as the apples slid across the plate in a gooey mess. Granted, it was still hot, but should there be so much liquid? The crust was a bit gummy on the bottom, and the apples were unevenly cooked.

"I guess this is going to be harder than I thought." Mary read the recipe again. Where had she gone wrong? It was another mystery she was determined to solve.

She took another bite. It tasted like apple pie, but something was wrong with the texture. She didn't really want to serve this to anyone, but she sure hated to waste all the good ingredients. And she couldn't leave the pie around for Betty to find. She was going to have to eat what she could and throw away the rest. Pie for breakfast? Well...apples were healthy, right?

Mary scooped out the best parts and then dumped the remainder in a plastic grocery bag and took it to the outside garbage. She returned to the kitchen, washed the dish, and tucked it in the cupboard. All evidence of her baking experiment was gone except for a slight odor of baked apples. She sprayed some cleanser on the counters and a lemon scent filled the room. Satisfied that a pie for Betty's birthday would still be a surprise, she got Gus's carrier.

"Come on, Gus. Time to go to work."

In more ways than one. With the discovery of how much the ball was worth and John's plans to help a child, it was time to take the investigation to an official level. It was finally time to talk to Chief McArthur.

SIX

Mary entered the reception area in the Ivy Bay Police Station. The sage-green walls and wide-planked floor made a cool contrast to the bright hot afternoon outside. She asked for the chief and was semirelieved when she was told he was in. What would he think about this?

As she waited, she started to have second thoughts about talking to him. Before she could leave, she was called back.

Chief McArthur sat behind his black steel desk, talking on the phone. He motioned Mary closer. His normally neat stacks of files were in disarray on the walnut desktop. His normally neatly pressed beige shirt was wrinkled and already sweat-stained. He hung up the phone with a sigh and settled back in his chair before giving Mary a small smile.

"I'm sorry if I came at a bad time," she said.

"No time today is a good time. It's been crazy. We've been running since midnight. Three traffic accidents all caused by impatient out-of-towners. We have one guy on the beach going around spraying people with window cleaner and a little old lady who attached herself to the lifeguard chair in protest of the fishing."

"Oh dear. Fishing of what?"

"Doesn't matter. She feels that fishing hooks are abusive and should be banned. People should fish with nets." He ran his hand over his head. "And those are just a few highlights of the morning. Now what can I do for you, Mary Fisher?"

"Well, after what you told me, I suppose my problem kind of fits the crazy category. Here's the gist: I loaned a 1970s signed Red Sox ball to the baseball exhibit in the town hall, and I think someone has replaced it with a counterfeit."

The chief raised his eyebrows. "Well, this is a new one. And what makes you think that?"

"There was a smudge under Sparky Lyle's signature, and now it's gone. And according to Lincoln King, the signatures on the current ball are likely forgeries."

"I...see." He stroked his chin, no doubt thinking that her story did indeed fall in the crazy category. He sighed and twirled his pen between his fingers. "Do you have any idea of how much the baseball is worth?"

"Rich Tucker did an initial appraisal on it, and it turns out that the ball may be worth over $2,000. Maybe $4,000."

The chief dropped his pen. "Well, you have done your homework, haven't you, Mary? But why would you just leave a valuable ball out in the open for anyone to take?"

"The area is cordoned off, and there is someone there to watch over things," Mary said, feeling the slightest bit indignant. "And I had no idea the ball was worth that much."

The chief laughed and picked up his pen. "Okay, I'll turn this over to Deputy Wadell, and he'll write up a report. He'll be by the town hall today to take a look."

Mary dropped Gus off at her shop and hurried up the street to the town hall. She wanted to tell Stephanie that the police would be stopping by. She stepped inside to find the wiry man she'd seen at the fish fry. He wore a navy-and-white Western-style shirt, jeans, and the Red Sox cap. He leaned back in the chair by Stephanie's desk, legs outstretched with one brown boot on top of the other. Stephanie had mentioned he'd been hanging around the display quite a bit.

Stephanie leaned forward over her keyboard as she concentrated on whatever was on the computer screen.

"Good morning!" Mary gave them both a smile.

Stephanie looked up. "Oh, hi, Mrs. Fisher. Can I help you with something?"

"Oh, I don't want to interrupt. It looks like you're busy. I just came over to check on the display and see if there is anything that needs to be done," Mary said, not wanting to bring up in front of a stranger that the police would soon arrive.

"Ah, so are you the one who put this intriguing slice of local history together?" the man asked. "I admire what you're doing to help the league and the children."

"Thank you. It was a group effort." Mary held out her hand to the man. "I don't believe we've met before."

The man pulled his lanky legs under him and stood. "Billy Halliday. Howdy, ma'am." He shook her hand. "Everyone calls me Bill."

"It's nice to meet you, Bill. I believe I heard you're a scout?"

"Sports agent now, although I've had other careers in my life."

"So have you discovered any new talent?" Mary asked, wondering how interested he was in Brent and Tyler, especially after the tense conversation he'd had with Brent at the fish fry.

"I may have. If there's potential around, I'll spot it." His smile stretched across his weathered, tanned face. "You never know when one might find the next Ted Williams or Pedro Martinez. I've been following some of these players' stats during their high school and college careers. The summer leagues are icing on the cake."

His enthusiastic tone caused Mary to smile again. "I bet it's exciting when you do make a discovery."

"Oh, it is. As some of my young clients would say, it's a real rush."

Stephanie clicked her computer mouse and rose from her chair. "I'll be right back with your documents, Bill. The printer is in the office."

Bill looked at Stephanie. "Sure thing."

"I'm looking forward to going to the game tonight," Mary said to Bill. "I know two of the players. Brent Bailey and Tyler Matthews."

"Both promising young players," Mr. Halliday said matter-of-factly. "I predict big opportunities for them if they keep up the good work." He gestured toward the tables. "So, are any of these things yours?"

"Just the Red Sox baseball. The team-signed one. My husband caught it."

"Ah yes, I was admiring it earlier and wishing it were mine."

"So you collect memorabilia?" Mary asked, watching him carefully and curious as to just how badly he wanted it. Enough to switch it with a forgery?

His grin broadened. "You should see my office. I have a great collection of trading cards as well as several signed balls. I have one signed by Ted Williams. But to own a team-signed ball like yours from that era is special. I got my start back in the seventies. Would your husband consider selling the ball? I'll offer a more than fair price," he said with a hint of shrewdness in his eyes, and Mary reminded herself that this man bargained contracts for a living.

"John passed away, and I'm not ready to part with it." Mary didn't add that she'd never part with it except to donate it to Loving Hearts.

Stephanie returned and handed Bill a stapled stack of paper. "Here's the demographic information on Ivy Bay that you wanted. If you think of anything else you need, just let me know."

"Thank you, Miss Stephanie. You're a very efficient young lady. This will be very helpful." He glanced at his gold watch. "I'd better go. I wanted to watch practice this morning. It was nice meeting you, Mrs. Fisher, and if you change your mind about the ball, I'll be around for the next week." He gave her a smile and headed out the door.

"He's doing research," Stephanie said, answering Mary's unasked question.

"What kind of research?"

"He asked for some copies of old town-council meetings a few days ago. And last week, he had me research some zoning laws. But mostly, when he comes in, he just goes over to the display. A couple of times, he talked to Bea too."

"Has she been in today?" Mary asked. Bea needed to be clued in on what was going on, especially now that the police were involved.

"Not yet," Stephanie said. "I can let her know you'd like to talk to her when I see her." She pulled out a neon-pink message pad.

"It's okay. I can stop by her office on the way back to my shop."

"I don't think she's in yet. She said something about having a buyer for her car. Is there something I can do for you?"

"Yes, you can call me when the police officer gets here to finish the report on my missing baseball."

"So that ball over there really is a fake?"

"It appears so, but we shouldn't let that information get around. We don't want to do anything to impede the police in their investigation."

"Like tipping off the thief?"

Mary nodded. She just hoped the police were discreet. If there was any chance of getting that ball back, they didn't want to scare off the culprit.

She tucked her purse strap higher on her shoulder. "Why did Mr. Halliday need demographics, if you don't mind me asking?"

Stephanie shrugged, her fingers poised over the keyboard. "Some project he's working on. He didn't offer any details."

The door opened, and three giggly girls entered and headed for the baseball display.

"Come on, Dad," one called behind her as a rumpled man shuffled after the girls. He passed the donation box without a glance.

"Before I forget . . . ," Mary said, "when we first opened the display, we considered putting out a guest book. We forgot about it, but having a place to sign in would be a great way to see who comes to visit."

Stephanie nodded. "Good idea. You can also get their e-mail addresses and use them to send announcements if you do another exhibit next year."

"Good idea." Mary glanced again at the visitors.

Stephanie made a note on her pink pad. "I'll take care of it."

Mary stepped outside and went down the stone steps. The sun had crept higher and beat down on her head, but an ocean breeze kept the temperature comfortable as she strolled to the bookshop. Down the street, she saw Mr. Halliday sauntering along. He paused by a parked red pickup and appeared to be hunting for his keys in his pocket. In his other hand were sheets of paper. He glanced down at them and then turned, spied a trash can, and dropped them inside.

She paused, looking in her shop window until Bill Halliday's pickup drove away. Then she hurried down the sidewalk. She peered into the trash bin. On top were typed sheets of paper with demographic statistics of Ivy Bay.

She picked up the stack of paper. Had he even read them? He'd just left the town hall a few minutes before she had. If Mr. Halliday wasn't actually using the information Stephanie got for him, then why was he spending so much time in the town hall and around the display?

Mary carried the paper back to her store, puzzling over it. An enticing, warm homey scent emanated from Sweet Susan's Bakery next door, reminding Mary of her dismal pie-baking attempt that morning. She had been looking forward to sharing the pie with Rebecca and Ashley. Well, maybe she could still share a treat.

She popped inside the yellow-fronted store and waited behind another customer. She surveyed the mouthwatering pastries, breads, muffins, cakes, and the signature cupcakes that Susan was known for.

"Earth to Mary," Susan Crosby said with a chuckle.

Mary blinked, startled. The previous customer had finished and moved on. She smiled at the attractive middle-aged woman with a round figure and dark hair tucked under a baker's hat. "Sorry. I zoned out there for a moment. Everything looks so yummy. I have no idea what to choose."

Susan chuckled again. "Glad to hear that. It's good for business." She leaned forward on the counter and lowered her voice as if sharing a secret. "The cinnamon muffins just came out of the oven and are still warm."

"Oh, that must be the scent that drew me in, although everything you bake smells wonderful."

"Part of my marketing strategy." Susan smiled. "Especially if it brings you in here more often."

"I'd come in here anyway." Mary smiled back. She studied the case again. "Okay, definitely three of those cinnamon muffins and three blueberry." Mary could barely resist the urge to take a dozen. She knew she'd be tempted to munch on them all day if she did.

Susan punched her order into the register. Mary reached in her purse for her wallet and then stopped. A perfect pie rested regally at the end of the case. It reminded her so much of the pies her grandmother and Betty used to bake, with its golden-brown crust with tiny leaves cut out of the top layer giving a peek at tantalizing blue filling below. She wanted to be able to make a pie just like that.

Susan reached for a white paper bag and added the blueberry muffins as Mary moved closer to the pie. She wondered how Susan got the crimping on the edges so even.

"Would you like some pie too?" Susan counted out three cinnamon muffins and tucked them gently in the bag.

"I was just trying not to drool over your work. What a great-looking pie. I tried to make one just this morning, and it was a disaster."

"Oh, that's too bad," Susan said. "What kind was it?"

"Apple. I followed the recipe, but I'm not sure what I did wrong." Mary sighed. "When I was young, my sister and I visited our grandparents here every summer. My grandmother and Betty would get up early before the heat of the day and bake lots of pies."

"How wonderful she got to spend time with her grandmother that way. I used to bake cookies with my aunt during the holidays. Every time I make Christmas pinwheels, I think of her."

"I want to make a pie to surprise Betty on her birthday next week. I know I can just buy one, but I wanted to do it myself for old times' sake." Mary gave a little shrug. "Maybe I'll have to do something else if I can't get one to turn out right."

Susan folded over the top of the bag and placed it beside the cash register. "Well, if you'd like some help, just holler. I can give you baking lessons, if you want."

"Really? That would be terrific," Mary said. "But I don't want to impose."

"I've been thinking for a while about offering baking lessons. You can be my test case. All you'll need to do is pay for the ingredients, and that won't be much because I already buy in bulk."

Mary's smile grew. This seemed like an answer to a prayer. She could learn to make a pie correctly, and she'd be away from the house so Betty wouldn't find out.

Thank You, Lord. With Him, all things were possible.

"I'll take you up on it, then," Mary said. "When would be good for you?"

"How about tomorrow afternoon? Around two when my assistant gets here."

"I'll be here." Mary paid for the muffins and went back to her shop.

She flipped the sign to Open. Gus sat on the counter with an indignant gleam in his eyes. His long tail swished.

"Took a little longer than I thought." Mary gave him a pat as she passed by.

Rebecca wasn't coming in until noon today. The young mother was taking advantage of some back-to-school sales with Ashley and wanted to get to the stores early. Mary couldn't believe how fast the summer was flying by. Soon, the tourists and summer residents would be heading back to their homes elsewhere for school and work, just like Betty and Mary used to do. Mary looked around her little shop and felt a thrill that she didn't have to go anywhere and now lived here year-round.

Mary carried the bag of muffins to the back room and set it on top of the microwave. She checked Gus's water dish and refilled it before returning to the front of the store. She turned on the computer and straightened a couple of bookshelves. Satisfied the store looked neat and inviting, she returned to the counter.

She picked up the sheets that Bill Halliday had thrown away. From the data printed, it appeared he'd been researching the ages of residents, average housing costs, growth over the last twenty years, and a list of current businesses. Mary's Mystery Bookshop was listed, among others. Anyone could get this information off the Internet, but maybe Bill wasn't comfortable with computers.

What would a sports agent want with this information? Stephanie had mentioned he frequently visited the display too. Was he just a big fan, or was he there for other reasons? Like scouting out valuable artifacts? Could he be requesting Stephanie to print reports to get her out of the room? He might have been able to get access to the display with no one else in the room. True, he had made an offer to buy John's ball, but did he already have it and the offer was a diversion?

She needed to find out more about this man. According to Brent, Bill Halliday was a big-shot sports agent, so why was he hanging around the town hall so much? And why have Stephanie do research for him only to throw it away minutes later?

She turned to her computer and typed his name into the search engine. Numerous links popped up for sports-magazine and baseball-information sites. She skimmed through a couple of them, noting most of the articles were over five years old.

The store door opened, and Henry strode in. He wore faded jeans and a short-sleeved green shirt. A Blue Jays cap covered his silver hair, and a warm smile lit up his face.

Mary returned his smile. Henry smelled of sunscreen and the sea, a mix that had Mary longing for the beach, an umbrella, and a good mystery to read. "Good morning. How's your day going?"

"It's off to a good start. I took a family of six out for a couple of hours of fishing."

"How'd they do?"

"Fish weren't biting as much as they were yesterday, but it didn't stop them from having a good time. They're from Ohio, and this was their first time deep-sea fishing," Henry said, his gaze stealing over to the New Arrivals display. Henry enjoyed a good mystery.

"I'm glad it went well," Mary said with envy. It'd been a while since Mary had been out on Henry's boat *Misty Horizon*, which Henry used for fishing and tours around the bay. She needed to get out on the water again before the cold set in.

"I was just stopping in to see if you and Betty are still planning on going to the game tonight."

"Betty said she'll go, and we're looking forward to it," Mary said. Actually, Betty had been a bit hesitant. Although she said she was feeling better, she didn't want to overdo it. Mary had reminded her of the fun times they'd had with their grandparents, and besides, it just involved sitting in the stands. It hadn't been hard to convince her.

"Me too!" Henry glanced at Bill's sheets beside the computer. "Doing some research?"

Mary updated him on her growing suspicions of Bill Halliday and his frequent visits to the town hall. And how maybe he was using the reports as a way to get Stephanie away from her desk. "I know it sounds far-fetched, but so does someone counterfeiting John's ball."

"I'd be suspicious." Henry tapped the computer screen. "Find anything interesting on him?"

"It mentions he's originally from Texas, been in baseball since the seventies, and it looks like he's been very active up until about five years ago or so. Lately, he's hardly mentioned online."

"Maybe business hasn't been so good, and he's having trouble getting clients that are newsworthy."

Mary nodded. "Or maybe he's planning on retiring soon and winding down his client list. He looked like he was in his late fifties to early sixties."

"Could be," Henry agreed.

She studied the page on the screen. "This article called him a shark and said he'd fight for his players to get exactly what they wanted despite what might be good for the team."

"That probably explains why he was so successful. What was your impression?"

"He seemed nice. Confident. Maybe *overly* confident. Relaxed and easygoing on the surface, but there's an intensity about him. It's difficult to really know because I've only talked with him once. I did notice Brent seemed upset with Halliday last night at the fish fry."

"Maybe Bill isn't interested in Brent for a client."

"That's possible," Mary said with a sigh. "I need to find out more about him."

"Anything new on Mr. Rigsby?"

"Bea has spent time with Charles, but I haven't had a chance to talk to her privately."

Henry glanced at his watch. "I'd better get back and get the boat stocked and ready for this afternoon. I had a last-minute charter booking, so I'll have to meet you out in front of the stadium at seven. Will that be okay?"

"No problem at all," Mary said with a smile, looking forward to spending time with her friend.

Henry reached into his pocket. "I'm going to leave these with you, in case I get delayed. And if you think of someone else who'd like to go, bring 'em along. The more the merrier." He passed over an envelope. He gave her a warm smile and headed for the door. "See you tonight."

"Thanks, Henry. Looking forward to it," Mary called after him and tried to think of a baseball fan who wasn't already going. Maybe her nephew, Evan?

She was tucking the envelope in her purse when the door opened and a middle-aged couple entered. They both sported dark hair with silver streaks and were dressed similarly in brightly patterned tropical shirts and brown shorts.

"What a cute shop!" the woman said and headed for the children's section. "Oh, look, James. Nancy Drew. I loved Nancy Drew. I wonder if Sofia would like it."

"She's only three, dear," James said and wandered over to the series section.

"I know, but it won't be long until she can read." She looked over at Mary. "Sofia's my granddaughter. She's very bright."

"I loved Nancy Drew. Still do," Mary said with a smile. "We have some books for younger children, if you're interested."

"She might like those better, Ellen." James pulled out one of Lee Child's novels and read the back cover.

Ellen reluctantly put the Nancy Drew back on the shelf and checked out the children's shelves. "Oh, this is cute." She picked up a book about a baby seagull looking for his mother. "The pictures remind me of Ivy Bay."

"That's one of the reasons I like that one too, plus the story has a great ending," Mary said. "There's also a book there about a sailboat and a little girl who explores the world." Mary pulled it off the shelf and handed it to her.

"Thank you. I'll look these over." The woman sat in Mary's grandmother's rocker.

"If you have any questions, just let me know." Mary stepped back. She glanced at James, who was still perusing detective novels, and went back to the counter.

Mary printed off the articles on Bill Halliday. She then searched Charles Rigsby. His Web site popped up, and Mary clicked through the merchandise. Having no experience with memorabilia, it was difficult to tell if the prices were fair or not. She put 1970 in the Web site search engine, and a bat came onto the screen. She thought that Charles had said he had a 1970 collection. Perhaps it wasn't for sale online.

She went back to the search page. Charles was mentioned in an article about a baseball convention, but just in general terms. How did one go about checking out the reputation of someone in Charles's profession?

Mary surfed a bit longer and found an article on profitable discoveries. There were several stories of great sports memorabilia finds, including one of an old Mickey Mantle jersey unearthed in a thrift shop in a small town in New Jersey. Charles Rigsby paid $50 for it and later auctioned it off for $25,000. He was quoted as saying he "got lucky."

There was no mention of the person he bought it from. Mary couldn't help thinking that although Charles was lucky, the person he bought it from wasn't.

Gus hopped down off the counter and stared at the front door with an intent gleam in his eyes. About thirty seconds later, Rebecca and Ashley strode in. Gus ran to Ashley. She wore pink overalls and a baseball cap, her expression glum. She scooped up Gus and buried her face in his fur.

"What's wrong?" Mary asked. "Didn't you have fun shopping?"

Ashley shook her head.

"Oh, yes she did, for the most part. She just doesn't want summer to end." Rebecca stowed her purse in the cubby behind the counter. "I keep telling her she has several more weeks."

"I thought you liked school," Mary said.

Ashley peeked over Gus's back. "I do, but I like being here all day more."

"Sweetie, you can come to the shop after school starts, like always. I'm counting on it," Mary said. "I'd miss you too much if you didn't."

"We'll make sure your dad brings you by after school when he can, okay?" Rebecca said.

Ashley nodded, gave Gus another squeeze, and set him down. She squared her little shoulders and marched to the children's nook. Ellen looked up from the book she was flipping through and smiled.

"That's a very good book," Ashley said. "The plot slows down in the middle just a little bit, but that's okay because it makes the ending really good."

Ellen blinked at the grown-up tone in the little girl's voice. "Thank you. I think I'm going to get it. It's for my granddaughter." She rose from the rocking chair. "James, we need to get going if we're going to meet the Littles for lunch. Did you find anything?"

"Yep." James held two of Lee Child's latest in the Jack Reacher series. One was open, and James continued reading as he came over to the counter.

Ellen grabbed the first book in the Nancy Drew series as she passed. "I'm still going to get this Nancy Drew. Even if Sofia is too young, I'll enjoy reading it again. I may be back to get a few more before we head back home."

"Where is home?" Mary rang up their purchases, including the one James continued to read, and Rebecca put the others in a brown paper bag with a Mary's Mystery Bookshop sticker in the center.

"Stoneham. It's a suburb of Boston," Ellen said, taking the bag.

"Oh, I know where that is. My daughter lives in Melrose, just a little ways from there. Nice area."

Ellen smiled. "It is, and it's close enough to the city to get in for special events like the symphony, and James likes getting to a game now and then."

"Are you big Red Sox fans?" Rebecca asked.

"Yep." James adjusted his reading glasses without looking up from his novel.

"He goes to the hockey games too," Ellen said. "And, by the way, we're going to a league game tonight with my daughter and granddaughter."

Mary handed Ellen a bookmark, wishing she could take her granddaughter to a game too. She glanced at Ashley and got an idea.

"I hope both you and your granddaughter enjoy the books and have a great time at the game tonight," Mary said.

"I'm sure we will." Ellen grinned. "Come on, James."

"Yep." James moved to the door. Mary admired the way he could read and still maneuver his way outside.

Ashley had set her backpack on the floor and replaced the books Ellen had been looking at before climbing into the rocker. Gus trotted over and rubbed up against Ashley's ankles.

Mary motioned for Rebecca to follow her to the back. "I didn't want to say anything in front of Ashley in case this wasn't okay with you, but I have an extra reserved seat to the game tonight and was wondering if Ashley would like to go."

"Are you kidding?" Rebecca grinned. "She'll be thrilled, and it's fine by me."

Mary felt giddy with excitement and started back to the front of the store. "I brought some of Susan's muffins. They're on the microwave. Help yourself."

Rebecca took a deep sniff. "That's what smells so good in here. Yum!"

Mary laughed. "That's what I said to Susan."

She approached Ashley, who was playing catch-the-paper-wad with Gus. "Ashley, would you like to go to the baseball game at the stadium tonight? It'd be with Henry, Betty, and me."

"Yes!" Ashley's blue eyes grew large. "Can I, Mommy?"

"As long as you remember to behave and mind your manners." Rebecca winked at Mary from across the room.

"I will," Ashley said. "I promise."

Mary smothered a grin at Ashley's serious expression. Ashley was a delightful child and easy to be around. Mary adored her. "I'm so glad you're coming. It's going to be fun!"

"I can't wait!" Ashley said with a clap of her hands that distracted Gus from his stalking.

"Mary, I think your cell phone beeped," Rebecca called. Mary hurried to the cubby and dug her phone out of her purse. She had a new text message from Stephanie: "The police officer is here."

SEVEN

The young Deputy Wadell, with his crew cut and crisply pressed dark uniform, stood in front of the display. Mrs. Leary stood off to the side, her arms crossed over her white blouse. Disapproval pressed her lips together in a thin line.

"He's been here about ten minutes," Stephanie whispered as Mary passed her desk.

"Deputy Wadell," Mary said. "Nice to see you."

He turned. "You too, Mary. I'm here to get your statement." He gestured with his pen. "Is this the baseball in question?"

"Yes, but I'm almost positive that's not the original."

"Uh-huh." The deputy made a note. "Has anything else been taken?"

"We don't know yet," Mrs. Leary said. "Stephanie is going to call people in to check their belongings."

He scribbled another note in his small notebook. "Anything look unusual to you?"

Mary surveyed the tables crammed with artifacts. "I can't tell."

"Everything looks the same to me," Stephanie offered from her desk.

Mrs. Leary didn't comment.

The officer flipped to a fresh page. "Okay...start at the beginning, and tell me what you do know."

Mary relayed the events from when she found the smudge missing to discovering the ball was worth much more than she imagined. "I had no idea the ball was worth that much."

"Someone else evidently did." He stepped back and surveyed the scene. "It's not likely anyone could just walk by and grab anything, seeing as they'd have to duck under the ropes first."

"I had them cordon off the area just for that purpose," Mrs. Leary said. "No one should have been back there unless they were working on the display. Stephanie is always out here when the hall is open."

"Most of the time." Stephanie's color deepened. "Sometimes I've had to go to the back for a few minutes."

Mrs. Leary's lips thinned even more as the officer turned to her. "Are the doors and windows secured at night?"

"Of course."

"I need to check them," the deputy said.

"As you wish," Mrs. Leary added with a slight huff. "This way." Deputy Wadell followed her down the hall to the ground-floor offices.

Mary heard Mrs. Leary saying, "I do hope that this matter is handled discreetly. I don't want to wake up tomorrow and open the newspaper to find our office blamed for theft."

"She's not happy, and she's going to take it out on me," Stephanie said with a shiver. She slumped back in her desk chair.

Mary patted her on the arm. "I hope not. This isn't your fault." At least she hoped not. Stephanie had more private access to the display than anyone, but with her aversion toward sports, Mary doubted she had anything to do with the theft.

Mary looked back over the table. Officer Wadell had brought up a concern. How would they be able to tell if some item was missing from the hundreds of items on the table? They needed some sort of visual record. She still had her camera in her purse from Allison's baseball game. She pulled it out and took shots up and down the tables. Of course, that wouldn't show if any of the other valuables had been swapped for fakes.

"Good idea," Stephanie said.

Mrs. Leary marched back down the hall, her chin lifted. "That was a waste of time."

"Security is never a waste of time, ma'am," Officer Wadell said.

"Of course not!" Mrs. Leary said. "But I told you that the hall was secure. None of the windows have been opened. They're painted shut, and the rear door has a dead bolt."

"What about the construction crew outside?" Officer Wadell asked.

"The foreman has a key, of course."

"I'll need to speak with him." He strode to the door, and Mrs. Leary had to hurry to catch up with him. After a moment, Mary followed, her curiosity getting the best of her.

Mrs. Leary cast her a withering look, but the police officer didn't seem to mind that she tagged along. They rounded the corner of the majestic building. The screeching sound of saws and hammering filled the air. Mary's nose tickled from the smell of sawdust. Mrs. Leary pointed to a short, dark-skinned man wearing a yellow hard hat.

"Max," Mrs. Leary shouted over the noise. He looked her way and gestured for them to follow him inside the maintenance shed. As Mary approached the doorway, she noticed a silver object just under the eaves. A security camera.

The noise lessened inside the temporary metal shed. Mrs. Leary introduced Max Lopez, and Officer Wadell asked him about keys to the building.

"No, no, the key to the building is either in my pocket or locked in the desk drawer. My boss, Mr. Baxter, is strict on security. I will get fired if I give that key to anyone but my employees."

"I noticed a security camera when I was coming in," Mary said. "Do you always use those?"

"We put those cameras up on projects when we have to leave equipment outside."

"Do you have any that face the building?" Officer Wadell voiced Mary's question.

Max shook his head. "Not this time."

The officer asked a few more questions, but Max hadn't noticed anything unusual or anyone suspicious hanging around.

When they returned to the assembly room, Officer Wadell took another look around. He agreed that Mary should leave the baseball in place so as not to tip off the culprit, assuming he or she was still around.

Mrs. Leary again asked for discretion. "We don't want to discourage people from visiting the display and supporting a worthy cause."

After Officer Wadell said he'd be in touch, and departed, Mrs. Leary suggested, "How about we pull the ropes out farther away from the tables. People will not be able to see as well, but we don't want someone with long arms to snag anything."

"Good idea." Mary helped them reset the partition, and Mrs. Leary went back to her office.

"Call me if anything new happens, okay?" Mary said to Stephanie. "I'm heading over to see Bea."

Stephanie straightened a stack of paper on her desk. "Good luck on catching her. When she called earlier, she mentioned she's leaving work early today. Taking some personal time."

"Is she still in town?" Mary asked, dismayed. She really needed to talk over what was happening with her friend.

"I think so."

Mary thanked Stephanie and headed out, turning down Meeting House Road. Stephanie was correct. Bea had departed early. Another woman was behind the counter at the county clerk's office.

Mary sighed. She'd just have to try to reach Bea later. She glanced at her watch. She'd make a quick stop at the library before she went back to the shop. She wanted to arm herself with as much information as she could get on baseball and memorabilia. As she continued on Meeting House Road, she glanced across the street at Cape Cod Togs, an upscale clothing store, and noticed through the window that Brent stood in front of the counter. He appeared to be paying for a large stack of clothing. That was interesting because he was broke enough yesterday to borrow twenty dollars from his mother.

Puzzled, Mary wasn't sure what she'd say to Brent if she were to approach him, so she kept walking toward the library, which was housed in a redbrick building with white doors and windows on the corner of Meeting House Road and Liberty Road. Mary liked the spacious impression promoted by the skylights in the high, vaulted ceiling. She passed the tables and chairs arranged in cozy nooks and made her way to the computerized catalog. She found three books on baseball history and a book on sports memorabilia, which was outdated and only had a limited section on baseball.

She headed toward the checkout, and as she passed the microfiche machine, she noticed the man with a Red Sox cap and Western shirt sitting in front of the screen. Bill Halliday.

She paused and looked over his shoulder. He was rapidly scrolling through old copies of the *Ivy Bay Bugle*, pausing every twenty pages or so. He paused again, leaning forward in his chair.

"Hi, Bill," Mary said with a smile.

"Well, hello, Mary. Did you come to tell me you changed your mind about selling your baseball?" He looked up at her with a shrewd grin.

"'Fraid not."

"Too bad." He glanced at the books in her hands. "Doing a little reading on baseball?"

She hitched the books higher in her arms. "Yes, I figured it might be smart if I brushed up on it because I'm involved with the display."

"Makes sense to me."

His gaze narrowed in on the memorabilia book, but before he could say anything else, a female voice said, "Mr. Halliday. I've been looking all over for you. You weren't answering your phone."

As Bill turned in his seat to talk to the young woman in a league polo shirt, Mary glanced at the screen again. The page he'd stopped on was the obituary section.

"Well, Tina, I wasn't answering because I didn't want to be disturbed."

The girl seemed undeterred. "Jeff Johnson is looking for you."

Mary gave him a wave as Bill and Tina continued to talk and checked out her books. After Tina had left, Bill was busy turning the nob on the microfiche machine again.

She left the building and headed down the street at a brisk pace. All the way back to the shop, she pondered possible reasons Bill Halliday was searching old obituaries and Brent Bailey was shopping at Cape Cod Togs.

EIGHT

◆◆◆

"Strike three!" the umpire called at the bottom of the sixth inning. The Blue Jays led the Mariners 3–2.

Ashley jumped up and down, clapping her hands. The usually reserved child who conducted herself like a young lady in the bookshop was brimming over with exuberance here, along with the rest of the fans.

She didn't seem to mind hanging out with older people, and Mary was delighted that Ashley was having a great time. Watching the game through Ashley's eyes brought back memories of her own childhood. She caught Betty's eye. Her sister smiled, obviously remembering the same good times.

"Popcorn!" a college-aged girl called, carrying a box strapped to her shoulders.

"Would you like some popcorn, Ashley?" Henry asked. He'd met them outside the gate and now sat on the other side of Ashley. He was great with kids and kept her giggling.

Ashley wiggled in her seat. "Yes, please."

Henry raised his hand, and the popcorn lady traded a red-striped bag for three dollars.

Mary had cleared it with Rebecca that they could buy Ashley treats, and Ashley had already eaten a hot dog and a bag of peanuts, and drunk a lemonade.

"The popcorn is really salty." Ashley sucked up the last of her lemonade.

"I have some water," Betty said, pulling a bag up on her lap.

Mary took a closer look at the woven straw bag with pretty daisies. "What a cute bag. I don't think I've ever seen it before."

Betty handed Ashley the water bottle. "I just got it this afternoon at a yard sale Bea was having. It's been going on for a couple of days."

"How fun!" Mary said, knowing how Betty liked to shop for bargains. "Did she say why she was having a sale?"

"No, but she had a lot of nice things. I saw a deck chair I might go back for. You ought to drop by. Her neighbor's been helping and Bea's going to keep the sale going over the weekend, to, as she put it, 'Get rid of most of this junk.'"

No wonder Bea seemed hard to get hold of if she had all that going on. Stephanie had mentioned Bea also had a buyer for her car.

The Blue Jays were up to bat again. The crowd roared. Brent's hit flew into the outfield, and he charged all the way to third base.

The prized seats placed them on the third-base line, and Mary could see Brent's intense expression of concentration as he inched off the bag.

The pitcher flung a ball at the third baseman, but Brent dove back, narrowly missing the baseman's glove.

"That was close," Henry said. "Whew!"

"Whew," Ashley echoed.

The pitcher threw a curveball, but the batter made a solid hit, and Brent raced home.

Mary shifted her attention to the fans sitting near the Blue Jays team. Joe Bailey held a video camera, taping his brother. The Bailey girls were paying more attention to Tyler Matthews in the dugout. They giggled frequently. Jamie kept flipping her auburn hair over her shoulder and leaning over to look at Tyler. The young man ignored them for the most part and concentrated on the game.

Mary leafed through the program and found the Blue Jays' biographies. The paragraph under Brent's name mentioned his pitching success in high-school baseball, his college scholarship, and the stats he accrued. As his mother had mentioned, he'd had a promising beginning. Hopefully, he'd get another career opportunity.

She found Tyler's bio. Raised in Boston, he'd gone to Westbow private school, where he made his mark on the baseball team. He then attended Douglas University, where he was first-string third baseman. He was majoring in business and going to be a senior the coming year.

Mary's gaze wandered over the rest of the crowd. There were a lot of Ivy Bay residents there she recognized, although she didn't know all of them by name yet. Bill Halliday sat behind the umpire by home plate. He had a notebook open on his lap and occasionally made notes. Mary again wondered what he'd been doing in the library searching obituaries. Did he have a connection to someone in Ivy Bay?

The Blue Jays' catcher flied out, and Brent was back on the pitcher's mound. He did well, striking out the first two batters on six straight fastballs. The Mariners' star player came up to the plate and drove the next pitch straight toward them. Tyler made an incredible diving catch for the third out. The crowd went wild, and the rest of the game progressed quickly with victory for Ivy Bay's Blue Jays.

"Is it over already?" Ashley asked.

"Already? It's almost ten," Betty said with a smile. "You must have had fun if you don't want to go home yet."

Ashley nodded. "Thank you for bringing me," she said to Mary and then looked up at Henry. "Thank you for letting me have one of your special seats."

"You're welcome. It's fun being with such an enthusiastic fan," Henry said with a wink at Mary. Mary smiled. Ashley seemed to enjoy the variety of food more than the game, just like Mary had when she was a kid. It made for a total experience.

"We don't have to go just yet. We can go down and congratulate the players," Mary suggested as she watched Bill Halliday talking to Tyler and the Bailey girls. Mary wondered what they were discussing.

"Awesome." Ashley led the way to the playing field.

A crowd had grown around Brent. Henry and Ashley were in the mix, waiting their turn to talk to him. They joined the line of youngsters holding programs for players to autograph. Brent's family lingered on the outskirts of the small crowd.

"One more winning game and we're in the play-offs," Brent was saying. He pounded a hand on Tyler's shoulder. "And we're going to do it!"

Tess caught Mary's eye. She beamed the proud smile of a supportive mother and stepped toward them.

"I can remember when he was just a little guy starting Little League," Betty said to Tess. "He has turned out to be quite the accomplished pitcher."

"He has," Tess said. "I'm so relieved. You never know what's going to happen, especially in sports. I sit through these games on the edge of my seat. Brent wants to play pro ball so badly, and I thank God he has another shot at it." Tears glistened in her eyes.

Mary patted Tess on the arm. "Well, Brent certainly looks happy tonight."

Tess looked over at her son. "He does." Bill Halliday shook Brent's hand and said something to Tyler and Brent that made them grin.

Tess leaned close to Mary and Betty and lowered her voice. "That's a sports agent talking to Brent, and from what I've picked up from the conversation, he seems to be very interested."

"That's wonderful, Tess," Betty said. "I'm happy for him."

Whatever argument Brent and Bill had been having at the fish fry must've blown over, Mary mused. She was glad Tess seemed so happy about Halliday, especially after sharing her worries over Brent's future, but Mary couldn't help but feel a twinge of worry. How honest was this man?

Tyler had moved off to the side, watching Brent and Bill Halliday talk. He caught Mary's gaze, smiled, and waved. Mary waved back.

Paige Bailey tugged on Tyler's sleeve and said something to him, motioning toward the parking lot where the crowd had started to drift.

"The girls sure like Tyler," Tess said, keeping an eye on her daughters. "He's been staying with Brent and us the last few days, and I have to make sure the girls don't overwhelm him with attention."

"He seems like a nice young man," Mary prompted, hoping that Tess would provide more information about him.

"He is. I don't mind him staying with us at all. And unless the girls are talking to him, he's so quiet I hardly know he's in the house. Unlike my two." She grinned. "The place nearly rocks on its foundation with them being home." Tess glanced over at Brent. "Stop by the shop if you'd like some ice cream. We've invited the players over." She slipped into the crowd.

"Look what I have," Ashley said as she returned with Henry. She held out a season program booklet with signatures on it. "I got autographs."

Betty nudged Mary. "Just like we did that one summer. Didn't we have a contest to see who got the most autographs?"

Henry winked at Mary, and she smiled. "Yep. I think you got the most autographs," Mary said. "I was wondering what happened to those autograph books."

"I think they were with Gram's things. They must be in the attic. We'll have to see if we can find them one of these days."

"It'd be fun to see those books again." Mary looked at Ashley. Her eyelids drooped. "It's getting late. We should start home."

"Okay," Ashley said with a sigh.

As they made their way to the exit, Tyler was already in the parking lot by a black BMW, leaning over and rubbing his leg, no doubt from the fantastic catch he'd made.

Brent passed them, carrying a blue-and-white duffel bag, and as he swung the long strap onto his shoulder, several things fell to the ground. Ashley picked up socks, a jersey, a candy bar, and a small bottle of glove oil and handed them to Mary.

Brent gave a wave to Tyler and climbed into a fancy red convertible. A pretty young woman with a blonde ponytail sat in the driver's seat.

"Brent, you dropped something," Mary called, but she was drowned out by the car's engine as it roared out of the parking lot.

"Here, I'll take it to him." Tyler unzipped his duffel bag and groaned. "He did it again. Grabbed my bag by mistake, and my wallet was in there!"

Ashley picked that moment to ask. "You played third base, right?"

"Yep," Tyler said, irritation still in his tone as he stuffed his belongings into the bag.

"Can I have your autograph?" She held up the season program and a pen that Henry had supplied and looked up at him with her big blue eyes.

Tyler's scowl lightened to a small smile. "Well...sure." He signed his name with a flourish. "Here you go, kid."

"Thank you." Ashley clutched the program to her chest.

"You're welcome." He caught Mary's eye, and she gave him a grateful smile.

They continued on to Betty's car. Henry's antique blue convertible was parked over in the next row.

Betty turned to Henry. "Thank you for a lovely evening."

"I'm the one who is grateful, spending the evening with such pretty ladies, especially this one." He playfully tugged the brim of Ashley's cap down over her forehead.

She pushed the cap back and grinned. "It was fun."

After they dropped a sleepy Ashley off with her parents, Betty turned her car onto Main Street. It was a pleasant evening, and many people strolled leisurely along. A line snaked out of Bailey's Ice Cream Shop, no doubt open late to accommodate the many baseball fans in town for the Saturday night game. Bea Winslow stood near the doorway, dwarfed between two robust men.

"Oh, there's Bea. I need to talk to her," Mary said.

Betty pulled over to the sidewalk. "Do you want me to wait?"

Mary opened her door. "I'll walk home, unless you want to get some ice cream or something."

Betty's expression brightened at the mention of ice cream. "That sounds really good, but I'm too tired to stand in that line."

"I'll see you in a little while," Mary said and closed the door.

Mary walked toward the ice-cream shop, but Bea wasn't in sight. Deciding Bea must already be inside, she joined the line. They inched forward, and as Mary stepped inside the door, she spied Bea. She was sitting at a table with a man, a cup of coffee in front of her. She laughed and placed her hand on the man's arm.

His face turned toward Mary, and she nearly gasped.

Charles Rigsby.

NINE

❖◆◆❖

Bea leaned back in her chair inside Bailey's Ice Cream Shop, a smile on her animated face. Charles threw back his head and laughed. They enjoyed each other's company as if they were old friends.

Bea and Charles? Mary didn't want to intrude. Besides, she wanted to ask Bea what she knew about Mr. Rigsby. That wasn't something she could do in front of him.

Obviously, Bea knew him a lot better than she'd let on when she'd first mentioned Charles was going to donate some memorabilia. Not that it was any of Mary's business, but what was going on?

Mary backed toward the door and was almost outside when Bea called, "Mary! Over here." She waved.

Mary waved back. She couldn't leave now without saying hello. She squeezed her way through the boisterous crowd over to their table.

Charles, in a dress shirt and striped suit pants, stood as she approached them. "Hi, Mary. Care to join us?"

"Please do." Bea gestured to the chair beside her. "It's been such a busy week. We really haven't had a chance to chat."

"Yeah, I'm sorry we keep missing each other." Mary sat on the chair Charles pulled out for her.

Bea glanced around at the energized crowd. "Everyone is so excited about the game." Bea had to raise her voice over the rising din. "I wish I could've been there."

"I wish you could've gone too," Mary said, also raising her voice.

"Next time," Bea said. "I'm hoping to drag Stephanie. She needs to try going to a game at least once."

"It was pretty exciting." Mary gave them some of the game highlights before the talk turned to the baseball display.

"We've raised over $1,300 in donations from those who've come to see the display. A huge thanks to generous people who donated their memorabilia," Bea said, her eyes sparkling as she looked at Charles.

Mary wanted to discuss her missing baseball and the police visit, but not in front of Charles. And it didn't look like he was going to leave anytime soon.

"I had a question about the value of memorabilia, and, Mr. Rigsby, you're the right person to ask with all your experience. Suppose something is flawed or damaged by a player. Would that increase the value?" Mary asked, watching Charles carefully.

"Depends on what it is." Charles set his ice-cream spoon down on a napkin. "If it makes the object really unattractive, then probably not. But then in other cases, like with my Dom DiMaggio cap that's on display, the value is increased by the fact that cap and the others that season were damaged at the factory. The stitching was off slightly, which caused the emblems to unravel. They only wore them for half a season before they had them replaced. That unique quality triples the value of the cap."

"Fascinating!" Bea said. "Too bad that principle doesn't apply to some of the junk in my garage."

A *whoop* went up from the crowd in the corner with Brent Bailey. The noise increase made talking difficult.

Charles leaned forward and asked Mary, "Did I answer your question adequately?"

Mary nodded, although there were still many questions she longed to ask but couldn't. Not until she was sure that Charles Rigsby hadn't stolen John's baseball.

Mary brushed a couple of bread crumbs off her navy-and-white striped shirt as she trotted up the steps to the town hall Monday afternoon. She'd barely had time to eat a sandwich for lunch. The morning had been busy with plenty of customers. Rebecca and Mary were kept hopping, and Ashley had enthusiastically pitched in by bagging up books and answering questions. Luckily, it had slowed down over lunch so Mary could slip out. Mary's appointment with Susan at the bakery was in half an hour.

Mary had planned to visit Bea first, but the door to the county clerk's office had been locked with a note they'd be reopening at two thirty.

Mary had hoped to catch up with Bea yesterday after church, but she and Betty had been surprised by an unexpected blessing. Her son Evan and Mindy needed to go visit a sick friend in Boston and asked if they could drop

Allison and Betsy off with their grandmother for the day. Betty had been thrilled to spend time with her granddaughters and she and Mary had spent the day driving down the coast and going beachcombing. Mary had a wonderful time and then had gone to bed early, exhausted from keeping up with the youngsters all day, but when she woke early Monday morning, her feeling of urgency to find John's baseball hadn't waned.

Mary walked into the assembly room, hoping to find Bea, but only Stephanie sat behind her desk.

"Afternoon," she said in a groggy voice. She'd pulled her hair up in a messy knot and a spot of mascara was smudged slightly under one sleepy eye. "I finished calling everyone and asked them to come in and inspect their items. One man got really grumpy and said he was just taking his stuff home."

"Well, I suppose that is to be expected," Mary said with a sigh. "We'll need to send him a nice thank-you note for the time he did give us."

Her footsteps echoed as she walked over to the display and scanned the tables. Everything seemed in its place except . . . what was that? She leaned forward trying to get a better view. Something white was poking out from behind a framed photo.

She ducked under the rope and had to stretch to reach the object. She pulled out a piece of waxy white paper with swirling red and white stripes. A logo of a bulldog wearing a baker's hat was printed in the corner, but the name of the business appeared to be ripped off. A sticky residue that looked like frosting came off on her fingers.

Stephanie had walked up behind Mary. "What's that?"

Mary held out the paper for Stephanie to see. "Appears to be a wrapper from a bakery or doughnut shop. It's still sticky. It was at the back of the display."

"That's just rude! People aren't supposed to eat in here, and now they are throwing trash. Mrs. Leary will have a fit."

Mary carried the paper over to Stephanie's desk and tossed it in her waste can.

"I—" Stephanie yawned and covered her mouth with her hand. "Oh, sorry. I didn't get much sleep."

Mary fought off a yawn of her own. After she'd gotten home last night, she'd done more online research, jotting down phone numbers of shops that sold sports memorabilia in Cape Cod and all the way to Boston. She'd also printed out the photos she'd taken of the display before fatigue overtook her.

"Late night?" Mary asked.

"Movie. Brent asked me out but…" She shrugged. "I don't want to date a guy with sports on the brain 24–7. There's more to life, you know?"

Mary nodded. Better if Stephanie stayed away from Brent until they were sure he didn't steal John's ball. "Has Bea come by?"

"Oh, sure. She got here before me. She was in a big rush as usual. In and out. Took the donation money to the bank."

"Thanks, Stephanie. I'd better go. Call if there are any problems."

Mary stepped outside. Thick clouds rolled away toward the eastern horizon, reducing the chance of rain forecasted for later in the afternoon. Ashley would be happy. She had been very vocal about hoping the weather lady was wrong because she and her father were going to play catch after he got home from work.

As Mary reached the sidewalk, Brent, Tyler, and Mr. Halliday rounded the corner at the intersection. They walked close together in animated discussion. Brent wore an attractive burgundy sweater, one they sold at the Cape Cod Togs. Tyler, as usual, managed to look both preppy and athletic in a polo shirt and team jacket. Halliday wore his uniform of aged jeans, Western shirt, boots, and Sox cap.

"Yo, dudes! Tyler! Brent!" A young construction worker with longish blond hair and muscles that stretched his tight T-shirt set down a board and ambled over.

Tyler stopped, but Brent merely gave a wave and kept walking with Halliday toward the town hall steps.

"Jace. Long time, no see," Tyler said with a wide smile.

Jace took off his helmet. "Heard you were playing ball again."

"Yep. Third base. If you get out to the stadium, I'll save you a seat near the dugout."

"Awesome!"

"Hey, Mrs. Fisher," Brent said, and Halliday gave her a nod of greeting as they passed her and turned up the steps.

"Gotta go," Tyler told Jace. He shot Mary a smile as he rushed to catch up with his companions.

Mary wanted to follow them inside to see what they were up to, but she was already late. She didn't want to keep Susan waiting. She picked up her pace and was slightly puffing when she reached Sweet Susan's Bakery and opened the door.

A teenager with carefully spiked hair, eyes lined with smoky liner, and fingernails painted green to match her poison-green blouse stood behind the counter. Multicolored bracelets jangled on both wrists as she counted out buns into paper bags.

"Mary, come on back here," Susan called from the doorway to the back of the shop. "Jasmine, if you need help, let me know."

Mary said hello to Jasmine and slipped behind the counter. Susan handed Mary a full-body apron and hairnet. She tied on the apron and tugged the hairnet over her head before stepping back into the bakery. On a stainless-steel table in the middle of the room was a large rolling pin, two baker's boards, and stainless-steel canisters.

"Welcome to Pie Baking 101," Susan said with a grin. "I think this is going to be a blast. You can wash your hands back here." Susan led the way to a sink. "Then we can dive in."

After Mary scrubbed and then dried her hands, she joined Susan by the table.

Susan set two mixing bowls in front of Mary. "I'm going to teach you as if this is your first time baking a pie, but if you feel like I'm making it too simple, just say so."

Mary smiled. "I don't mind starting from scratch."

"So tell me what was wrong with the pie you made at home."

"The apples were runny, and the crust was kind of gooey on the bottom. The crust looked uneven and not quite put together," Mary said. "But it still tasted good."

Susan chuckled. "Taste is what really matters, but we can easily fix the other problems. I thought we would try making apple pies side by side and see if we can pinpoint where things went wrong."

"Sounds like a great plan to me."

"Let's start with the crust. You said your crust was a little tough?"

Mary nodded. "A bit chewy and not flaky."

"That comes from overworking the dough. You want to handle it as little as possible." She demonstrated how to mix the flour and ice water, and sprinkle butter cubes over the flour mixture.

Susan grinned at Mary. "I hope you don't mind using your fingers to work the dough."

"Not at all." Mary dropped her butter cubes into her bowl and followed Susan's example of rubbing her thumb against her fingertips to make the flour mixture resemble cornmeal. The mixture felt cold under Mary's fingers and reminded her of when Betty and she would make drip sand castles on the beach. They mixed sand in a water bucket with their hands until it was really smooth and goopy and then dripped the wet mixture off their fingers onto hot dry sand.

Susan sprinkled out flour on two large bread boards, and they dropped their dough on them. "Just knead three times or until it's cohesive." Susan flipped the dough over and pushed it down. "We don't want to overmix."

"Just three times?" Mary asked with a little laugh. "Well, that explains why mine didn't turn out well. I must've mushed it at least twenty times." Mary laughed again.

Susan chuckled. "Lots of people make that mistake. Now, what kind of apples did you use?"

"I think they were Red Delicious. That's all we had in the house."

"Red Delicious make great eating apples, but for pies, texture is important. We want apples that will retain their shape during baking and not be too sweet since we need to add sugar for a thickening agent. I have Granny Smith and Braeburn, which we will mix together to get a nice flavor and texture."

After Susan got a bowl of apples out of the refrigerator and handed Mary a peeler, the door swung open and Jasmine poked her head into the kitchen. "Susan, there's a customer asking about ordering lots of cupcakes for tomorrow."

Susan wiped her hands on a towel. "I'll be right back. Keep peeling."

As Mary worked diligently on the apples, she thought how fascinating it was to be in a professional bakery. The entwined smells of spices, vanilla, chocolate, yeast-baked breads, and pastries were intoxicating. It reminded her of a mystery from Joanne Fluke's Hannah Swensen Mysteries, which were titled after baked goodies. The novels featured recipes in each book. Her gaze shifted to a pan of cupcakes on the counter waiting to be frosted. Susan's specialty was her cupcakes, which gave Mary an even better idea for a thank-you gift for Susan.

By the time Susan returned, Mary had finished slicing the apples. They sprinkled the apples with sugar, nutmeg, and cinnamon, and then Susan taught Mary how to roll the dough and explained that adding sugar and flour to the bottom of the pie would help prevent sogginess.

They rolled out the top crusts, trimmed the excess, and crimped it with the bottom dough. Susan said, "Cut some slits for the steam to escape in the top crust, and voilà, you have a pie."

"Voilà!" Mary echoed and stepped back, pleased with the results. "Not as good as yours, but I like it."

Susan beat an egg, and they each brushed it over the top crust and then sprinkled it with sugar. They put the pies on baking sheets and slid them into the hot oven.

Susan brushed back curly tendrils of hair that had escaped her baker's hat. She opened the refrigerator. "I feel like some iced tea. How about you?"

"Sounds perfect." Mary wiped her brow.

Susan poured the tea into two paper cups. "Want to sit?" She gestured to her desk in the small office.

Mary sat on one of the metal chairs, and Susan took the other. She pulled out an order book from under the pile of recipe sheets on the desk. "I need to make three dozen cupcakes by lunch tomorrow. The development committee is meeting."

The development committee reviewed any growth expansions to the community and protected the historic aspects of their little community, for which Mary was grateful. She loved the fact that parts of Ivy Bay were beautifully preserved and looked the same as when she came here as a child.

"Am I in the way?" Mary asked. "I can leave and come back."

Susan looked up. "Oh no, you're fine. I won't do these until tomorrow morning. I just wish they wouldn't contact me so last-minute, but of course, this isn't their usual time to meet."

"Must be something important going on."

"I heard a rumor that someone proposed another condo development south of town along Mason's Creek."

"I thought they couldn't build there because of the natural watershed." Mary recalled an *Ivy Bay Bugle* newspaper article on the subject. "At least that halted the last proposal."

"Maybe they worked out the kinks or have new data to share," Susan said with a shrug.

"Susan?" Jasmine called from the storefront. "Mrs. Greene is here."

"Excuse me." Susan rose. "This may take several minutes. She entertains a lot, and her orders are usually complicated. Can you turn the oven down fifty degrees in five minutes?" She crossed the kitchen.

"Sure. Do you mind if I make some phone calls?" Mary held up her cell phone.

"No problem. Go right ahead." Susan pushed open the door. "Well, hello, Mrs. Greene! What can I do for you?"

Mary thought about the demographic data Bill Halliday had collected from Stephanie Doyle. Could he be involved in the new development? Why would a sports agent settle here? All the action was in Boston. But if he was planning to move here, that would mean her suspicion that he was using Stephanie to gain access to the artifacts would be ungrounded and she could check him off her suspect list.

The panicky sense of time and her chance of recovering John's ball slipping rapidly away tightened her stomach. Mary pulled out the sheet of phone numbers she'd copied from the Internet the previous night and dialed the first memorabilia store on the list: Bob's Sports. A man answered, and Mary asked if they had a Red Sox ball from 1970.

"Nope. But I have a nice Red Sox '79 ball, or how about a World Series '04?"

"Those sound nice, but I'm really looking for that 1970 ball. It's important. Could you call if one comes in?"

"Yeah, yeah, lady. Give me your number." He jotted down her name and cell number and then asked, "Anything else you're looking for?"

"That's all. Thanks." Mary popped up and turned the oven down.

She returned to the chair and looked at the next number on her list. Cold-calling was probably a long shot, but at least she felt better doing something to find John's ball.

As she punched in the next store number, Luke 11:9 flowed through her mind: *Ask and it will be given to you; seek and you will find; knock and the door will be opened to you.*

And she'd keep knocking on heaven's door until the mystery of John's ball was solved.

"Pie!" Ashley exclaimed as Mary walked into her bookshop, holding the glass pie plate with a towel. The golden-brown pie was a vast improvement on her previous effort, although not quite as nice as Susan's. Thrilled with the results, Mary's hope was renewed that she'd be able to create something special for Betty's birthday.

"Did you make that?" the little girl asked.

"I did." Mary smiled. "Miss Susan helped me. I know it's getting close to supper, but would anyone like a taste?"

"I would!" Ashley said, setting down the book she was reading. "Can I, Mom?"

"We both can," Rebecca said with a laugh as she ran the dust mop over the floor.

Mary carried the pie to the back room and cut slices. The juices ran, but the sauce would thicken as the filling cooled.

She put the slices on paper plates and added forks. "Careful, it may still be a little hot." She set the plates on the counter.

Ashley climbed on the stool and took a big bite. "This is awesome."

"It's very good," Rebecca added as Mary took an experimental taste. The apples were still slightly firm with a pleasant flavor, and the bottom crust wasn't soggy like her first attempt.

When they'd all finished, Mary asked, "Do you want to take the rest home with you?"

"Oh, we couldn't do that," Rebecca protested. "Not after all your hard work."

"You'd be doing me a favor. I can't take it with me. I'm making a pie for Betty's birthday, and it's a secret. This pie was just practice. It'll go to waste if no one eats it."

"We don't want to waste food, Mommy," Ashley said firmly.

"When you put it that way, we'd be happy to help out," Rebecca said with a big grin. "Russell loves pie, especially with ice cream."

Ashley nodded. "Daddy can eat a whole pie just himself."

"Yeah, well, he shouldn't do that, but he can. He has," Rebecca said with a slight blush, "which is why we don't keep it around the house much. This will be a treat."

Mary smiled and handed the pie to Rebecca. "Enjoy."

Ashley skipped out after her mother, and Mary checked the lock on the back door and turned off the lights. "Gus?"

The cat came out from behind a bookshelf, rubbing his back along the wood. Mary opened the door to his carrier and set it on the ground. Gus poked his head in the doorway and twitched his tail before slinking the rest of the way in. Mary picked up the carrier and stepped outside into the balmy evening air.

Mary still hadn't been able to connect with Bea and wondered if there was still a chance to catch her at work, so instead of heading straight home, Mary hurried up Main Street and turned left on Meeting House Road. Even though Mary had left a few minutes before the usual closing of the clerk's office, the building was shut up tight again.

Mary sighed. She'd really prefer to talk to Bea in person about Charles so she could better discern Bea's reaction to her questions. If those two were indeed close friends, Mary wanted to tread softly about bringing up her suspicions about Charles.

Maybe Bea was still around the downtown area. Mary set Gus's carrier on the ground and called Bea's cell phone. When there was no answer, she left a message. She called Bea's home phone, and it just kept ringing. What was going on with her friend?

Betty had mentioned Bea was having a yard sale all week. Maybe she was outside and didn't hear her phone. Mary could just drive by and see if Bea was in her yard. She picked up the carrier and hurried home to get her car. She took Gus inside and then climbed into her silver Impala. She had time before supper for a quick visit and to see what else she could learn about Charles, assuming Bea was available.

She cruised back up Main Street and turned right on Meeting House Road, then continued past her church and Ivy Bay High School.

A homemade sign on the corner of a side street advertised a yard sale. Mary turned. Cars lined both sides of the narrow street, and Mary pulled in the first vacant spot under an old elm, one house down from Bea's.

The yard in front of Bea's cute blue shingled Cape Cod cottage was filled from one end to the other with boxes of books, kitchen appliances, shoes, blankets, and sheets. Several card tables held lamps and one, a television set. A rolled-up burgundy carpet leaned against a brown couch. Framed paintings of all sizes covered the couch.

Half a dozen people milled around the merchandise. Bea stood on her porch, chatting to Bernice Foster, a member of Mary's church. Bernice was holding a brass floor lamp and pointing at the tasseled shade.

Mary was opening her car door when an older-model black Cadillac rolled past her and swung into a spot in front of the house that had just been vacated. Charles Rigsby exited the driver's side and walked around the back of the car. He tucked a long brown box under his arm and waved at Bea.

Mary sank back down in her seat. Charles again. Mary couldn't very well talk about the baseball display and her suspicions with Bea if he was standing there. Bea greeted Charles with a bright smile as he handed her the long, narrow box.

Mary pulled out and did a three-point turn. As she headed home, she again wondered what kind of relationship Bea had with Charles. She was worried about her, especially if Charles turned out to be dishonest. Was she experiencing financial trouble and Charles was helping her in some way? Mary shook her head. She trusted Bea, but she had been acting somewhat odd lately.

Mary parked her car and went in the house. The pungent smell of garlic greeted her, and she followed the scent to the kitchen. Water boiled on the stove, and Betty chopped broccoli to add to a large green salad bowl on the counter. "There you are. I was wondering if you'd make it for supper. I noticed your car was gone when I got home."

"I drove over to Bea's house."

"Oh, is she still having her yard sale?" Betty glanced at her face. "Is something wrong?"

Mary shook off her unease. "I hope not. Bea had a lot of stuff out there. Is she planning on moving?"

"I haven't heard anything. Why didn't you ask her?"

"She looked busy."

"And?"

Mary smiled at Betty's gentle prodding. "It's just that the last two times I've tried to talk to her privately, Charles Rigsby has been there."

"Is he wearing a wedding ring?" Betty turned back to the stove.

"I didn't notice. Oh—" Mary said, catching on to what Betty meant. "I don't think so. Do you think he's interested in Bea?"

Betty gave a slight shrug. "These things happen."

Charles and Bea? Mary considered the idea of them dating. "I just got the sense that they are friends, but that's something to think about."

Mary hoped Bea wasn't going to get hurt if Charles Rigsby did turn out to be a thief or at least an unscrupulous businessman. She wondered what was in the package he'd brought her.

"I was in the mood for spaghetti tonight. I hope that's okay with you."

"More than okay. It smells delicious in here." Mary lifted the lid of a pot on the stove. Thick red sauce bubbled inside. "What can I do to help?"

"How about putting some ice in the glasses and get us whatever you want to drink. I thought we could eat on the deck since it's such a nice evening."

"Great idea." Mary filled the glasses with ice and added cranberry juice and soda. She took the sparkling drinks to the table on the deck. Betty had already set out eating utensils and cloth napkins. A vase of white daisies was set in the center. Betty came out carrying a basket of bread.

"Pretty flowers. This is so nice. Is this a special occasion?"

Betty smiled. "I just had a great day and felt like celebrating summer. You remember how Gram made spaghetti almost every Friday night that one summer?"

Mary smiled at the memory of Gram's table laden with good food and surrounded by people she loved. "Remember how Gramps would put so much garlic in the salad dressing it would take all weekend to wear off? But it was so good we didn't care."

"And seeing how we all smelled like garlic, we could stand to be with each other," Betty added with a chuckle. "But don't worry, I didn't put in *that* much garlic."

126 CRK SECRETS of MARY'S BOOKSHOP

They dished up the food in the kitchen and took their plates outside. Mary let Gus out with them and sat down with a sigh. This was really nice. The sea breeze, the setting sun, the delicious food, and being with her sister brought feelings of contentment and being home.

As they bowed their heads and Betty said a blessing, Mary silently sent up a prayer of thankfulness for being blessed to live this part of her life with family.

"Did you have a good day?" Betty stuck her fork into the crisp salad.

"It was really busy, but we made some great sales," Mary said, wishing she could share her adventure at Sweet Susan's with Betty, but that would have to wait until after her birthday surprise.

"That's good. Any news about John's baseball?"

"Nothing new. Chief McArthur hasn't called me back, which I don't take as a good sign," Mary said. "I have started to make some phone calls and leave my number with stores in case someone does try to sell it. It's a long shot, but you never know."

Betty gave her a sympathetic smile. "We can hope and pray."

Mary nodded, feeling blessed to have such a caring sister. She took a sip of her drink and decided to change the subject. "How was your lunch get-together?"

As Betty talked about her lunch with some church friends and later working on a volunteer project, Mary leaned back in her chair and felt herself relax. After dinner, they lingered on the deck, enjoying a slice of lemon cake and coffee.

"Guess what? Allison's team won today. They have a chance at the Little League play-offs," Betty said.

"How exciting!" Mary said, thinking about how thrilled Isabella would be too.

"Oh, and before I forget, Evan told me he got reserved seats for the Blue Jays on my birthday. It will be a play-off game, although we don't know who will be playing yet. He said he got one for everyone in the family. We're going out to dinner after the game, and then we'll come back here for birthday cake."

"Sounds fun. Maybe you and I can have lunch before the game? I'll make it." And she'd serve pie for dessert, she thought with a twinge of excitement. She couldn't wait to see Betty's face.

"I'm going to feel really spoiled."

"You deserve it," Mary said. "And because you made dinner, I insist on cleaning up. Come on, Gus, you can keep me company in the kitchen."

She gathered up the dishes and took them in. Betty was a neat cook, and the task of cleaning only took a short time. Betty came in and said she was heading to her room with a good book. Mary and Gus settled in the living room. She put the TV on low volume. A rerun of *Monk* was coming on later, and she was in the mood for a humorous mystery before she went to bed.

Meanwhile, she'd search for John's ball. Maybe whoever took it would offer it for sale online, especially if they thought they'd fooled everyone with the forged ball. She turned on her laptop and plugged in autographed baseballs into the search field. Dozens of Web links popped up, so she narrowed the search down to autographed Red Sox baseballs. She was again amazed at the wide range of asking prices. Jayne was right. The market for these balls had to be very subjective. Imagine paying hundreds of dollars for a little ball just because it was signed by a favorite player. She looked carefully at the team-signed balls on each site. She spotted a couple of balls with Sparky Lyle's signature on them, but there were no smudges under his name. She e-mailed several sites, telling them what she was looking for.

She tried searching for Bucky Swarnson, and one ball popped up. It was a single-signed ball from 1969, the year before Bucky had quit and joined the military. The owner was asking $1,000. That seemed to fall in line with what Rich had found. John's ball had been team-signed and used in Bucky's last game, which would account for its increased value.

She searched a bit more until a yawn overcame her. It had been a long day but a productive one. She'd search some more tomorrow. She turned off the TV, shut down her computer and put it back in its case. With Gus tucked under one arm, Mary climbed the stairs to her room and set him on the bed. Gus was already asleep by the time she snuggled under her grandmother's quilt. She read through her devotion for the evening. The lesson was on Psalm 23, a favorite of hers and John's. They'd hung a framed picture of a mountain range and the psalm in their Boston home.

Thank You, Lord, for Your promise that Your goodness and love will follow me all the days of my life.

She reached for her bag of books and flipped through the volumes of baseball history, pausing now and then to read when she saw an item similar to one from the display, like baseball jerseys. She picked up *Obscure Facts of New England Baseball* and turned to the Red Sox section. She learned that the Red Sox had won five World Series, but then after the sale of Babe Ruth to the rival Yankees, it took eighty-six years before the team won their sixth World Championship in 2004. Some called it the "Curse of the Bambino." That would explain why the Sox's 2004 memorabilia was valued so much more. Of course since this book had been printed, the Red Sox had won in 2007. John had been so excited about the championship.

She flipped over the page about uniforms, and on a sidebar was the story Mr. Rigsby had told her about Dom DiMaggio's cap. The Red Sox caps manufactured for the team for the 1952–53 season suffered a mistake in the manufacturing process and stitching around the emblem, causing the corners to pull loose and curl. The caps were replaced midseason.

Mary moved the book closer to her bedside lamp so she could see the cap in the photo. The emblem and color matched the cap in the case at the display, only this one wasn't signed.

She went back to reading, but her eyelids kept sliding shut, so she finally set the book aside and turned off the light. As she drifted off to sleep, images of baseball uniforms, balls, bats, and gloves swirled through her brain.

TEN

· ◆ ◆ ·

Russell loved your pie," Rebecca said after she arrived at the bookshop the next morning, carrying the empty pie plate. "He took the leftovers with him for lunch. He said he was going to share, but somehow I doubt that will actually happen."

"I'm glad he enjoyed it," Mary said with a smile, imagining the gruff fisherman out on the ocean eating her pie.

"He said to tell you that if you need someone to sample your baking attempts again, he'd be happy to volunteer."

"Me too," Ashley said. She wasn't wearing her baseball cap this morning, and her blonde hair was tied back in a cute ponytail. She hoisted her backpack up higher on her shoulders and headed for the children's section.

"I'll keep that in mind." Mary smiled. She was looking forward to another pie-making lesson that afternoon. She just hoped that when she struck out on her own, she'd make something as edible.

The morning passed quietly with only a few customers coming in. Mary worked on her inventory spreadsheet, put in a new order, and then checked in a shipment of hardcovers. Rebecca decided to reorganize a bookshelf, something Mary had suggested earlier. Gus supervised the growing stack of books on the floor, occasionally leaping on top of the stacks to get a better view.

At noon, Rebecca and Ashley headed home for lunch. Mary's stomach gurgled, reminding her of the spaghetti waiting for her in the refrigerator. Gus jumped up beside her on the counter and stared at her intently as if saying he was ready for lunch too.

The spaghetti container went into the microwave. She scooped kitty tuna into a small bowl and freshened Gus's water dish. She washed her hands, took the spaghetti from the microwave, and settled behind the counter by the computer with her lunch.

The spaghetti sauce had an even richer flavor than it had last night. She'd brought along a baguette instead of the leftover garlic bread to avoid the shop smelling like an Italian restaurant.

She opened *Obscure Facts of New England Baseball* again and continued her research on the history of baseball and learned that trading cards, called cabinet cards, were actually first made in the 1840s, but they weren't commercially mass-produced and sold nationwide until the mid-1880s. She thought about the hundred or so cards on display in the town hall, but she didn't think any were from before 1900.

She read a story about a signed Texas Tyler card that had been traded between brothers in the early 1900s. Fifty years later, a new owner of that home found it wedged behind a baseboard. It was sold for $5,000, and three years later, it was sold again for $50,000. She thought about the article she'd read about Mr. Rigsby's find of the baseball jersey and how he'd tried to buy her ball for a lot less than it was apparently worth. Trying to undercut the seller was a seemingly common practice.

She pulled out Charles Rigsby's business card from her purse. She wondered again at his relationship with Bea.

A thought crossed her mind. For someone to forge John's baseball, they'd need time to make a copy. Mary had been in the town hall every day. Surely, she would've noticed if the ball was missing. But if someone went in after hours, they could've taken the ball and returned the fake by morning without anyone noticing. Besides the construction foreman having a key to the town hall, Mrs. Leary, Stephanie, and Bea each had one. Charles had mentioned Bea gave him a private tour. Could Bea have let Charles in after-hours again?

She located Charles Rigsby's Web site on her computer. Again, she was astounded by how much some of his memorabilia was worth. The offer he'd made on her baseball was peanuts compared to some of the things he already had. But he did say he loved to discover bargains. Maybe he thought John's ball fell into that category. Bea could've told him the history about the ball, and perhaps he figured Mary wouldn't sell and decided to take it anyway. But did that make any sense for someone as established and refined as Charles?

She pulled out her cell phone. Bea hadn't tried to call her back.

Mary turned back to the screen and searched through his list of baseballs. If Charles had stolen the ball, what would he have done with it? Sell it? But where? He certainly wouldn't try to sell it online unless...Did he think he'd successfully fooled her with the counterfeit?

Maybe she was jumping to conclusions. She focused back on other possible suspects. Brent Bailey had been down on his luck and needed money. He'd had to borrow money from his mother but then had enough funds to buy expensive clothing at Cape Cod Togs. Where was he getting the money?

Ivy Bay compensated their players to help with their expenses, but it wasn't much. Certainly not enough for expensive tastes. Even if his parents were helping Brent out, she still couldn't eliminate him. Brent was a sports fanatic and had worked in sports merchandising. Perhaps he knew someone who could copy the ball. He'd openly said he wanted a great collection someday. Maybe he'd started with her ball.

Tyler and Joe had been by the display but didn't seem that interested in the memorabilia. They both seemed well-off financially with good futures and no apparent motive to steal the baseball. Tyler was an LA Dodgers fan too, which made his interest in the ball even less likely.

Again, the thought crossed her mind that Stephanie had more access to the display than anyone else, but she didn't even like baseball. She didn't seem to be financially strapped and liked her internship.

What about Bill Halliday? He'd been at the top of the agent game for a long time, negotiating contracts for some of the best players in baseball, until about five years ago. Was his career in a slump? He seemed to have a lot of spare time to be able to hang around town and the town hall. And why was he researching Ivy Bay?

Then, of course, there were the hundreds of other people who had come through the town hall in the last few weeks. That was the worst possible scenario, because the thief could be anyone. But then again, if it was one of the visitors, that person would have to get behind the display ropes without being noticed or get into the hall during a time when no one else was around.

Mary rinsed her dish in the back room and brushed her teeth. When she returned to her computer, she heard her cell phone ring. She picked it up and answered.

"You said to call if something happened." Stephanie spoke in almost a whisper. "It did."

ELEVEN

——◆◆◆——

"Look, I just know this isn't my bat. It looks like my bat, but it's not! You asked, and I said no; it's not mine," a stocky, balding man said to Mrs. Leary, who stood in front of the display. A red tinge seeped into his shiny scalp and bulbous nose. In his thick hands, he held a black bat autographed in silver by David Ortiz.

"I'm not arguing with you, Mr. Dorchester. I'm just trying to clarify what you are saying," Mrs. Leary said calmly.

Mary stopped next to Stephanie by her desk. Stephanie leaned close and whispered, "That's Stanley Dorchester. I called him to come in to check his stuff."

"I want to know what you're going to do about this," Stanley demanded.

Mary gestured to Mrs. Leary if it was okay to join the conversation. She nodded in relief, and Mary stepped forward.

"Mr. Dorchester, I'm Mary Fisher. I'm on the Artifact Committee and helped organize the display. Why don't you think it's your bat?"

"See the handle? There was a chip out of it. It wasn't very noticeable unless you scratched your hand on it, but it was there."

"So you bought the bat that way?" Mary asked, thinking it might've gotten damaged while being used in a game.

"Well...no, my son banged it on some concrete, but what does that matter? Am I going to be reimbursed or what?" His chest puffed up, and he sounded out of breath. "This bat is worth a couple hundred bucks."

"You signed a release," Mrs. Leary said. "But we'll call the police and get a report taken. Maybe your insurance will cover it."

He held up his hand. "Whoa, there. The police? No way. I don't think so." He shook his head. "I don't want the police involved."

"But we have to report it if you wish to have any chance of compensation," Mrs. Leary said, looking perplexed.

"Forget it. I don't need this hassle. And if the police ask, I'll just say it's mine." He stormed across the floor, swinging the bat by his side, and went out the door.

The three women looked at one another.

"That was strange," Stephanie finally said. "Maybe the bat was genuine and he thought he could get some money out of us."

Mary nodded. "Or maybe he was telling the truth but doesn't have a good relationship with the police, if you know what I mean."

"Like unpaid parking tickets," Stephanie said.

Yet Mary had a feeling the man was telling the truth. Had the bat truly been switched when the thief took her ball, or had the switch occurred more recently?

"I'm just grateful no one else was here to witness that scene." Mrs. Leary stared at the display. "Maybe we should just shut down the exhibit. I don't know how to keep it any more secure. I'd hire a security guard, but if we did that, then any donations we collected would be gone."

Mary didn't like the idea of shutting down, but Mrs. Leary had a point. She didn't want anyone else to lose their things. Maybe there was a way to keep going and trap the thief at the same time.

"Could we put up some sort of surveillance camera?" Mary asked. "Like the one the construction company uses outside. We could put one up in an inconspicuous place and maybe catch someone red-handed."

"That would be another expense unless..." Mrs. Leary appeared deep in thought. "Let me see what I can do. I might be able to get them to loan us one of their cameras. Security of the whole site is important."

The door opened, and Brent, Tyler, Joe, and two girls came in.

"Hey, Steph," Brent said. "We're all going to lunch at the Black & White Diner. I'm treating everyone."

"Better take him up on it," Joe said. "It might be years before he offers again."

"Well, I don't—"

Tyler flashed her a smile. "You've got to eat anyway, right?"

"I guess," Stephanie said faintly.

"Go ahead," Mrs. Leary said. "I brought my lunch and will eat it out here."

Stephanie opened her mouth as if to protest but then shrugged. She grabbed her purse and followed them out.

"I'm glad she's getting involved with some of the young people around here before she goes home," Mary said, although she hoped the girl continued to be leery of Brent. "She doesn't seem to have any family close by."

Mrs. Leary nodded with a faraway look. "She's shy like her mother."

"You know her mother?"

"Actually, her mother's aunt. They lived here for a while, long ago. I was working at the DMV at the time. Her aunt left Stephanie's mother her cottage. I didn't realize the connection until Stephanie came to work here."

The phone rang on Stephanie's desk, and Mrs. Leary went to answer it. Mary turned her attention back to the display. She straightened the area where the bat had been and decided to take another round of photos for documentation. This time, she took some close-ups of the more valuable pieces, which consisted mostly of Charles Rigsby's collection.

Feeling like she'd done all she could for the moment, Mary caught Mrs. Leary's attention and waved good-bye. She stepped out the door just as Pastor Frank Miles came up the steps, holding the hand of his eight-year-old grandson Trevor.

"Good morning, Mary!" Pastor Miles said with a big smile. "How are you?"

Mary hesitated on the stone step. She was tempted to blurt out her troubles and emotional turmoil to the kind leader of her church, but now wasn't the place or time. She wished again she could talk her problems over with Bea. Her friend still hadn't returned her calls, and Mary couldn't help but start to feel Bea might be avoiding her.

"I'm doing okay," Mary finally said and then leaned over so she could be face-to-face with Trevor. The pastor's beloved grandson had been diagnosed with autism, and Mary knew

Trevor well from their visits to her bookshop. "Are you going to go see the baseball stuff?"

Trevor pointed to the door, his gaze avoiding hers.

"That's great. Have fun!" Mary said with a smile and gave him a wave.

She reached the sidewalk and turned down Main Street, her steps dogged by the feeling of time running out. The Loving Hearts auction date loomed, and she hadn't made any real progress on recovering the baseball. Now another item appeared to have been stolen. Which meant the thief might still be around and so might John's ball. But where? And who?

Lord, I know You provide for all our needs, but please help me find John's ball and help fulfill a need for that poor little girl needing a heart operation.

The words of one of her favorite songs flooded her mind, and she softly sang, "His eye is on the sparrow, and I know He's watching me" as she picked up her pace heading into the downtown area.

⸻

"You're doing really well," Susan said during Mary's second baking lesson. "Feeling better about the process?"

Mary nodded. "I feel like I have a better grip on what I'm doing."

"The more you practice, the more confident you'll get," Susan said and went to check the oven. "We're going to do a crumb topping this time, so we need to crimp the bottom crust."

Mary placed her dough in the pie plate and smoothed the dough over the edge. She followed Susan's example and crimped the edge so it looked pretty and then added the peaches.

"Okay, now for the crumb topping. It's very simple," Susan said. "We just combine flour, light brown sugar, and butter. Pinch it until you have large crumbs."

Mary followed Susan's example, and by the time she slid her pie into the oven, she was very pleased with how the pie looked.

"We went much faster today, so there's time to show you an easy pie that is great for those last-minute times when you need a dessert."

"Easy sounds good to me," Mary said with a little laugh.

"You use an oil crust and canned cherry pie filling. I can show you how to use fresh cherries another time, but like I said, this is the fast way." Susan added oil and boiling water to a mixture of flour and salt.

"The dough is hot," Mary observed as she patted hers into a ball.

"And the beauty of it is that you don't have to chill it. We can roll it out right now. In fact, you could even just press it into the pie pan, but it's nicer if you roll it."

Mary picked up her roller and set it on the dough ball, and the dough almost spread itself. "Wow, this rolls out very easily."

"That's why I showed you this recipe second," Susan said with a laugh. "Both piecrusts are good, but you can decide for yourself which you like better. And of course, this one saves time, if you're in a hurry."

Mary put the dough in the pie pan and added the canned cherry pie filling. Susan dotted the filling with butter, and the dough still felt warm under Mary's fingers as she crimped the top and bottom together and cut slits in the top.

"Voilà!" Susan said when they were done.

"Voilà!" Mary echoed. "That was super easy." She was feeling so much more optimistic about her baking skills that she suggested, "Next, I'd like to try a blueberry pie. My grandmother and Betty used to make a lot of them when berries were available."

Susan smiled. "I actually have fresh blueberries already in the refrigerator, and we can attempt one tomorrow."

They put Mary's cherry pie in the oven, and as Mary assisted Susan in cleaning up the table, she asked, "Did the development committee enjoy their cupcakes?"

"I think so," Susan said. "The secretary that cut me a check said there weren't any left, despite the hostility."

Mary raised her eyebrows. "Hostility?"

"It seems there was quite a loud discussion and some heated opinions. They had to postpone the decision concerning whatever property they were discussing until the next meeting."

"Maybe they'll buy more cupcakes."

"Maybe." Susan smiled. "I think I'll suggest double-chocolate next time. Chocolate seems to soothe people."

"I know it does me." Mary turned the water on in the sink and rinsed the mixing bowls. "For years, I'd only wanted chocolate when my grandfather treated Betty and me to an ice cream. It wasn't until I got to be about seven or eight that I discovered that there were other good flavors as well."

"And you should know. Big fan of your ice cream here. I always look for your newest creation at Bailey's."

"Thanks." Mary's face warmed. "Now if I can only get my pie-making skills up to par with my grandmother's and Betty's."

"You're doing terrific, and I'm not just saying that because I'm your teacher." The buzzer sounded. "The peach pies are done." Susan carefully extracted them from the oven and placed them on cooling racks before running out front to assist Jasmine with something.

Mary glanced at the clock. It was almost five already. Rebecca was planning to stay until closing, so she had time for another errand. She wondered if Jayne and Rich were back from their trip and called the antique store.

"Gems and Antiques," Jayne's cheerful voice answered.

"Hi, Jayne. Mary Fisher. When did you get back?"

"Last night. It was a quick trip, but we found some wonderful treasures."

"That sounds fun," Mary said. "Are you busy right now? I just made a peach pie and would love to share. It will be my way of saying thank-you."

"Oh, that sounds so good. I haven't had peach pie in years. Come on over. I have coffee going already."

"See you in a little bit." Mary clicked her phone off as Susan returned.

"If you don't want to wait until the cherry pie is done, I can bring it over to your shop later," Susan said.

"Thanks. That would help me out." Mary glanced at the cooling pie. "Can I take the peach pie with me?"

"It's still hot, but we can put it in a box." Susan got out a bakery box with Sweet Susan's stamped on the side.

"Remember to keep the lid up until the pie is cool, otherwise the steam will make the piecrust soggy."

Mary thanked Susan, paid her for the ingredients, and walked over to the antique store. Two customers were in the store standing by a beautiful cherrywood armoire, talking to Jayne.

Mary carried the pie to the counter where Rich stood with his back to her, while talking on the phone.

"I'm afraid I can't let it go at that price." He paused, irritation etching his forehead. "No, because that is a ridiculously low offer. If you change your mind and offer me a fair price, I may reconsider. Good-bye, Charles."

He hung up the phone and turned with a roll of the eyes. "Unbelievable. You'd think he'd learn," he muttered and then caught sight of Mary. "Oh, I'm sorry. I didn't see you."

"By chance, was that Charles Rigsby?" Mary asked.

His eyes flickered affirmation, but he said, "I really can't discuss it. Sorry."

Mary held up a hand. "That's okay. I understand. It's business." She set the pie on the counter, her mind whirling with this new information. So Charles had been trying to lowball Rich too.

"I brought you a treat. And I also came to settle up about the baseball. I really appreciate your checking on its value."

"Oh, you don't owe me a thing. I only made a couple of calls."

"Are you sure?" Mary asked.

"Tell you what, if you ever decide to sell it, consider letting us make an offer."

"I will, and thank you," Mary said, thankful to have such kind friends.

Jayne joined Mary at the counter. "That smells fantastic."

"I just hope it tastes as good as it smells," Mary said. "I've been taking some lessons over at Sweet Susan's."

"What gives women that urge to bake?" Rich asked with a grin. "My wife seems immune."

"That's not fair. It's not just women who bake. Some great chefs are men," Jayne teased back.

The door opened, and the couple interested in the armoire left. Rich gave Jayne a questioning look. She shook her head. "They want to think about it."

"Unless they are regulars, most people don't come back when they say that," Rich said to Mary.

"But you never know," Jayne said. "They probably want to comparison shop, but I told them that they won't find an armoire of that quality for that price anywhere in the area." Jayne took a deep sniff of peach pie and said with a laugh, "Let me get some plates from the back."

"So how was the trip?" Mary asked Rich.

"Productive. We came back with several sets of silver napkin holders. They are very ornate and will be spectacular when I clean them up."

"And we found a rolltop desk, which I'm having shipped down," Jayne said, returning with three china plates, silver forks, and a pie server.

Rich popped to his feet. "I'll get the coffee."

Jayne handed Mary a gold-plated pie server with a curved handle.

"This is pretty," Mary said.

"Found that in England when we were over there." Rich returned carrying a tray holding three cups that had a delicate blue flowery design and a silver bowl with packets of creamer and sugar. "Liked it so much, we decided to hang on to it for a while. This is the first time we've used it."

"Here we go." Mary cut into the pie, pleased to see it wasn't as runny as she feared. "It's still warm." She slid a slice onto a plate.

"I love warm pie," Rich said, reaching for the plate.

"And warm doughnuts, scones, and cake," Jayne teased. She pulled up a chair for Mary.

"I can't help it if I have excellent taste." Rich forked up a peach and took a bite. "And this is good. Well done, Mary."

Mary felt her cheeks flush as she lifted out two more slices. "Thanks go to Susan too. She walked me through it." Mary tried the pie. It wasn't as good as her grandmother's peach pie, but it still tasted fresh and flavorful.

"I'll have to get the recipe, although chances of me baking a pie are very slim, for the next few years anyway," Jayne said.

Rich smiled at his wife. "I'll forgo homemade goodies as long as my lovely wife can continue to travel the world with me."

Jayne gazed at her husband, affection in her smile.

Mary cleared her throat. "I appreciate your researching John's ball."

"I thought that was really incredible about Bucky Swarnson," Rich said. "We saw several signed baseballs at one estate sale. None were the Red Sox unfortunately, but I did talk to another customer who was interested in the balls. He told me that memorabilia can bring in a great deal of money, if you know what you are doing. He recently paid a couple of dollars for a set of old baseball cards at a garage sale and was able to sell the set for one thousand dollars because of a Jackie Robinson card. I may reconsider expanding our stock of sports memorabilia."

"I was just reading about baseball cards last night too," Mary said. "Of course, not all are worth that much."

"Are you interested in collecting trading cards?" Jayne asked.

"No, but if you happen to see any more 1970 Red Sox balls, I might be interested," she said, hoping that maybe they'd spot John's ball somewhere.

"We'll keep a lookout," Rich said, eyeing the pie again. "*Hmm*, I think I know what I want for dinner."

TWELVE

—◆◆◆—

That evening, the house smelled like lemon-scented furniture polish instead of garlic. Mary set Gus's carrier down and let the cat out as she looked around. The house was generally kept neat, but today, the floors and furniture shone. What was going on? Mary and Betty usually shared the cleaning on Saturday mornings.

In the kitchen, Betty was putting the mop and bucket away.

"Hi! It looks like you've been very busy," Mary said.

Her sister smiled, pulled out a kitchen chair, and sank into it. "I wanted everything nice for Friday."

"But I would've helped you," Mary said, refraining from pointing out that it was only midweek. "You shouldn't be cleaning for your own birthday."

Betty let out a contented sigh. "I woke up feeling restless, and this was a perfect antidote."

"In that case, I will make dinner," Mary said, and added as Betty started to protest, "I insist. You just relax."

"All right. I am a bit tired."

Mary hoped Betty hadn't overdone it and her arthritis wouldn't flare up for her birthday. She opened the refrigerator door. "What are you in the mood for?"

"Something simple. I'm not that hungry."

"How about a fruit salad and tuna melt?"

"Sounds perfect." Betty slowly got to her feet. "I'm going to take a shower and change."

"Supper will be ready when you get back." Mary got a can of tuna from the pantry and opened it. Gus bounded into the kitchen, his nose in the air. He slid to a stop at Mary's feet.

"So, you smell something good," Mary said with a laugh. She drained the can into Gus's cat dish, which had a small amount of dry cat food on the bottom. "There you go."

While Gus ate his dinner, Mary assembled the sandwiches, cut up cantaloupe and watermelon, and added a generous sprinkling of blueberries.

The sound of running water shut off, which indicated Betty was done with her shower. Mary dropped the sandwiches on the griddle and let the bread toast. She flipped them, checking to see that the cheese melted.

Gus slunk to the middle of the kitchen floor and looked the picture of tuna-induced contentment as he proceeded to take a bath.

Mary had the sandwiches and the bowl of fruit salad on the table by the time Betty returned.

"Looks wonderful!" Betty's eyes shone brighter, and she looked fresh and pretty in soft-blue slacks and a silky white blouse. As always, Betty looked refined even when relaxing. She took her place at the table. "Should I say the blessing?"

They bowed their heads.

"Dear Lord, we thank You for the blessings You have bestowed with good food, shelter, and family. Please bless this food to nourish and strengthen us to continue to do Your will. Amen," Betty said.

"Amen," Mary repeated. She helped herself to the fruit salad, placing it in a bowl by her plate.

"How was your day?" Betty asked. She took a bite of her sandwich.

"Interesting." Mary told Betty about Stanley Dorchester's bat and her visit with Jayne and Rich, leaving out the part about the pie.

"This is so bizarre," Betty said. "I can see someone wanting John's baseball if it is indeed worth thousands of dollars, but why the bat? And why not just take the items in one big haul?"

Mary chewed her sandwich, thinking about it. Did the thief have more of a motive than money? Like keeping artifacts for him- or herself?

"Mrs. Leary is going to obtain a security camera, so if it happens again, we will know who it is," Mary said.

Betty stopped eating. "You think something else will get stolen?"

"I hope not. I'd hate to think of someone losing something they love," Mary said and then grimaced. "Well, I guess it would make things easier if they did try. I keep feeling like I'm not making any headway. Just waiting, hoping for a new clue or that the ball will turn up at one of the places I called." Mary rubbed her temple, her frustration building to a small headache. "I'm sorry. I think I'm just tired. We can change the subject."

Betty gave her an understanding smile. "I thought of something fun we can do this evening. After supper, we should look for those autograph books we had as kids. I was going to do it earlier today but got sidetracked with cleaning. I'm pretty sure they are in the attic."

"Good idea." Mary stood and picked up her plate. "Would you like some cookies for dessert? I saw a package of macadamia nut–chocolate chip in the cupboard."

"I love those cookies, but I think I'm fine with just fruit. Now, if it were ice cream..."

They both laughed. It was strange not to have ice cream in the house, which reminded Mary she needed to think about working on a new flavor for Bailey's Ice Cream Shop. Searching for clues about John's ball and making pies had totally distracted her.

"I almost forgot...," Betty said. "This is sort of last-minute, but Tess Bailey called. We're invited to a barbecue potluck at the beach tomorrow night. It will be people from the church, and Brent's teammates are invited."

"Sounds fun." And it might be productive if her suspects showed up. "What are we supposed to bring?"

"Tess said any side dish that would go well with barbecue chicken. I offered coleslaw, and she said that would be great. I think we should take some sliced tomatoes too, since we have a bunch of ripe ones in the garden."

They quickly cleaned up the kitchen. Then Betty and Mary climbed the stairs to the attic with Gus trotting after them.

Like the rest of their home, the attic was neat and tidy with just a fine layer of dust that was expected because the room was rarely visited.

Betty surveyed the room with her hands on her hips. "I believe the autograph books were in the trunk with the toys. The last time Jean was here looking for some napkins of Gram's, she said she saw a trunk with our old toys tucked under an eave."

She walked the perimeter of the attic and finally stopped in a shadowy corner and shoved two bar stools out of the way, revealing a medium-size trunk deep under the eave, with a box wedged between the lid and the attic ceiling.

"Here it is." Betty started to move the box, and a groan escaped her lips.

"Let me do that," Mary said, hurrying over. She didn't want Betty to strain herself, especially after her full day of housecleaning.

Betty stepped back. "It's a bit heavy. We should probably both handle it."

"I haven't seen this up here before," Mary said.

"With it stuffed in the corner, I'd forgotten that it was here too."

Mary lifted the latch on the trunk. The hinges creaked, and Mary had to push harder to open the lid.

The flashlight beam flicked over a ghostly white face with staring blue eyes. Mary let out a screech. Betty jumped and dropped the flashlight. Gus scampered away.

Mary picked up the flashlight and took a closer look. "It's just Molly." She giggled and placed her hand over her pounding heart. "Your old doll."

Betty came closer, her knees touching Mary's back as she leaned over. "Sure enough. I thought I had lost Molly decades ago." She lifted the doll dressed in a long, faded pink dress and tiny white cloth shoes. "I loved this doll. I looked forward to playing with her every summer."

"How come you never took Molly home to Boston?"

"Gram suggested that Molly liked living in Ivy Bay and would miss her home." Betty laughed lightly. "She was just trying to keep something special for me here when we visited. Of course, now I realize that just being with them was special enough. We were so lucky to have that experience."

"We were," Mary agreed with a longing for those carefree days secured with family love. "And now we get to experience being together all grown up."

"Who would've guessed when we were young that we'd end up back here together?" There was wistfulness to her smile, and Mary knew she must be missing Edward. With her birthday looming, Betty was probably feeling the loss of her dear husband even more than usual. Mary could understand. Sometimes she'd get a whiff of a certain scent like bay leaf or hear a sound like a heavy male step on a hardwood floor that would bring back a memory of John. She missed him so much sometimes it hurt to breathe. Being here with her sister made the days pass more easily, and for the most part, the constant ache that she'd carried since John's death eased.

Thank You, God, for bringing me back to Ivy Bay and Betty. It wasn't even close to the first time she'd prayed that very prayer.

Betty pulled out blocks in a mesh bag and a little tin blue bucket with a seagull painted on it. "Didn't Mom paint this bucket?"

"I think so." Mary's heart tugged at the memory of playing with that bucket when she was small. "Wasn't there another one with a sailboat on it?"

"Yes, but I don't see it in here," Betty said.

A memory flashed across Mary's brain. "Didn't that bucket disappear one Fourth of July? We'd gone down to Hyannis. Mom and Dad were there with Gramps and Gram."

"Oh, I remember now. Dad helped us build sand castles. We were down by the water's edge, and I think the bucket got washed away. I don't remember being upset about it."

"That's because it was *my* bucket," Mary teased.

Betty looked stricken. "Was it? I'm sorry."

"I'm teasing." Mary patted her on the arm. "That was a great Fourth of July. Mom and Dad were there. Gram still had her vision."

"And she helped us collect a bunch of shells," Betty said as she pulled out some doll clothes, two Barbie dolls, and a Candy Land board game. "There's a box on the bottom." She handed a heavy shoe box to Mary.

Mary opened it to find an assortment of card games including Old Maid, a devotional book for children, and on the bottom two small albums labeled autographs. One was red and the other blue.

"There they are!" Betty said with delight. "The red one was yours. Let's take them downstairs."

Mary carefully opened the little book, and waves of summer memories washed over her. The pages had yellowed, but the signatures were still clear. She set it aside and helped Betty repack the trunk.

"I think I'm going to give Molly a good cleaning and wash her clothes. She can live in my room," Betty said. "She doesn't deserve to be cooped up in the attic. Of course, if she had been downstairs all these years, she might not even be here. I had some other dolls I used to keep on a shelf downstairs, and Evan cut all their hair off one day when he was four. He wasn't supposed to use grown-up scissors, but the temptation was too great. I used to wonder what kind of father he'd make. There wasn't a sentimental bone in his body, not that you expect boys to be sentimental."

Mary smiled as the image of Evan at Allison's game, running around with the video camera and cheering crazily for his daughter came to mind. "You needn't have worried. He's a great father."

"He is." Betty smiled and tucked the doll under her arm.

Mary stood. "Come on, Gus. Let's go."

She heard a scratching sound from the depths of the attic.

"I don't think he's going to come willingly," Betty said. "He's probably having a terrific time stalking spiders."

"Gus?" Mary leaned over an old desk and could see Gus crouched down low to the ground, tail twitching. He did indeed seem happy and preoccupied. "Gus, we're leaving." He glanced up at her with bright eyes for a split second and then crouched even lower, every muscle poised to catch whatever he was seeing in the dark.

Mary caught him as he sprang into the air. He squirmed for a moment and then stilled, not happy but interested in where they were going. Mary paused by a tall basket by the entrance that held a baseball bat and a couple of old yellowed balls.

"Mind if I take one of these balls?"

"Go ahead. I think those were Evan's. That's where I got the stuff to decorate the shopwindow."

Mary followed Betty to the kitchen and set Gus down. He stalked off in the direction of his water bowl.

Betty set her doll in a chair and then sat at the table. She opened her autograph book. "Look at all these signatures. We sure made pests of ourselves, didn't we?"

"I think the players must've enjoyed it," Mary said, thinking of Tyler's smile after Ashley asked for his autograph. Mary flipped through her book. "You know, if any of these players made the major leagues, their signatures might be worth something now."

"I wouldn't know anything about that," Betty said with a laugh. "All I cared about was getting their autographs, and then I promptly forgot about them after the summer was over."

"The fun is in the hunt," Mary said, thinking of Gus in the attic. He might not catch anything but cobwebs up there, but he always had a great time stalking them.

Mary turned a page and gasped with delight. "Oh, look, here's Henry's signature. I forgot I'd gotten him to sign his name after we decided that we didn't just have to get the ballplayers. He's the one who reminded me of our contest that summer."

"Did we really have a contest?"

Mary grinned. "Yes, and I think you won by getting the most."

"Did I?" Betty said with a playful gleam in her eye. "We could count them now."

Mary laughed. "All right." She flipped through her book. "I got forty-seven."

"I had forty-nine, but this last one doesn't count. It's fake," Betty said, pointing to the last signature.

Bolt Travers.

"Betty Nelson Emerson! You forged a signature?"

"I know, I know. But I wanted to win," Betty said. "I meant to confess…eventually. It didn't matter anyway, since I was two autographs ahead."

Mary gave Betty a mock look of reproach, then studied the autograph. "Who would ever know? It doesn't look like your writing."

"It was easy. I traced it from the autograph Jane Portland got."

"Betty and her secret life of crime. How do I know the other signatures aren't fake? Maybe I won our contest, after all. Maybe you should give me Molly as a prize."

Betty laughed. "No way. Molly is going to get a place of honor in my room." She looked fondly at the doll. "Just seeing her makes me feel years younger."

Mary was glad to see her sister smile. They chatted about old times a bit more, and then Betty retired to the sunroom to read a bit as the sun set.

Mary sat in the kitchen, rocking the baseball from the attic back and forth with her finger. Tracing a signature from one paper to another was simple, but how would one do that with a baseball and still make it come off looking authentic? If you goofed up with just one of the autographs, you'd have to start all over. Lincoln said it had to be done by someone skillful. And it had to have been done quickly so the ball wouldn't be missed from the display. There were many artists in Cape Cod. Maybe Mason Willoughby at the local gallery could help her.

Her gaze returned to the ball. Time was seeping away. The Loving Hearts fund-raising auction loomed, and she so wanted John's donation to help that little girl. Where could the ball be? Still no luck from the calls and e-mails she'd put out. She thought about Charles's Web site. Of course he wouldn't put John's ball on there if he stole it, but what about at his shop?

She walked out to the sunroom. "Betty, would you like to go to Hyannis tomorrow morning?"

THIRTEEN

❖◆❖

Mary hurried down Meeting House Road wanting to stop in at the art gallery and then hopefully talk to Bea privately before she headed out of town. She'd opened her shop and waited for Rebecca and Ashley to come in. Rebecca had agreed to run things while Mary and Betty drove over to Hyannis.

Mary looked in the window of the county clerk's office. Bill Halliday stood at the counter. Bea was flipping through a record book as she talked with him.

Mary sighed. That man sure got around town. She wondered what he was doing now. Three people stood in line behind him. She lifted a hand to wave at Bea through the window, but Bea didn't see her.

The Gallery was next door, housed in an old Victorian. A tiny, melodic chime sounded as she opened the door. Mason Willoughby, a dapper elderly gentleman with a silver-white mustache, was at the counter sorting paperwork.

"Good morning, Mason."

Mason looked up, a preoccupied expression on his face. "Hello, Mary. How can I help you?"

"I have a quick question for you since you're the expert on art around here," Mary said.

Mason set down the stack of paper. "Well, I'd be happy to be of help, if I can." Mason loved to talk about art.

"This may be an odd question, but you know a lot of the artists around here. Is there anyone who specializes in reproductions? Say, reproducing images from a photograph or another object."

He frowned slightly and stared at her for a long moment that bordered on uncomfortable. "Well, now, I'd think just about any skilled artist can copy still life. The genius is how their unique talent and interpretation shines through." His focus narrowed on a wall painting beside Mary, his expression growing more animated. "That's what I look for. You can see it in that painting there where she took simple objects like pennies on the bottom of a fountain and turned it into an intriguing thought piece."

Mary gazed at the painting he was referring to. She couldn't see the pennies, just copper shadows under the rippling streaks of blues and whites of what must be the fountain water.

"I was thinking more of reproduction than interpretation," Mary said before Mason could continue. She knew from past experience that eccentric Mason could be long-winded on the subject of art.

Mason's lips tilted down again. "There are a couple of artists I know who are adept in that more simplistic medium, but they are in the Boston area. If you are looking to reproduce something, perhaps a commercial artist would better fit your needs."

"Possibly," Mary said, trying not to blurt out that she was searching for someone who could do forgery and commit a crime.

"As you know, I paint as well. Perhaps I can help in some way."

"I appreciate that. I'll keep it in mind," Mary said as she noticed a stack of paintings with vivid colors behind the counter. She'd seen something like them on the couch in Bea's yard.

Mary gestured to the canvases. "Those are interesting."

"Ah yes, I just acquired them this morning. I haven't had a chance to evaluate them yet."

"I think I saw something similar at a yard sale."

"Actually, the artist is Carol Moore, a relative of Bea Winslow's. They do have a uniqueness to them that might appeal to some of my clients, although she is an unknown. Are you interested in them?" He reached for the first one.

"They wouldn't fit the decor in my home, but they are colorful."

"It appears Carol liked to create unique combinations of color. Her use of broad strokes makes a bold statement." He placed a painting with an explosion of oranges and reds on the counter.

"It's very bold."

"But she was also adept at fine, detailed work, as you can see by these." He picked up a cardboard box off the floor and set it on the counter. It contained several smaller prints of flowers and plants that were indeed more lifelike. "*Hmm*, actually this Carol may have the skills you are looking for. You said you wanted a photograph reproduced in another medium?"

"Something like that," Mary said, wondering if someone who had taken photos of John's ball like she had for Lincoln

King could reproduce them accurately enough that most wouldn't notice. "Do you have a phone number for her?"

"Actually, no. Bea brought these in."

"Thanks, Mason." Mary glanced at her watch. "I wish I could chat more, but I'm on my way out of town right now. I appreciate your time. Have a great day."

She scooted out the door, hoping she wasn't being rude, but once Mason started talking art, sometimes it was difficult to get away from him.

She stood on the sidewalk, waiting for traffic to subside. So Bea had a relative who was an artist. She wondered if Charles knew Carol. Of course, that didn't mean this woman could or would forge signatures, but it did bring up the point again that for someone to reproduce John's ball accurately, he or she would have to take it from the display, copy it, and return the fake unnoticed. Or perhaps take photos of it. Either way, that person risked discovery. Surely it had to have been done when the town hall was closed and no one was about.

Mary took a couple of steps back to the clerk's office. Bill Halliday had left, but two other women had joined the long line. Bea looked up, and Mary waved. Bea smiled and waved back and then turned her focus back to the woman standing in front of the counter.

Mary decided it was getting too late to wait for Bea to get free. She needed to get some cash for her trip to Hyannis. She could see the ATM machine across the street in front of the pharmacy. A man was using it, but luckily there wasn't a line.

As she waited on the sidewalk for cars to pass, she realized Tyler Matthews stood at the machine. His blond hair glistened in the sun as he leaned closer to the screen and stabbed at the number pad with his index finger. He paused and then pushed buttons. Finally, he ripped out the receipt, wadded it, and threw it on the ground before stalking away up the street to his BMW.

Mary walked over to the ATM machine and picked up the receipt, wondering what had made him so angry. "Insufficient funds" was printed across the front of the receipt. Well, she could understand his frustration. She hoped the ATM wasn't on the fritz. She put in her card, and after giving the required information, it spit out bills. It was obviously working, at least for her. She put the cash in her purse and turned to head back to Main Street and home.

As she strolled along, worried thoughts about Bea swirled in her mind. The yard sale, selling her car, and the fact that Bea had been seen frequently with Charles Rigsby worried Mary. Was Bea in some kind of financial trouble? Mary didn't want to hurt her friend's feelings. She had always trusted Bea and couldn't imagine her stealing anything, but still... people sometimes acted out of character if they were desperate.

Betty was ready to leave as soon as Mary reached the house, and they took off for Hyannis, the largest of the seven villages in Barnstable, Massachusetts. The town was noted as a popular tourist destination and provided ferry service to Nantucket. Shopping was good too, with a district in the historic downtown and along the highway.

Mary drove past a museum dedicated to John F. Kennedy that also had a section devoted to Cape Cod baseball, and turned onto a side street. There were two sports memorabilia stores not far from the museum: Rigsby Sideline Sports and Hyannis Sports Equipment. Mary had already called Hyannis Sports and inquired about their baseballs, but she figured it wouldn't hurt to check out the shop while she was here.

"Okay, let's see what they have," Mary said, setting the brake. They'd already discussed their strategy and were hoping to glean information without making anyone suspicious.

A bell rang as they entered the shop, and they walked down a narrow aisle. The shop was crammed to the ceiling with new sports equipment on one side of the aisle and collectibles on the other. Betty paused to look at a New England Patriots jersey as Mary continued to the counter.

A robust man, who made the cramped area around the register appear even smaller, gave her a hearty greeting. "What can I do for you lovely ladies?"

"Good morning." Mary smiled. "I called the other day to inquire if you had any 1970 Red Sox team-signed baseballs. You said you'd call if anything would turn up. We're here in Hyannis for the morning, and I thought I'd drop in."

"Ah yes." He rubbed the dark stubble on his chin. "As I mentioned on the phone, I haven't seen any like that for a while, but I have a nice 1972 ball in pristine condition." He took a small step over to a cabinet. "Want to see it?"

"Actually, it has to be from 1970. Do you know how much a ball like that might cost?"

"Team-signed? Anywhere from $150 to $500, sometimes more, but it's hard to say without actually seeing the ball. Depends on the condition, who signed it, and how rare it is."

Betty had been checking out the autographed bats and came up behind Mary. "What about a Bucky Swarnson–signed ball?"

Interest flickered in the man's eyes. "Those are rare and will go for a lot more. I certainly can keep my eye open for you. You never know what will come on the market from day to day."

"I really appreciate that." Mary gave him her name and phone number again, just in case. "Do you know of any other dealers that might carry balls from that decade?"

"I wouldn't know," the man said.

"What about the store across the street?" Betty asked Mary. "Should we look there?"

"You can try Rigsby's," the man said, "but don't expect to find any bargains. I can set you up with a much, much better deal."

"So their items are more expensive?" Mary asked. Was he insinuating the other store jacked up prices?

He lowered his voice. "A word of advice. Check with me if you want a comparison before you buy anything from there."

"I'll remember that," Mary said, then thanked him before going out the door with Betty.

"He certainly didn't seem to have a very good opinion of Mr. Rigsby's store," Betty said, heading for the crosswalk.

"Well, they *are* competitors, so it could be expected," Mary said, but she wondered if it was something else motivating his attitude toward Charles.

"I didn't see any David Ortiz–signed bats while I was in there either," Betty said as they crossed the street.

Charles Rigsby's shop was bigger than Hyannis Sports, so Mary didn't get the impression she was going to be swallowed up as she made her way into the interior. Unlike the other store, Rigsby only sold memorabilia. She looked around for the owner but with relief saw that the only employee in the store was a pretty young woman with her thick dark hair pulled back in a ponytail and looking sporty in a stylish jogging suit. Her name tag indicated she was Kim. Kim invited them to browse and to let her know if they needed assistance.

"Look at that. JFK's putter," Betty said, staring at a golf display. There was a Not for Sale sign on it. She tore herself away and followed Mary to the baseball section.

Uniforms from various teams were displayed on the wall above glass cases containing balls, gloves, and trading cards. Rigsby also had an extensive collection of signed baseball caps and bats hanging from a ceiling rack.

"I'll check out the bats," Betty said quietly.

Mary continued on to the display case where team collections were grouped by decades. She moved down the case, descending through the years from the 2000s, 1990s, '80s, and finally to the '70s.

"Are these the only bats you have?" Betty asked Kim.

"Yes, but of course we can always look for a specific one, if you'd like."

"Thanks. I'll keep that in mind." Betty turned her attention to the cap collections as Mary searched the 1970s case.

Some years contained just a few items, but others had more, with memorabilia priced as a collection, although items could be purchased individually. She reached the end of the seventies, passed the Cincinnati Reds, New York Yankees, and then on to the Red Sox in 1970.

Her mouth went dry. There was a collection for 1970 with various caps of team members, a shiny signed bat, a Jose Santiago glove, a team photo, programs, pennant, and right in the center on a little stand was a 1970 Red Sox team-signed baseball.

FOURTEEN

Mary's heart fluttered as she leaned over the glass, trying to read the signatures.

"Would you like to take a closer look?" Kim asked from right behind her.

Mary jerked upright, her heart thumping. "Yes, please."

Kim produced a key from her pocket and opened the case. "You can see what good condition it's in, considering it's over forty years old. The signatures are still very clear despite the yellowing of the ball." Kim gave the ball to Mary.

Mary held her breath and turned it over. There was Sparky Lyle's signature but no fingerprint smudge, and there was also no Bucky Swarnson signature.

She blew out a sigh and glanced at Betty. It wasn't John's baseball. "How long have you had this ball?"

"Um...for a while. Mr. Rigsby has been adamant about selling these 1970 items as a set, but of course anything can be negotiated for the right price."

Mary handed the ball back. "I noticed that this one doesn't have a Bucky Swarnson signature."

"So you know about Bucky?" She smiled. "Those are rare, but Mr. Rigsby mentioned the other day to a collector that he knows where to get one. I can take your name and number if you'd like me to check into it."

Mary hesitated. She didn't want to make it obvious that she'd been here. "Thank you, but I'll give you a call if I'm still looking."

Betty bought a couple of antique postcards featuring some league players that went on to the pros. As they stepped back out on the busy street, she said, "I'm looking forward to lunch at the marina. I'm glad we came, although I'm sorry we didn't find John's ball."

"I'm glad we came too," Mary said. "I do find it interesting that Mr. Rigsby told me he needed John's baseball to finish his collection when he already had one."

A shop awning down the street caught her attention. Red and white striping reminded her of something, but what? Then as they got closer, Mary saw the sign for Ivan's Bakery. The logo was a bulldog wearing a baker's hat. Just like the wrapper she'd picked off the display table.

"Do you mind if we stop in here?" Mary asked when they reached the door.

Betty looked at Mary and then the shop. "Sure. We can get a snack for the drive home."

The store reminded her of Bailey's Ice Cream Shop with its old-fashioned decor. Mary went up to the register and ordered six miniature cherry popovers.

"Here you go." The salesgirl handed her the bag, and Mary pulled out the wrapper. It was identical to the one she'd found in the display. "Are there any other Ivan's Bakery shops?"

"Nope, we're the only one, although I think the boss is thinking of opening another."

Mary carried the bag outside and examined the wrapper.

"What are you doing?" Betty said with a laugh.

Mary explained about finding a similar wrapper at the back of the display. "Someone had to have dropped it back there behind the partition ropes."

"Someone who had been in Hyannis," Betty said, catching on.

"Yes, and I think I know who." Mary looked up the street at Charles Rigsby's shop.

<hr />

Mary stuck her fork in a slice of the blueberry pie she'd made at Sweet Susan's. She'd barely made it back from Hyannis for her lesson, even though they'd changed the time to four o'clock.

The pie she'd made with Susan that day was very simple, utilizing blueberries, a little lemon juice, quick-cooking tapioca, and butter. The warm berries burst on her tongue, filling her mouth with tart sweetness.

"I like it," Mary said as she took another bite. "But it's different from my grandmother's. I don't know what it is. Of course, after all these years, I could be mistaken."

"There are lots of different variations on blueberry pie. Do you have your grandmother's recipe?" Susan asked, sampling her own slice.

"I've looked, but it wasn't in Betty's recipe collection," Mary said. "It's possible that my grandmother and Betty made so many pies they didn't need a recipe anymore. I may ask my cousin Jean and see if she copied it. If not, this will do. Do you mind if I come by the day after tomorrow to bake another?" Mary asked. "It will be Betty's birthday."

"Sure thing. You don't want Betty catching on." Susan tossed her blue-stained paper plate in the trash can. "Afternoon is best because we're in a lull between baking periods, but come anytime you need to."

"Thank you," Mary said with a spurt of excitement. Betty was going to be so surprised. "This was so much fun."

"It was for me too. I'm seriously thinking about advertising baking classes this fall."

"I'll be happy to recommend you to any wannabe bakers." Mary took off her apron, grabbed her purse, and followed Susan to the front of the shop. Susan had offered to let the pie remain on the counter until it cooled thoroughly and she'd store it in the refrigerator until Mary could get it later.

Mary glanced at the assortment of cookies for sale in the case. The Bailey beach party was in a few hours. "Can I get a couple dozen cookies?"

"What kind?" Jasmine looked up from a textbook she was reading on the counter. "There's peanut butter-chocolate chip baked this morning, and oatmeal raisin, white chocolate-macadamia nut, spice, and shortbread."

"They all sound so good. I can't decide. Just give me an assorted two dozen."

Mary paid for the cookies and pie ingredients. "I'll see you later. Thanks again." She pulled open the door, stepped outside onto the sidewalk, and almost bumped into Betty.

"I was just going to pop into the shop and see if you needed anything from the market. I ran out of cabbage for the slaw." Betty glanced at the bag in Mary's hand.

Mary lifted it up. "Cookies for tonight."

"Good idea." Betty leaned closer, her eyes narrowing slightly. "Is that a bruise on your lip?"

Mary lifted her fingers to her mouth, and a purple smudge came away on her fingers. "Blueberry."

"Oh, is Susan giving out samples again?" Betty looked in the window with interest. "I love her blueberry scones."

"If your car is here, can I put the cookies in it?" Mary said, trying to change the subject and keep Betty from going in the bakery. "I'll close up the shop and be home in about an hour. It should be a nice night."

Betty turned her face to the sun and the clear, deep-blue sky. "It's days like this that I thank God I can live here where it's so beautiful." She took the bag of cookies from Mary. "See you in a bit, then."

Mary breathed a sigh of relief after Betty got in her car to drive to the market up the street. She'd be glad when Betty's birthday arrived and she could stop keeping secrets from her sister. She'd be even more glad if she could discover what happened to John's baseball. Maybe she'd find more clues tonight.

FIFTEEN

The sand squished up between Mary's toes, still warm from the sunny afternoon, as she carried the beach-chair bags and her platter of cookies. She slowed for Betty, who tramped after her with their container of coleslaw.

A canopy had been set up, and the white fabric flapped gently in the breeze. Smoke rose from a round portable barbecue, and sweet-savory smells greeted them.

Nearer to the shore, youngsters were playing volleyball. Jamie Bailey played referee, and their laughter punctuated the air above the steady *whoosh* of the waves and screams of seagulls.

"Mary, Betty!" Tess Bailey exclaimed. "Welcome. Come on over."

Mary and Betty walked under the canopy and set their food down on one of two tables underneath.

"I'm so glad you came. Chicken and burgers will be ready in about half an hour. Soda, tea, lemonade, and juice are over there." Tess gestured to two blue coolers by a large white jug labeled Water. "Just help yourself."

Mary pulled the plastic wrap off her cookie tray and then joined a group gathered near the fire pit. Jill Sanderson, a member of Mary's prayer group, looked up with a smile. "Mary, long time no see."

"You're back!" Mary pulled the chairs out of their bags and set them up by Jill. "How was your trip?"

Jill tucked a strand of windblown blonde hair back behind her ear. "Harry and I had a blast introducing the boys to Italy. Benjamin liked the Colosseum and fountains, but Luman was mostly interested in the food," she said, referring to her two towheaded sons, ages ten and eight. Jill rubbed her flat stomach. "Can't blame him, especially while we were in Tuscany. I put on five pounds."

"You can't tell by looking at you." Mary grinned as Dorothy Johnson strode over with a glass of soda in her hand. Dressed in white slacks, a navy-and-white striped blouse, and her pearls, she managed to appear sophisticated even on the beach.

"Hello, Mary. I was hoping you'd be here." Dorothy sat on the other side of Jill. "Now that Jill's back from her trip, the prayer group can start meeting again."

"We could," Mary said slowly, "but the rest of the group probably won't be available for two more weeks. Of course, if you have a special need, we can try to get them on the phone for a conference call, like we agreed."

Dorothy sniffed, looking put out. "Well…I don't have anything urgent, but there are people in the church that we can be praying for. Perhaps I can check with the other members to see if we're ready to start again next Friday?"

"Dorothy, there you are," Betty said, placing a hand on Dorothy's shoulder. "Are you still in charge of Saturday afternoon at the park? I read in the paper that this week's theme will be baseball."

"Yes, that's the plan. We're going to have a baseball celebration, even if the Blue Jays don't win. We're expecting a big crowd," Dorothy said as her cell phone rang.

"Excuse me." She rose gracefully and headed toward the water, away from the party noise.

Mary shot Betty a grateful look for the interruption. Dorothy was a sincere, very active worker for the church who tended to take charge in almost every situation. When Mary had started a prayer group, Dorothy had been there from day one and had a tendency to try to take over.

Last month, the ladies had voted to suspend the prayer group's weekly meetings until the first of September due to members being on vacation or unusually busy during the summer. The members agreed to carry one another's phone numbers in case there was a special need. However, Dorothy hadn't approved and felt the event should have stayed on the church calendar even if only two people showed up.

Mary turned to Jill. "So, tell me more about your wonderful trip."

"Florence was breathtaking," Jill began and shared highlights of their Italian tour as more people continued to arrive.

Suddenly, there was a *whoop* from the parking lot and a swarm of younger folks emerged from a half dozen cars. Brent parked a red convertible. His passenger was the blonde young woman Mary had seen him with at the ball game.

"Looks like the ballplayers are here. Practice must be over," Tess said with a laugh. "I suggest you all get in line for the food before they get here."

Mary joined Jill and Betty as they made their way down the length of the table, filling their plates with coleslaw, potato salad, baked beans, and other goodies. Then they stopped by the grill where Mr. Bailey flipped hamburger patties and chicken.

Mary decided on a chicken breast and returned to her chair. As Tess had predicted, the area was suddenly swamped with players, and food rapidly disappeared off the table. An excited hum sizzled in the air. The team was energized and excited, no doubt from their recent wins and chance at the play-offs.

"Tyler, sit with us over here," Paige Bailey said, waving. Jamie and some other girls giggled as he ambled over.

Brent collided elbows with another player as they reached for a hamburger. "Hey, watch it, Jeffries," Brent said good-naturedly.

"Sorry. Don't want to bruise the star," Jeffries said with a touch of sarcasm in his voice.

Brent didn't seem to notice. He sat on a bench, and a group of guys and girls surrounded him like he was a king. Mary hoped for Tess's and his sake he wasn't getting himself into any trouble. She wondered again about where he'd gotten the money for such nice clothes and being able to treat his friends to lunch.

Betty sat next to Mary and leaned close, causing her chair to sink in the sand. "Brent Bailey reminds me of Sal Buckner from high school. Remember how he played ball for the league too? I had such a crush on him."

"I think I got his autograph before you did," Mary said with a grin.

Betty laughed and bit into her hamburger. Mary leaned back in her chair, enjoying people-watching as Betty started a conversation with Jill and others that wandered over.

Mary got up to get seconds on potato salad, and Stephanie Doyle walked up. "Hi, Mrs. Fisher."

"Stephanie, nice to see you here."

"Brent invited me to drop by." She cast a glance over at the crowd that had grown around the team's star pitcher. "I'm late because Mrs. Leary had me hunting down a report she'd misplaced."

"There's still plenty of food. How did it go at the town hall today?" Mary asked. "Did anyone else come to check their memorabilia?"

"Just Mr. Meade. He said everything looked okay to him, and he was fine with leaving his trading cards out. He said they weren't much. He just had fun collecting them."

"That's good," Mary said as Stephanie looked over at Brent again. "Have you talked to Mr. Rigsby lately?"

"Not since the other day when I mentioned we were doing a security check, and he said that his stuff was all insured and he wasn't worried."

"Well, he was warned, at least," Mary said with a shrug. "You're doing a good job."

"Thanks," she said with a sigh. "I just hope Mrs. Leary thinks so because she will be giving me my evaluation next week. My grade depends on her."

"I'm sure she recognizes how hard you've worked," Mary said, hoping that was true. "Did she get the security camera up?"

"Yep. It's small, and you wouldn't even know it was there unless someone told you. I turned it on when I left."

"I guess that's the best we can do for now," Mary said. Too bad they hadn't had a camera earlier when someone swiped John's ball.

"Hi, Stephanie." Bill Halliday grabbed a plate, and Mary stepped aside so he could reach the table. "And good evening, Mary."

"Good evening," Mary said after Stephanie gave Bill a smile. Stephanie walked over to the grill where Blake Bailey was still grilling.

"This is quite a spread." Bill piled potato chips on his plate and spooned up onion dip. "The Bailey family knows how to throw a good party."

"They do," Mary agreed. "Do you have family in Boston, Bill?" There had been no mention in the articles she'd looked up.

"I did. Blew that," he said. "One of my regrets as I get closer to my retirement years."

"Are you thinking of retiring soon?" Mary asked, curious as to why he was researching Ivy Bay.

"Not anytime soon," Bill said with a chuckle. "For better or worse, baseball has been my whole life. I'd miss it too much. And I'm good at what I do." He ambled over to the group around Brent and said something to Tyler Matthews that made him smile. Brent was talking to Stephanie now but kept glancing over at Bill and Tyler.

Mary refilled her plastic cup with water. So if Bill wasn't interested in investing here, then why all the information gathering from Stephanie? Again, she wondered if that was just a pretense to allow him moments alone with the baseball display. Being in baseball so long, he probably knew about the value of a baseball with Bucky Swarnson's signature.

A figure moved along the shore. Dorothy was still out there on the phone. What had she meant that there were other prayer needs? Mary felt guilty about being so wrapped up in her own problems. Did someone need assistance?

She kicked off her sandals and walked toward Dorothy. The sand turned cool, almost chilly, under her feet as she approached the water.

"I don't appreciate your canceling at the last minute, Daniel. Who am I going to get to fill your spot at this point?" Dorothy said.

Mary paused at a discreet distance, waiting for her to finish her call.

"Fine. I'll call them. But you owe me a favor." She clicked the phone shut and saw Mary. "I just had the brass quartet cancel on me. Apparently, there was a mix-up on the dates and the trumpet player can't make it for Saturday afternoon."

"That's a shame," Mary said.

"It is, but it will work out, God willing. They gave me the phone number of another group. If they can't make it, I'll just have the guys in the string group play longer. I like having more variety, though."

"I'm sure it will be wonderful, whomever you get. You do such a great job organizing the park events."

"I try very hard to be of service to the community as well as the church," Dorothy said in her usual prim voice.

"That's what I came over to talk to you about. I know you didn't want us to put the prayer group on hold, and I can see your point," Mary said, although the group had discussed and voted on the matter. "Is there someone we should be praying for that I don't know about?"

"Yes, yes, there are several in need. I was going to bring them up at prayer group this week, but of course we aren't meeting. And I just don't feel that it's as personal or effective on the phone."

Mary bit her tongue from arguing that God would hear them whether at the church or praying on a conference call. She missed the prayer group too, but it was only for a few weeks. "Who is in need of prayer?"

"Well, I don't have my list here in front of me, but Mrs. White had a fall, Tom Bartholomew lost his job, and oh, Bea's sister had surgery."

"Bea's sister?" Bea's sister lived in Rhode Island. Bea rarely mentioned Bonnie and had never said anything about her being ill. Poor Bea. Could that be the reason she seemed so preoccupied? But why the yard sale? Did she need money to help her sister out?

"Is it very serious?" Mary asked.

"I assume so or Pastor Miles wouldn't have put her on the church prayer list."

"When was the surgery?"

"I think it was earlier this week, but I don't know the details. I tried calling Bea but never got through."

Mary's heart squeezed. "Maybe we should pray for all of them now."

"Yes, I think that would be wise. 'For where two or three gather in my name...,'" Dorothy said, quoting Matthew 18:20. "I'll get Jill."

"But..."

Dorothy was already gone. Mary didn't want to disturb Jill when she was having a good time. She had meant that the two of them could pray.

Dorothy bent close to Jill's ear, and she got to her feet and headed over to Mary with a concerned look on her face. "Dorothy says there are some people we should pray for?"

Mary nodded and let Dorothy update Jill.

"Before we begin, do we have any other prayer requests?" Dorothy asked.

Mary hesitated. "This seems a little insignificant compared to other people's problems, but—"

"Nothing is too insignificant for God," Dorothy said.

Mary suppressed a sigh. She hadn't meant that. Yes, she wanted to get the ball back and give it to the charity, but they should focus on other people's more serious problems first.

Dorothy continued to wait for Mary to reply.

"I lost something that belonged to my husband. It meant a lot to him, and I'm hoping to recover it."

"That's terrible," Jill said. "I'm sorry."

Before Mary could respond, Dorothy turned to Jill. "Anything you wish to pray about, Jill?"

"Just a prayer of thanks that God granted us traveling mercies and we arrived home safely."

"Let's walk farther down the beach where we can have some privacy." They moved along the shore until they were just beyond the lights from the party.

"Let's join hands," Dorothy said. "I'll start and then Jill, then Mary." She bowed her head. "Good evening, heavenly Father. We're having such a nice time out here by the beautiful shore You created. We come to You with some problems our beloved church members are having." Dorothy prayed for Mrs. White, Tom, and Bea's sister, and then spoke of Mary. "Our friend Mary lost something that belonged to her husband, and she is sad about it. You know where it is and how important it is to her. Please help her find it. We thank You for Jill and her family's safe return, and we ask that You continue to take care of us daily. Amen."

Mary's throat choked up a little by the sincerity of Dorothy's words. Dorothy could sometimes be bossy and snooty with Mary, but when she prayed, the formality she carried herself with disappeared.

When it was Mary's turn to pray, she lifted a simple request that those hurting would be healed, that Tom would find a job, and for her to recover what was lost. She thanked Dorothy and Jill, and they all returned to the party feeling less burdened.

Betty gave her a questioning look, and Mary indicated she'd explain later.

A fire had been built in the fire pit. Several of the children already had marshmallows on long metal roasting sticks. Joe Bailey pushed the wood to one side, revealing a mountain of coals.

"Hey, Tyler, wanna play catch with us?" Jamie asked, holding a glove and repeatedly dropping a ball in it, reminiscent of her pitcher brother.

Tyler threw his paper plate in the fire. "Sure. Hey, Brent, where's my duffel bag?"

Brent looked up from talking with Stephanie. "How would I know?"

"I took yours by mistake, and I want my glove."

Brent shook his head. "We need to quit doing that. It's in Jess's car. The red Lexus."

Tyler took off in a jog.

Mary smiled at Brent. "Great game the other night."

"Thanks." Brent nudged Stephanie with his elbow. "See? You should've been there."

She rolled her eyes. "I went to a movie and then had reports to finish. Some of us have to work a real job."

"Hey, I'm going to have a real job soon. Playing ball."

"That's just a game. What about a backup plan? What happens if you don't get chosen?"

"Picked. Don't worry I *will* get picked up," Brent said, irritation edging his tone.

Stephanie stared at him for a long moment. "Right. Um, I think I'm going to get dessert." She slipped away.

Brent looked at Mary. "If I don't believe in myself, then no one else will. I only need to hang on for a little while longer."

The cute blonde Lexus owner strolled up. She twirled her hair around her fingers and smiled at Brent. "Want to go for a drive? It's getting lame around here."

Brent glanced in the direction where Stephanie had gone. She'd disappeared. He smiled at the blonde. "Only if I can drive."

The girl dangled the keys in front of his nose. He snagged them in his fist. He turned and nearly bumped into Mary.

"See you, Mrs. Fisher."

As Mary walked back to her chair, she noticed Tess standing by the canopy, hands on her hips as she watched Brent drive off. She glanced at Mary and shook her head before turning and heading back over to where her husband, Blake, was eating.

Someone nudged Mary's arm. Henry held three metal roasting sticks with a marshmallow on each. "Hey,

Mrs. Fisher," he teased. "Care to try your skill at roasting marshmallows?"

Mary smiled. "When did you get here?"

"Just a few minutes ago." He offered Betty a stick. "Care to give it a try?"

Betty looked up. "I haven't done this since Edward and I took Evan camping. The last time must have been when he was sixteen."

"Then you are long overdue." Henry gave the marshmallow holder to Betty and looked at Mary. "What about you?"

"More recent. It was"—Mary swallowed hard—"just last year." A few months before John passed away, they'd gone to visit their son Jack, his wife Christa, and granddaughter Daisy who lived in Chicago. Jack had rented a cabin on a lake, and they'd had a lovely but cold weekend enjoying nature and, of course, the cozy fireplace in the cabin. Daisy, who was fifteen then, wasn't too old for roasting marshmallows. They'd also made s'mores, drunk hot cocoa, and talked long into the night.

Henry seemed to sense Mary's sudden flashback of emotion. He gave her a warm, encouraging smile. "Bet you burn your marshmallow before I do."

"Oh, you think so?" Mary took the marshmallow stick and scooted her chair closer to the coals. "We'll see about that."

Betty actually beat them both in roasting skills, turning her marshmallow patiently and slowly until it was a golden brown.

"You used to not be able to wait to eat your marshmallow," Mary protested.

"I grew up." Betty blew on the treat and then popped the whole thing in her mouth.

"Or maybe not." Mary laughed. She loved these moments when the Betty she knew as a child rose to the surface.

Henry lowered his marshmallow closer to the coals, and it erupted with fire. He pulled it close and blew the flames out. "I actually like mine with charcoal flavor."

Mary scooted her chair closer to Henry's to get out of the smoke. She noticed Dorothy staring, and Mary smiled at her. Dorothy turned her head without smiling back.

"Hey, Mrs. Fisher, watch your feet." Tyler squeezed through the chairs and put another log on the fire.

"When do you have to get back to school, Tyler?" Betty asked.

"Practice starts in three weeks. School starts in four," Tyler said. He turned and his foot caught on the chair leg.

"Careful!" Henry grabbed Tyler's shirt as he tripped, keeping him away from the fire as he fell to his knees.

"Whew. Thanks!" Tyler picked himself up and brushed the sand off his jeans. He limped for a couple of steps.

"Are you okay?" Betty asked.

Tyler leaned over, unfastened the Velcro on his sandal, and reattached it. "I'm fine."

"He's a ballplayer. He's tough," Henry teased, and Tyler grinned.

"You bet. Big game coming up." He straightened and walked back to the other young adults.

Henry leaned back in his chair and groaned. "I think I ate too many marshmallows. I'm going to take a walk. Anyone care to join me?"

"I think I need a walk too." Mary looked at her sister. "Want to go?"

Betty shook her head and snuggled back in her chair. "I'm going to stay right here and enjoy the fire."

Mary returned the roasting sticks to the table with the marshmallows for others to use and headed toward the firmer wet sand with Henry. The moonlight was bright enough that they didn't need a flashlight.

"How is the pie baking going?" Henry asked.

"Good. Susan is a great teacher. I actually produced something edible. If you want a sample, I have leftovers. I'm going to make a blueberry pie the day after tomorrow for Betty's birthday. I hope it turns out okay." Mary stopped when she saw a glowing white shell in the sand. She bent down. It was half a clamshell, worn shiny by being washed up onto the beach. She rubbed the sand off and tucked it in her pocket.

"I'm sure it will turn out great, and I'd love a sample." Henry tossed a piece of driftwood into the bay. "I talked to Kim today. She's going to bring the boys down for a long weekend before school starts."

"That'll be fun. You're a good grandpa."

He grinned. "Being a grandpa is much easier than being a parent. I get to do all the cool stuff and leave the hard work of raising them to their parents."

"Isn't it great? I try not to spoil mine, but it's so fun being the doting grandmother." Mary smiled, thinking of her three darlings, Emma, Luke, and Daisy. "I only wish—" She caught herself before saying how much John would've enjoyed seeing them grow up.

"Any developments on finding John's ball?" Henry asked after a bit, intuitively sensing where her thoughts had gone. "I just wish I could help."

"I thought for a few seconds that maybe I'd found it today," Mary said and told Henry of her trip to Hyannis with Betty.

"Weren't you worried that Mr. Rigsby might've been there?" Henry asked, concern in his voice.

"Yeah, but I figured he'd just think we were in the area and popped in to see his place. Besides, he doesn't impress me as the dangerous type, just—"

"A crook."

"I don't have any real proof, just little coincidences that make me suspicious." She told him about the wrapper.

"You think he might've dropped it while stealing something?"

"Well, there's only one Ivan's, and it's in Hyannis. Coincidence? I'm not so sure. And then there's his relationship with Bea," Mary said. "But, I do realize it could feasibly be someone else." She updated Henry on seeing Charles at Bea's, delivering a package that was long enough to contain a baseball bat, and then the trip to the Gallery where she discovered that Bea's relative was an artist. Someone who might be able to duplicate signatures.

"I know this may just be my imagination going overboard. I can't even imagine that Bea would do anything to hurt me, but I'm worried about her. It's almost as if she were avoiding me. She's been having a yard sale and selling her things. And I just learned tonight that her sister needed surgery this week. I feel terrible to even suspect Bea of any wrongdoing, but what if she's in trouble?"

Henry thought for a few moments and then said gently, "People sometimes do things for family they would never do otherwise. But I'm thinking it's more likely that if Bea is involved, Rigsby is using her somehow and Bea doesn't even know what he's up to."

"Maybe," Mary said, still worried for Bea but liking Henry's suggestion. Maybe Bea was just a pawn in Rigsby's scheme. She sure liked that scenario much better than thinking Bea would steal from her, even if desperate.

She gazed up at the moon. *Thank You, God, that I have friends like Henry to talk to.*

"Hey, do you remember that night after Betty's birthday when we were around ten?" Henry asked in a light tone, suggesting he was making an effort to distract her.

Mary nodded. "We had the celebration out here on the beach."

"Yeah, that's the one. It was really hot that day, and you came down to the water to wash cake off your fingers."

The memory was cemented in Mary's brain.

"Don't you dare, Henry Woodrow!" Mary scooted back. "We're too grown-up for that."

"Oh, you don't really think I'd splash you now! Although that *was* a fantastic water fight. Even your grandpa participated."

"Oh, well, if Gramps could play, then..."

Mary used her toes to flick water at Henry's jeans. He looked down at the salty drops soaking into his knees.

She turned and broke into a run, feeling like a carefree child again with the surf splashing on her feet. It was exhilarating...until she ran out of breath.

Henry stopped behind her. He was breathing hard too, but not puffing like Mary. "Okay, so it was easier to play back then."

"Whew! Still feels good, though." She glanced at the group down the beach, glad no one seemed to have noticed their antics. Betty probably wouldn't approve if she had gone back into her prim-and-proper mode. Mary smoothed her hair and brushed the sand off her capris.

"Thanks, Henry. This was fun. I feel ten years old," Mary said.

Henry's smile widened. "Only no pigtails for me to tug."

SIXTEEN

Mary climbed the stairs to the attic, trying not to trip on Gus, who kept circling around her feet. After she'd gotten home from the party, Mary had called her cousin. Jean, who had helped Betty move some of Gram's things, suggested the recipes might be packed in the cedar trunk in the attic.

Mary opened the door. The air smelled dusty, and the ocean breeze set the roof to creaking whenever there was a gust. She grabbed the flashlight by the door and advanced in. Gus raced past her and leaped upon the stack of boxes he'd haunted before.

"Just don't get too engrossed," Mary said. "We're getting out of here as soon as we can."

The cedar trunk with Gram's wedding dress and other cherished items was in the middle of the floor. Mary knelt in front of it, and as she lifted the lid, Gus let out a yowl. Mary nearly dropped the lid on her fingers.

Her heart pounded as she stood. "What is the problem?"

Gus was on the uppermost stack of boxes, his gaze glued on a moth that circled the lightbulb overhead.

"Oh, silly, you can't have the moth."

She turned her attention back to the trunk and opened it. She carefully felt through the neatly folded clothes until her fingers touched something hard. She pulled out a small book wrapped in plastic. On the white cover was the title *Godly Tips for Mothers*. She was delighted to see it was actually a diary of sorts. Between the Bible verses and antidotes was space left for writing down thoughts. Gram had made notes in the designated spaces, and in the margins of passages she'd liked through the first three quarters of the book. Then the notes abruptly ended. Had she tired of the book? Or was that when Gram lost her sight?

A lump rose in Mary's throat. Her grandmother had never felt sorry for herself, and she kept active, so active that Betty and she had barely kept up with her at times. But still, not to be able to read or write must have been horrible. It would be for Mary.

Her eyes stung, and she wiped them with her hand. Back to what she was here for. She turned the book on its end and gently shook it. Several index cards fell out of the back of the book.

Recipes!

She searched through them. Mary recognized the meat loaf and cake recipes that Betty had copied. She gave a gasp when she came across the cards labeled apple, pecan, pumpkin, rhubarb, and blueberry. As Susan kept saying, "Voilà!"

She gathered up the cards and pushed them gently back in the devotion book. She wrapped it again in plastic and stood. Gus was still plotting on how to capture the moth.

"Let's go," Mary said and was ignored. She opened the attic door, and after a moment, she heard a thud. Gus brushed her ankle, and she gently encouraged him in the right direction with her foot, which he promptly turned into a game, rolling on his back and grabbing her shoe.

She gave up and tucked the cat under her arm until they were outside the attic. She was halfway down the stairs when she heard Betty's voice.

"Mary?" Betty came around the corner and stared up at her on the steps. "What are you doing up this time of night?" Her gaze lowered to the book Mary clutched. "Oh, you found Gram's book. I meant to show that to you years ago, but it got misplaced while we were organizing things one spring."

"I was bringing it down to read." Mary stepped the rest of the way to the second floor.

Betty nodded. "I read through it long ago. Made me feel closer to her."

"Did you need something?" Mary asked. Betty didn't come up the stairs often, especially if her arthritis was flaring up.

"Eleanor called a few minutes ago, and I've been summoned," she said with a wry smile.

"Summoned?" Mary asked. Eleanor Emerson Blakely was Betty's snooty sister-in-law, a widow, and self-proclaimed family matriarch. Mary wasn't particularly fond of her because of how Betty changed when around the family. Betty was gracious and kind as always, but she took a formality with that family, so unlike her young unconscious self. The self that Mary had glimpsed on the beach stuffing a marshmallow into her mouth.

"Yes, she wants me to go to brunch at the Chadwick Inn with her on my birthday. I told her I already had plans, but she was quite insistent. She said that some of the book-club ladies would be there."

"She's probably throwing a little birthday celebration for you."

"I suspect that too, but we're already having a family get-together in the evening."

Mary nodded. She guessed that Eleanor's motive was to be seen as the kind, generous sister-in-law treating Betty to brunch. Eleanor prided herself on being involved in the community. She headed up Ivy Bay's chamber of commerce, was a supporter of the Old State House historic organization, the oldest surviving public building in Boston and now a museum, and Eleanor ran an exclusive book club in Ivy Bay that Betty was in too.

"She insisted I think about it and call her back. Would you like to go? If not, I'll tell her again that I have plans."

Mary kept herself from blurting out an emphatic no. Spending an afternoon with Eleanor was like spending an afternoon at the dentist. "If you really want me to, I will, but seriously, it won't hurt my feelings not to be included. I can work a couple of extra hours and be ready for the ball game and dinner later. It will all work out well."

Betty nibbled her lower lip. "Are you sure? I'd much rather be with you, but it would keep Eleanor happy for the rest of the day."

Somehow Mary doubted that. "Then you should do it. And I'll be with you the rest of the day."

Betty let out a sigh. "You'd think at my age, birthdays should just slip by without any fuss or notice."

"Now you're not being any fun," Mary teased. "Remember you get cake and ice cream." And pie.

"That does ease the pain some." Betty laughed. "I can be bribed with my sweet tooth."

Mary smiled. "Then just relax and have a good time. Let Eleanor treat you to some goodies. It's your day."

Betty gave Mary a quick hug. "I feel better about the whole thing." She turned and slowly made her way back downstairs.

Mary went into her room and sat on the bed. She was glad she wasn't Betty. Of course, Betty marrying into a rich family had afforded her this lovely home near the water, which she now shared, so Mary wasn't going to complain.

Mary opened the book. She found the worn and stained card with "blueberry pie" written on it. She compared the recipe with the one that she had done at Sweet Susan's. Gram's recipe called for grated lemon rind, nutmeg, and cinnamon to be added to the blueberries. The spices must have been what she had found lacking in the other pie.

She'd follow this recipe when she made Betty's surprise. And now that Betty would be gone for part of the day on her birthday, Mary could make the pie at home instead of over at the bakery. Eleanor had actually done her a favor. She'd present the pie to Betty before they left for the ball game. Perfect!

Mary set aside her grandmother's book. She'd keep it on the nightstand and read parts of it before she fell asleep for the next couple of nights.

Right now she was eager to get back to working on the mystery surrounding John's ball. She lay back against the pillow and thought about Rigsby's collection at his shop. He had an amazing collection of baseball caps.

Gus had stretched on top of her baseball book, one back foot in the air while he licked it thoroughly. He hadn't caught the moth, but it didn't seem to bother the great hunter.

She tugged the book out from under Gus, and photos of the display fell out. She smiled. Gram wasn't the only one in the family who tucked things in books.

She spread out the photos she'd taken of the display. With the security camera in place now, she really didn't need these. Or did she? She paused over the two shots of Mr. Rigsby's glass cases. Was something different with the Dom DiMaggio cap? It was impossible to tell from the photo.

She scooted off the bed, got her laptop, and brought up the two images. She zoomed in on the cap. It was slight, but the two images of the cap differed. One cap was tilted at a smaller angle than the other one. No one would notice unless they were looking at the two images. Maybe someone had bumped the table and the cap shifted, but just to be sure, she'd head over there first thing in the morning.

Mary picked up the baseball book again, studied the picture of the 1952 cap on the page, and compared it to the one on the computer. The close-up photo images were too blurry to determine if anything on the cap was amiss, but she had a strong feeling something was wrong. She sighed and put everything away. She'd have to wait until tomorrow to go investigate for herself.

Clouds gathered overhead as Mary left the house and headed up Main Street. The storms they'd been predicting all week were coming in earlier than anticipated, which reminded her that she'd forgotten her umbrella. Her arms were loaded already with Gus's carrier, her purse, and the bag of baseball books. She hurried along, glad she was wearing her usual khakis and not a skirt as wind gusted around her legs. The first drops started as she crossed Water Street, and she made a dash for the steps of the town hall and knocked.

Stephanie came to the door and let her in. "Thanks for meeting me early," Mary said as she set down Gus's carrier.

Stephanie yawned. "No problem, but I was half asleep when you called, and I didn't understand you. What do you want to do?"

"I need to examine Dom DiMaggio's cap."

"Okay." Stephanie trailed after her. "I'm going to get some coffee from the back. Do you want some?"

"Sure," Mary said automatically as she scooted one of the holding posts to the side and stepped inside the cordoned-off area. She scanned the items on the tables until she found the small glass case holding a Red Sox baseball cap.

Her breath quickened as she got closer to the case. Dom DiMaggio's autograph was on the cap, but it was the information card propped against the case that grabbed her attention. The cap was one of the last ones he wore; he played for the Red Sox from 1940 to 1953. The hat was dated as being from the 1952 season.

She opened the book and flipped to the page she'd bookmarked and studied the picture of the hat and then bent so close to the glass case her breath fogged it. She backed up. The autograph covered a good portion of the bill, but the stitching on this cap was even and intact. No curling of the ends. Either the date was wrong on the cap or it wasn't authentic.

She examined the case. The glass was free from fingerprints, but the cap definitely sat at a different angle. She used a finger to rock the case gently, but the cap didn't move on its stand. Someone must've manually moved the cap.

"What's so interesting?" a male voice asked, startling Mary. Bill Halliday and Brent Bailey stood on the other side of the rope.

"I-I was just checking something. A little research." She moved down the table with the pretense of straightening things and trying not to let her breath hitch every time she looked at Dom's cap.

"Oh, I forgot to lock the door. Sorry, Mrs. Fisher," Stephanie said, coming out of the back office, carrying two mugs of coffee.

"Are you trying to lock me out?" Brent teased.

"Not you specifically. We aren't open for another twenty minutes," Stephanie replied primly as she set the coffee on her desk.

"Want to go to lunch with the gang again today?" Brent asked.

"Which gang?"

"You know," Brent said. "Tyler, Russ, Jessica, Lauren, and some of the other guys."

She chewed her lower lip for a second. "Um, no, thanks."

Bill nudged Brent again with a look of encouragement.

"Well, how about we go out just the two of us?" Brent asked.

"I don't think I can. I'd have to get Mrs. Leary to cover me again, and besides, I brought my lunch."

"Then it's settled. I'll bring my lunch over here. See you at noon." He headed swiftly for the door before Stephanie could protest again.

Mary gave him points for persistence. She just hoped his motivation and his character were noble. After observing his flirtations with the other girls after the game and the beach party, she didn't want Stephanie getting hurt.

"See you ladies later," Mr. Halliday said and followed Brent out.

Stephanie locked the door after them with an expression that wavered between exasperation and amusement. "I didn't mean to be rude, but I really don't want to get involved with a ballplayer. I don't want to repeat my mother's mistake."

"You know, not everyone is the same," Mary said gently. "Although, I think it's wise to be cautious until you know someone well."

Stephanie nodded, not looking at her. "I know."

"Okay, we need to get Mr. Rigsby on the phone." Mary dug out her cell phone and dialed the number on Charles Rigsby's card.

"Hello?" a groggy voice answered.

"Mr. Rigsby, this is Mary Fisher from Ivy Bay."

"Yes, yes, Mary. What can I do for you?" Bedsprings creaked in the background.

"You need to get over to the town hall. I think your Dom DiMaggio cap was stolen."

SEVENTEEN

——◆◆◆——

"My Dom DiMaggio cap is gone?" Charles's voice went from groggy to loud and clear.

"Not exactly." Mary hesitated. How could she explain this? "Well, yes, *your* cap is gone. Someone replaced it with another."

"Replaced it," he stated faintly.

"Yes, I think it's a counterfeit."

There was a long silence punctuated by Charles's breathing. "I'm on my way."

"Do you want me to call the police?" Mary asked.

"Yes, of course, but wait until I get there. Give me an hour."

Mary clicked off the phone. Did this mean Charles didn't steal John's ball? Or was his surprised voice an act? Maybe he'd stolen his own cap to throw anyone off the trail. Maybe he was going to collect the insurance money. If other items had been stolen, then why would anyone doubt his was too?

Stephanie came over to stand by Mary. "The cap was stolen?"

"Looks like it was switched with another." She explained about the manufacturing error.

Stephanie twisted her hands together. "What should we do?"

"What about the security camera?"

"Oh yeah. Mrs. Leary put it up there." She pointed to one of the wall lamps where the security camera was partially hidden.

"Better get Mrs. Leary."

Stephanie groaned. "She's not going to be happy." She picked up her phone. "Mrs. Leary, we have a problem out front." She paused and glanced at Mary. "No, it can't wait." She set down the phone and let out a deep breath.

Seconds later, Mrs. Leary marched out of the back room. Dressed in a gray suit, she matched the weather outside. She glanced from Stephanie to Mary. "What is so urgent?"

"I think we have another theft," Mary said.

Her lips pressed together. "You think? How do you know?"

As Mary explained what she'd discovered, Mrs. Leary's lips lost any color provided by her lipstick.

"We need to check the security camera," Mary finished.

"I'll get the cord to hook it up to the computer," Mrs. Leary said. "Stephanie, get the camera."

Stephanie blew out a breath as she dragged her chair over to the wall and climbed on it.

"Careful." Mary stepped forward to steady the chair. By the time Stephanie undid the wire holding the camera and brought it down, Mrs. Leary was back. She hooked the cord up to the computer on Stephanie's desk, and an image blinked onto the screen. The camera covered the room from Stephanie's desk to the display but not the hallway to the offices.

They ran the camera in fast-forward and then slowed it down when people appeared on the screen.

"Oh, I didn't realize my hair looked so bad yesterday," Stephanie said and earned a look from Mrs. Leary. She moved back a bit.

"Can we go through it faster?"

Mrs. Leary pushed a button, and the people began darting around the room at a rapid rate.

"Mr. Halliday is here a lot," Mary said absently as he appeared on the screen with a man Mary didn't recognize. They walked the length of the display and then left.

"Yeah, he does come almost every day," Stephanie said. "He doesn't talk to me much unless he needs information."

"What kind of information?" Mrs. Leary asked.

"Just stuff on the county. Historical and current statistics."

"Did he ever mention why he needed it?" Mary said, carefully watching the screen.

"Something about investing or retirement options. I don't really ask; I just find what he wants. I figure it's none of my business."

"That's understandable." When Mary had spoken to Mr. Halliday at the beach party, he had said he wasn't retiring anytime soon. But maybe he was looking to invest in property for the future. Or maybe he'd come in here for other reasons, like expanding his memorabilia collection with a Bucky Swarnson ball.

They reached the end of the day on the recording. Stephanie could be seen turning lights off, and first she, and then Mrs. Leary, left the building. For a long space of time, nothing moved in the room. Then a janitor came in and mopped the floor but didn't go near the display. He turned off all the lights except for the lamp on Stephanie's desk. The camera sped forward, continuing to show an empty room until Mary saw something strange.

"Wait. Go back," Mary said. "Stop. There!"

"I see them too," Mrs. Leary said.

Stephanie leaned forward. "What?"

"The wet footprints going across the floor. They just appeared."

"How weird," Stephanie said with a shiver.

Mrs. Leary looked at Mary. "Someone must've turned the security camera off and then back on."

"But how come we didn't see whoever did it?" Stephanie asked.

"They must've come in from the back of the building through the offices," Mrs. Leary said. "They could reach the camera without going in front of it. But how did they know the camera was there? It wasn't obvious. Of course, I guess if someone were looking for the camera, they'd find it."

"Or knew it was there," Mary added. "Who else knew about the camera?"

"Just us, as far as I know."

Mary walked over to where she'd seen footprints on the screen. Only a few smudges remained. The person must've had clean shoes. "Where did you get the camera from?"

"The foreman of the construction crew. He called his boss, so that would be two more people who knew about it."

"I think it's time we called the police again," Mary said. Regardless of what Mr. Rigsby said about the baseball cap, someone had broken into the town hall and had literally covered their tracks.

———

Mary sat on a wooden spindle-backed chair near Stephanie's desk, Gus in his carrier by her side, as Chief McArthur and Charles Rigsby conversed. Officer Wadell was there too, making notes.

Charles stood beside the opened glass case on the table, the Red Sox cap in his hands. He had his reading glasses perched on the end of his nose as he studied the photo in Mary's baseball book.

"Where did you find this book?" he asked Mary.

"Some yard sale, years and years ago. I can't remember exactly when, but my children were probably still in elementary school."

"I'd like to find a copy." Mr. Rigsby reached into his pocket and pulled out a magnifying glass. Mary remembered Brent mentioning that a cap like Charles's would be worth somewhere around $3,000. For having such an expensive cap stolen, Charles was acting rather calm and professional and not throwing blame around like some people might.

Stephanie still seemed nervous, twisting her fingers as she took her seat. Mary had tried to assure her earlier that none of this was her fault and no one would blame her, but they all felt unnerved.

Stephanie leaned over and looked at Gus. "Can I pet your cat?"

"Of course," Mary said, although she wished she'd dropped Gus off at the shop earlier. She had been so focused on getting here, she really hadn't thought things through. Of course, she hadn't expected to be here over an hour. If they didn't wrap this up soon, she'd have to once again call Rebecca and get her to open the shop.

Stephanie opened Gus's door and put him on her lap. Gus just seemed glad to be out of the carrier and let Stephanie ooh and aah over him.

While Charles examined the rest of his memorabilia to determine if it was authentic, the chief strolled over to Mary. "Who would've thought someone would pull this kind of stunt in Ivy Bay?"

"Not me." Mary shook her head. "We should've shut down earlier."

"If we'd done that, we wouldn't have raised another $1,000 for the league and the children," Mrs. Leary said, supervising the proceedings. "Besides, we contacted everyone to give them a chance to pick up their things."

"My items are insured, so I'll recoup," Charles said. "Just a shame, though. I was fond of that cap."

"Here, kitty," Stephanie said. Gus had jumped off of Stephanie's lap and run over to the display table.

"Gus, come back here." Mary chased after him. Gus leaped onto the table near Charles.

"Scat, cat. Get off," Charles said, making shooing motions with his hands.

"I'm sorry. He shouldn't even be here." She reached for Gus, who turned over on his back. "I don't think he did any damage."

"The most valuable cards are the ones in the individual cases, but he stepped on Josh Beckett." Charles picked up a card from the display. "What the—" He rubbed his thumb over the card, and the surface wrinkled. "The top of this card is glued on. Look, there's a new Yankee card under it. This is a fake."

EIGHTEEN

❖

Chief McArthur examined the fake baseball card. "Looks like someone scanned a photo of the original and glued it on top."

"Unbelievable!" Charles said. "Someone replaced my card worth twenty bucks with one worth less than twenty cents."

"You probably wouldn't have noticed for a while if the cat hadn't damaged this one," Officer Wadell said. Mary gave Gus a hug and put him back in the carrier.

"Here are two more fakes," Charles exclaimed, holding up the cards between his index finger and thumb.

"I'll have to take the counterfeit items as evidence."

Charles looked up. "Throw mine away when you're finished. They're worthless."

The chief stuck the notebook back in his pocket. "I'm going to talk to the construction foreman who loaned you the camera."

"That would be Mr. Lopez. I'll go with you." Mrs. Leary headed for the hallway. "Let me get my umbrella."

"Looks like it has stopped raining," Chief McArthur said. He pushed the door open and went out, and a few seconds later, Bea burst in the door.

"What's going on? The chief said he wanted to talk to me later." Bea looked past Mary, and her smile widened. "Charles, I didn't think you'd be back until tomorrow. How was your trip to NYC?"

"Productive but long. I didn't get home until early this morning, and then as soon as I'd lain down for a nap, I was called to come here."

"Why did you have to come? I'm afraid I'm in the dark here." Bea looked at Mary, Bea's eyes wide with alarm.

"There have been some thefts," Mary said. "My baseball, a World Series bat, Dom DiMaggio's cap, and some baseball trading cards."

"You're kidding. Why wasn't I called?"

"I did call," Stephanie said with an indignant tone. "I left two messages on your voice mail."

"I've been trying to call you too, Bea," Mary said. "I was getting worried."

Bea's eye's brightened as if she wanted to cry. "I'm sorry. It's just been crazy. I got a new phone last week, and for some reason, it doesn't notify me when I have voice mail." Bea sighed. "And with everything going on—my sister, my cousin, the yard sale, work—I forget to check, let alone answer. I have been a bad friend."

"No, you haven't," Mary exclaimed, touching Bea's arm. "I just wish I could've helped you more."

Bea placed her hand over Mary's. "I'm still the independent sort, I guess. Always handling things on my own. My cousin Carol passed away, and for some reason, she left me a storage locker loaded with a lifetime of stuff and her car. I've been trying to clean it out for the last couple of weeks. I figured if I was going to sell her things, I might as well clean out my attic and basement too. I had no idea how involved the process would be. And then my sister..."

Mary squeezed Bea's hand. "How's she doing?"

"As well as can be expected, I guess. I'm worried about her." Bea looked over at Charles still examining his artifacts and shook her head. "And to think I was too preoccupied to help here. I can't believe someone stole these things right under our noses."

"This is more complicated than just theft," Mary said quietly. "The items were replaced with counterfeits."

"Counterfeits," Bea repeated. "Seriously? Do the police have any idea who's behind this?"

"Not yet," Mary said. "We're going to close the display because it appears we can't keep it secure, even with a security camera."

Bea groaned. "This couldn't have happened at least a day later? The big game is tomorrow. There'll be swarms of people in town." She shook her head. "But I guess it can't be helped."

"No, it can't," Charles said grimly. "I'd better pack up my things. I need to get my bins out of the car." He headed to the door.

Bea watched him leave and said, "He's taking this better than I would've expected. He really is a nice man." Her lips lifted in a half smile. "We've been conducting some confidential business together, which is another reason I haven't been in touch much." She glanced at the display table. "I just hope that we still can."

Bea had Mary intrigued, and she wanted to tactfully ask what kind of business they were in together, but Bea moved to help as Charles came in with a large roll of bubble wrap and stacked bins.

"Before I forget, Mary, I got a message from my assistant at my shop. Someone came in inquiring about wanting a 1970 baseball. I was wondering if you'd reconsidered selling," Charles said as Bea helped him pack. "I'm willing to up my offer, say, $600."

Six hundred? Was Charles trying to cheat her, or did he not know the value? "I was thinking it was worth more."

"How much more?" Charles asked cautiously.

"Say, $3,000?" Mary said.

"Oh…so you know why the ball is so special. I was surprised too." A flush crept up his neck. "Well, you can't fault a fellow for trying to turn a profit. Tell you what. We can just forget this little conversation, and I can refer the buyer on to you."

Mary shook her head. "I can't sell it. The ball is counterfeit too."

"What?" The shock on his face appeared genuine. He may be unscrupulous at times, but Mary supposed she could cross Charles Rigsby off her suspect list or at least move him to the bottom. Charles had been in New York City the night before, so those couldn't have been his wet footprints on the floor.

"If it wasn't for Sparky Lyle's fingerprint missing, I wouldn't have known it was a fake either." She explained the smudge to Charles and how John thought that it made the baseball special.

"Ah, so that's why you asked me at the ice-cream parlor about flaws affecting the value of memorabilia." He frowned. "It's such a shame there are so many crooks in the world."

The door opened, and the police and Mrs. Leary returned.

"Okay," Chief McArthur said, "Deputy Wadell is going to collect the counterfeit items. I'd put a sign on the door that you're closed. Make sure the doors are locked tonight when you go, and I'll have a patrol car come periodically just in case you don't get everything out of here by this evening. Call the station if you notice anyone suspicious or think of anything that might be helpful to the investigation."

"I will," Mrs. Leary said.

After the chief left, Mary turned to Mrs. Leary. "Find out anything from Max?"

Mrs. Leary shook her head. "He says he didn't notice anything suspicious when he shut down last night, and the only key he has for the place is locked in the maintenance shed. I think I'm just going to have to get the locks changed."

Mary glanced back at Officer Wadell as he bagged the baseball. "I'd better get going too. Please do have Stephanie call me if there are any more problems." She noticed the guest book by the donation box. "Can I borrow this? We won't be using it now."

"Sure. Not everyone signed it, even though I tried," Stephanie said.

Mary picked up her purse, her book, the guest book, and Gus's carrier and stepped out into the soggy weather. She decided to walk around the building before she left. Her sandals sloshed through puddles, but she hardly noticed. They were still putting siding up, and some of the inner wall was exposed beneath huge sheets of thick plastic. Could someone have removed the inner boards and slipped through to the inside and then replaced the boards coming out? She took a closer look. Multiple nails lined the top and bottom of the boards.

Several young workmen and a woman swarmed out of the shed, carrying tools. She assumed the chief would have questioned them. She saw the young man that Brent and Tyler had stopped to talk to. He didn't seem to notice her as she turned the corner at the back of the building.

The rear door stood open, and a workman walked inside carrying a nail gun. A pink sheet of paper lay on the ground. It was a discarded shipping label addressed to Baxter Construction. She picked it up and slipped it in her pocket. It wouldn't hurt to find out more about this company who had access to the town hall.

She trudged back to the front of the building.

So, now what? If Charles was innocent, who stole John's ball?

NINETEEN

◆◆◆

The chime on the shop door rang, and Ashley bounded in. "Good morning," she sang as she skipped over to Gus on the rocking chair and grabbed him for a hug.

Mary smiled. "Hey, kiddo. Where's your mom?"

"Oh, she stopped to get something in the hardware store. Daddy has to fix my window when he gets home tonight."

"What happened to your window?"

Ashley plopped down on the floor and let Gus go.

"Softball?" Mary guessed.

Ashley shook her head. "Bat. I wasn't supposed to swing it in the house, and I really didn't mean to, but . . . it broke the window. And now Mom says I have to work to help pay for it. I need a job."

Mary nodded solemnly, although she found Ashley adorable and wanted to give her a hug.

Rebecca came in. "Sorry I'm late." She glanced at her daughter. "Did she explain what happened this morning?"

"She said it was her fault that the window broke, and she needs a job," Mary said.

"Oh." Rebecca's lips twitched. "I was thinking more along the line that she'd do extra chores at home."

"I have some things she can do. The garden in the back needs weeding. The ground should be soft after the rain this morning."

Rebecca considered the offer for a moment. "Okay, as long as it doesn't put a burden on you."

Mary smiled. "Ashley's never a burden."

Rebecca stowed her purse in the cubby behind the counter. Mary asked Ashley if she wanted the job, and she agreed after some hesitation when she heard it involved weeding.

Mary got a garbage bag from the back room and led the way to the backyard. Betty's wonderful green thumb had turned the back area into a relaxing oasis to read or think. Mary wished she could spend more time back here.

"Okay, sweetie. Do you see all these little weeds that are low to the ground?"

Ashley nodded.

"It's your mission to capture the bad weeds before they grow up and strangle the good plants in the garden."

Ashley gave her a look that said she was much too grown-up for such talk. "I'll pull the weeds."

"You can put them in this bag." Mary glanced at the sky, which had thickened with even more gray clouds. "If it starts to rain, come on in."

"Okay."

As Mary lingered by the door while Ashley knelt and got to work, the parable of wheat and tares came to mind. Sometimes, you had to let the weeds grow with the wheat or you risked pulling out the good with the bad. It was just so hard sometimes to distinguish between the two kinds of people out there. Confusing, like when it came to someone like Brent, who had moved to the top of her suspect list. If he did turn out to be guilty, would that tear his family apart?

Troubled, Mary went back in, leaving the door ajar so they could hear Ashley if she needed anything. She looked in the front room, and Gus was asleep in a patch of sun. She really didn't want him going outside without her. He was pretty good about sticking around, but he was way too precious to her to take a chance on him wandering off.

When John was in the hospital, Gus kept showing up on the back deck of her house, especially during the rain. Mary started leaving bits of food and a water bowl for him. She eventually took him in. He had been her buddy through the hardest period of her life, and if that meant she was overprotective, so be it. Gus dealt with it well. Cats seemed to thrive on attention, even when they pretended they didn't need it.

Rebecca was chatting with a short, redheaded boy, one of their frequent visitors this summer.

"Hi, Jason, did you finish that Encyclopedia Brown?" Mary asked when there was a pause in their conversation.

He nodded as he moseyed along the shelves of teen mysteries. "Yesterday."

"What did you think?" Mary asked, always interested in getting feedback, which stemmed from her days of being a librarian.

"It was okay." He lifted a shoulder in a shrug.

"Just okay? I guess you wouldn't be interested in the next one in the series. I ordered it just in case, but I can find something else, if you don't want it. "

"Well, if you ordered for me, I can take it," he said quickly.

214 CL>2 SECRETS of MARY'S BOOKSHOP

214 SECRETS of MARY'S BOOKSHOP

Rebecca shot Mary an amused look. As Rebecca took care of Jason, Mary checked the store mail but couldn't concentrate and set it aside. She got out the guest book and looked over the names of people who had visited the baseball display. Stephanie had made columns for names, hometowns, and e-mail addresses. Mary recognized a lot of names from in town. The Bailey boys, Tyler, and Bill Halliday had all signed in. Again, she wondered why Bill Halliday was spending so much time around the town hall.

She went back to her list of people who had been involved in setting up the display, which included Charles Rigsby, Tess, Brent and Joe Bailey, Bea Winslow, Stephanie Doyle, and Mrs. Leary. Frequent visitors included Bill, Brent, and Tyler. Tess hadn't been in since last week, but then it would have been her turn next week to check on the display.

She again wondered who would have motive to steal John's baseball. Stephanie and Joe appeared not to have that much interest in the display nor any real motive to steal. Neither did Tyler. The memory of his frustration at the ATM crossed her mind. She wondered if he'd gotten that straightened out.

Brent had been in trouble before, in high school. He'd lost his job, home, and car. He was at a major crossroads in his life and trying for a spot in a very competitive field. He certainly had motive if he was feeling desperate and needed money.

Bill Halliday's career seemed to be on the decline, although he didn't seem desperate for business. He did know baseball and could have recognized the value of John's ball.

A clap of thunder shook the building, yanking her out of her pondering. Ashley came running in from the backyard, water dripping down her face. She'd dragged the trash bag in with her.

"Are you okay?" Mary asked. "Did the thunder frighten you?"

Ashley wrapped her arms around herself and shivered. "Just a little."

Rebecca grabbed some paper towels and handed them to Ashley, and she wiped her face and hair. "I didn't know we were going to have thunderstorms. I thought it was just rain. Do you want to go home to change?"

"I'm not too wet," Ashley said.

"Well, if you feel chilled, tell me," Rebecca said, a worried look on her face.

The lightning passed over, and a softer, steady rain followed. Mary didn't have much time to ponder the situation at the town hall because the rainy weather brought a deluge of tourists and locals to the shop, looking for something to do.

Mary loved having lots of customers in the store, listening to their chatter and talking books. The afternoon sped by, and soon, Mary and Rebecca prepared her shop for closing.

"Ashley, aren't you forgetting something?" Mary asked.

Ashley looked at the floor around her. "I don't think so."

Mary took three dollars from the cash register. "Your pay."

"But I didn't finish."

"But you put in forty-five minutes' worth of work, and I'll pay you for your time. You did a good job and can work on it again tomorrow. And trust me, the weeds will be back."

Ashley took the dollars and promptly handed them to her mother. "For the window. I will make more money tomorrow."

Rebecca gave her daughter's shoulder a squeeze. "I'm going to tell your dad that you earned this money to help fix the window. He's going to be proud of you for taking responsibility."

Ashley stuck her hands in her pockets, looking unsure. "Can we take him more pie? That makes him happy."

"He'd like that, but I'm not sure it's a good idea."

"Bummer." Ashley turned back to the children's area and started returning the blocks and other toys Mary kept around for small children to the basket. There had been lots of children coming in today with their parents, and the area was unusually messy.

Mary moved closer to Rebecca and said softly, "There's a partial blueberry pie over at Sweet Susan's that I baked yesterday. You mentioned that Russell should cut back on sweets, but it's there, if you want it."

Rebecca looked outside. "Considering that he's going to have to replace the window in the rain, pie might be justified in this case."

After they finished cleaning the store and returning books to their proper places, Rebecca pulled her purse and an umbrella out of her cubby. "Ready, Ashley?"

Rebecca opened the doorway, and the sounds of pattering rain rushed into the room. She unfurled her umbrella. "Guess what? We can get pie, after all."

"Awesome," Ashley said.

Mary reached into her pocket to get her keys and pulled out the ripped pink invoice. She didn't know now why she'd bothered to pick it up, but she was curious about the company that had been working on the town hall for months.

The foreman had said that no one had access to the key, but was he trustworthy? What about his half dozen employees? How hard would it be to access the key or maybe even make a copy? Mary recalled that Brent and Tyler knew one of the workers. What was his name? Jace? Was there a connection there?

She turned her attention back to the label. There was a phone number under an address for Lumber Exporters. She put her keys on the counter and dialed the number.

When a nasally female voice answered, Mary said she had a question about a shipping label.

"Shipping number, please," the woman said.

Mary read off the number in the corner, and the sound of fingers tapping a keyboard filled the phone.

"I show that the shipment was delivered on the second. Is there a problem?"

"The label got ripped. I see Baxter Construction, but the address is a Boston zip code."

"That would've been the accounting department at Manning," the woman said, starting to sound impatient. "Why? Didn't they get the billing invoices?"

"I'm sure everything is fine. You were a big help. Thank you very much." Mary hung up.

Who or where was Manning? She did a search on the computer and discovered there was a Manning Enterprises in Boston. She tried several links until she found a brief company profile. Manning Enterprises consisted of several companies, including Baxter Construction.

Interesting, but she wasn't sure how it was useful. The information gave her nothing new about Baxter Construction. She wondered how they got the renovation job.

Feeling a little deflated, she glanced at the time in the corner of the computer screen. It was already after six. Betty was probably wondering where she was. She gazed out the window at the pouring rain. Somewhere out in that dreary gray world was John's baseball. Would she ever see it again?

TWENTY

-◆◈◆-

"You didn't really think Bea stole John's ball, did you?" Betty asked from her chair at the kitchen table as she watched Mary reheat tomato soup on the stove. Mary had just finished updating Betty on the day's events.

"I couldn't imagine her stealing anything, especially from me, but I was afraid she may be mixed up with a shady man. If you think about it, she has a key to the building and Charles could have used her to get into the building during off-hours. But it appears he's not guilty of forgery and theft. He may be guilty of cheating people if he can, but that's not illegal."

"No, but it's not nice. What about Bill Halliday? Is he still visiting the display a lot?"

Mary nodded. "Maybe he's just nuts about baseball enough to want the stuff for himself. I haven't eliminated him from my suspect list yet."

The soup bubbled. Mary stirred it and then removed it from the heat. She poured it in a bowl and took it over to the table.

By the time Mary had gotten home, Betty had already eaten, but she had saved some soup she'd made from tomatoes from the garden. Mary took a sip of the hot, tangy soup, which was the perfect antidote for a gloomy evening.

Betty yawned. "My! I'm really tired. I'm going to turn in early and read for a while."

"Sounds like a good idea. You have a big day tomorrow. Happy, happy birthday"—Mary glanced at the clock—"five hours early."

"Thank you," Betty said. "Unfortunately, it starts with brunch with Eleanor. I love Edward's family, but even after all these years, she still makes me nervous."

"You shouldn't be. The Emerson family is lucky to have you." Mary smiled. Betty was always kindhearted and generous. She'd worked hard to fit in with her husband's family, even though her sister-in-law sometimes made it difficult.

Betty put a hand on her lower back as she slowly made her way across the floor.

"You okay?" Mary asked, concerned.

"I think it's the weather. I've been feeling stiff since the rain started. Don't worry. I'll be fine by tomorrow if I take it easy."

Mary bid her sister good night and finished eating. Tomorrow was going to be a busy day for Mary as well. Mary was going to make the blueberry pie for Betty and then accompany her to the baseball game before going out to a family dinner.

She remembered that the Baileys were still waiting for her flavor of the month. She could make a special ice cream for Betty's birthday.

Mary explored what was in the refrigerator. She had cream left over from her last project. Betty had been shopping, and there were still strawberries, blueberries, and raspberries in the refrigerator left over from Betty's fruit salad. Perfect! She'd make an ice cream that complemented the pie she'd bake.

She put the berry cartons and cream on the counter. Now for flavoring the custard. Because the pie and berries would be sweet, perhaps something with citrus. She opened the fruit bin in the refrigerator and took out a lemon. The recipe would need vanilla. She reached deep into the cupboard and found her stash of vanilla beans. She took one out and put it on the cutting board.

Gus woke up and yawned while Mary separated eggs and then whisked yolks with sugar, lemon peel, and lemon juice in a large bowl and set it aside. She split the vanilla bean lengthwise and scraped out the seeds.

She combined the vanilla bean and seeds with milk and heavy cream in a saucepan. She set the flame low and brought the liquid just to a simmer. She gradually whisked the hot cream into the egg-yolk mixture and returned it to the stove and cooked it until thick. She strained the custard and put it in the refrigerator to cool overnight.

For the berry swirl, she combined the raspberries, blueberries, and strawberries in a saucepan and added sugar, lemon juice, and cornstarch. She let it heat to a boil, mashing the berries with a potato masher. She wanted the berries to be a little chunky so she decided not to strain them.

The berries smelled wonderful. Like Gram's kitchen when she was making berry cobbler. Mary poured the sauce into a bowl and put it in the refrigerator. She'd run the ice-cream maker tomorrow morning before going to the shop.

She quickly cleaned up her mess and then headed for the stairs, feeling much more relaxed and glad she'd accomplished something worthwhile today. Creating unique ice-cream flavors came easy for her. She liked to experiment. Sometimes she'd just try new variations of common ingredients, but she wasn't afraid to throw in something strange and new. New flavors, textures, and combinations were all waiting to be discovered.

It was like the mysteries she tried to solve. She'd add a clue here, random facts there, mix in intuition and a little bit of luck, and voilà, the whole thing came together to solve the case.

I'm not ready to give up on this, Lord. Please show me the way.

She just had to find that one important ingredient that would finish the recipe that led to John's ball.

———

"Yum, you outdid yourself again, Mary," Tess Bailey said, holding a dish of Betty's Triple Berry ice cream. "I love how the touch of lemon in the custard contrasts nicely with the berries."

"I wanted something that would go well with berry pie," Mary said. She'd popped over to Bailey's Ice Cream Shop with the quart of ice cream on the way to work.

"I think it's perfect for pie." Tess spooned up another bite. "Girls, you have to come try this."

Paige and Jamie were sitting at one of the tables, their heads bent over sheets of paper and colored pencils strewn out between them. Tyler and Brent were slumped in the other two chairs. Brent was drinking coffee, but Tyler had a tall glass of something dark green in front of him. Both had red-rimmed eyes and sleepy expressions.

"In a couple of minutes, Mom. We have to finish these drawings by noon, or it'll be too late," Paige said, a whine in her voice.

Tess sighed. "Well, hurry, please. We are opening in twenty minutes."

"Drawings?" Mary asked Tess.

"They're entering an art contest this weekend at the park. They're supposed to come up with designs that best depict baseball and summer on the Cape," Tess explained. "The winning entries from each town with a league team will move on to a final round voted on by the Cape League administration. The winning entries will be used as the advertising theme for next year's league."

"Does this mean you might get your drawing on a billboard?" Mary asked the girls.

"They don't care about that," Brent spoke up. "Grand prize is an iPad."

"Ah, that's a good prize," Mary said, moving closer to the table so she could see the drawings. Jamie was busy coloring sand around a family picnicking at the beach. Baseball equipment lay on the ground beside them. Paige's drawing portrayed a ball field with the ocean and sailboats in the distance.

"Dorothy said the theme at the park this weekend would be baseball. I didn't know about the contest."

"She's going all-out with decorations and trying to get the vendors to follow the theme too," Tess said. "We're going to have a booth if Blake can find us another portable freezer by tomorrow. Ours went on the fritz. I was going to serve scoops of vanilla with mocha strips to resemble baseballs."

"Sounds fun. I'd try one," Mary said with a smile.

Paige ran a hand through her dark hair. "I can't seem to get this right."

Jamie glanced at her sister's drawing. "Quit complaining; yours looks way better than mine."

"No way." Paige looked up at Tyler and Brent. "Help! My pitcher looks like Ernie from *Sesame Street*."

Tyler grinned. "That's because you drew his head too big, but you could leave it that way and name him Brent."

"Hey, dude. When you sign with Halliday, I'll say the same about you."

Mary looked at him in surprise. "Are congratulations in order?"

"Yep," Brent said. "Actually, I've been negotiating for a few days, but last night, I told my friends that I was going to sign with him."

"So did you guys celebrate?" Mary asked. Where were these guys last night when the mysterious footsteps had appeared?

"Yep. We spent the night celebrating with the gang at Jessica's house."

"I just hope Mr. Halliday is the right choice," Tess said as she checked the napkin holders on the tables.

"Don't worry, Mom," Brent said. "Baseball is in Halliday's soul. He knows what it means to be a player." He poised a red pencil over Jamie's paper.

"Cut it out." Jamie swatted his hand away. "Mom, he's going to ruin it."

Paige giggled and reached for a black pencil. "I still can't enter my drawing in the contest like this. People will laugh. Can you fix it?" She handed the pencil to Tyler.

"That's cheating." Jamie glared at her sister.

"It is not!"

"Hey, I'll help you get Brent's, I mean, Ernie's fat head right, but you have to do the rest on your own," Tyler said, leaning back so Brent missed punching him on the arm.

"Oh, then I guess it's okay." Jamie smiled at Tyler who didn't seem to notice the stars in the young girl's eyes.

"Do you think you'll get a contract?" Paige asked Tyler.

"Don't know yet," he said, concentrating on reshaping Ernie's head.

"Tyler has another year of school anyway," Tess said.

Paige looked up. "Would you quit school if you could play pro ball?"

"In a second."

"I would too," Jamie said.

Tess gave all of them an exasperated look. She cleared her throat loudly. "Hurry now. I'm not paying you to sit and draw. You have ten minutes."

"I'd better run and open shop." Mary picked up her purse.

"Thanks for the new creation. I can't wait to whip up a batch," Tess said, waving the recipe card Mary had given her. "See you at the park tomorrow?"

"I'm planning on it, and I'll be at the game this afternoon, cheering for Brent and Tyler."

"Wonderful!" Tess beamed, looking as excited as a mother should be when her son was going to be a star. "We're going to shut down early so we can all go."

"Are your folks going to the game, Tyler?" Mary asked.

Tyler looked up from Paige's drawing. "Probably not. They aren't big baseball fans."

Tess patted Tyler on the shoulder. "We'll be cheering for you." She narrowed her gaze on her offspring. "Up! There's work to be done."

"Gotta get to practice." Brent heaved himself out of his chair. "Can I catch a ride with you, Tyler? My clunker died on the way home last night. I'm going to get a fancy car like Tyler's as soon as I get back to Boston."

Tess shook her head. "You'd better wait until you're sure this Mr. Halliday negotiates you a decent job. You haven't even signed a contract with him yet."

He pecked her on the cheek. "Don't worry, Mom. It's in the bag, especially after tonight."

Tess patted him on the arm. "I sure hope so, honey."

"I'm low on gas, and I don't know where I left my wallet," Tyler said as they went out the door.

"Dude, you'd forget your big head if it wasn't attached. We're going to be late," Brent said. "Give me the keys. I'll drive."

"I'll see you all later. I'd better get back to the shop," Mary said.

"Thanks again for the ice cream," Tess said. "You made another winner."

Mary stepped outside into the shade of the elm tree as Tyler and Brent sped off in Tyler's BMW. As a mother, Mary could understand Tess's worry for her son. Even when they were all grown up, they were still your children. And what a shame Tyler's parents wouldn't be at the game. Even if they didn't like baseball, wouldn't most parents want to be there for their child?

Mary stepped out from under the shade, and bright sunshine blinded her for a moment. Already the humidity was rising as moisture left by the rain evaporated. She shut her eyes for a moment and then blinked until she could see safely to cross Main Street.

Gus greeted her at her shop door. His tail swished, clearly not happy about being dropped off alone. Because Rebecca would be filling in all afternoon, she wasn't due till eleven. She put her purse behind the cubby as a delivery truck pulled to the curb and a driver brought in a box.

Gus leaped on the counter to inspect the newly arrived books as she unpacked them. Mary loved getting the book shipments. It was like Christmas. She hummed as she added the new titles to her inventory. At the bottom of the box was a cozy mystery from Jenn McKinlay's series, Cupcake Bakery Mystery, that Mary had gotten for Susan in appreciation for the baking lessons. She hoped Susan would like it.

After shelving the new books, the next hour seemed to creep by. A couple of customers came in to browse but didn't buy. Mary had time to ponder the disappearance of her baseball and the other artifacts from the display. She wondered how Stephanie was doing with getting people to pick up their memorabilia. Such a shame to close early. She wished they could have something permanent at the town hall. A display that revealed the history of Ivy Bay shown through the sport of baseball. Bea, Tess, and she had once discussed rotating different themed historic exhibits throughout the years, but now after the problems with theft, the idea would probably be rejected.

Gus sat on the counter, his tail wrapped around his paws as he stared at the door. "Don't worry, Ashley will be in later," Mary said. Her pet loved the little girl, and he wasn't going to be happy when school took her away most of the day. Neither would Mary.

She looked around for the pen she'd been using and spied it under Gus's paw. "Gus, you're in the way."

She tugged the pen free and noticed Gus was also sitting on the file she'd been compiling with articles on Bill Halliday and Charles Rigsby. She flipped it open to the short article on Bill Halliday.

So now, Bill Halliday was going to sign Brent as a client. If Bill was as successful at spotting and nurturing talent as he had been in the past, then Brent's future looked bright. Brent desperately wanted fame and the lifestyle that came with being a pro ballplayer. She'd seen him getting out of expensive cars driven by other people. Did he want his own Corvette like in the magazine so badly he'd risk counterfeiting memorabilia? Or would he just want the memorabilia for himself? He'd said he wanted a collection of his own someday. He seemed impatient, overly confident, and slightly desperate. Not a good combination when temptation arose.

She glanced down at the article again that called Bill a shark, but that was ten years ago. How was his business now? Both he and Brent seemed to have spent quite a bit of time at the town hall around that baseball display. Bill had shown an interest in John's ball too. Did he know its value?

Perhaps Bill's career had slowed to the point he needed additional funds until he got his next big find. He was very knowledgeable about baseball and maybe knew that her baseball was worth several thousand dollars. He could've convinced Brent to help him steal the artifacts in exchange for a cut or maybe even a shot at a contract. Or perhaps...

Gus meowed and rubbed up against her cheek, bringing her back to the present. This was the problem of reading too many mysteries. She was adept at concocting them in her head. Too bad she couldn't put those thoughts down on paper fast enough. She thought about her unfinished mystery manuscript languishing in a drawer back home.

Much as she wanted to find the baseball, she hoped for the Bailey family's sake that Brent was innocent and would get his life back on track. She also hoped that Brent would realize soon that fame and fortune were not guarantees of a happy, stable life. A verse she'd memorized came to mind. Isaiah 33:6: *He will be the sure foundation for your times, a rich store of salvation and wisdom and knowledge; the fear of the Lord is the key to this treasure.*

Mary gazed out the window. Ashley skipped up the street, carrying her backpack on her shoulders. A gust of wind tugged at the baseball cap resting on her blonde locks. Rebecca hurried behind her.

Mary popped up from behind the counter and grabbed the cat carrier. "Come on, Gus. We have a pie to bake."

TWENTY-ONE

---◆◆---

Mary nervously wiped her hands on a towel. She'd run by the market and bought more berries. She'd had enough to make two pies, and her creations were cooling on a shelf in the pantry. She didn't want Betty to see them when she walked in.

She glanced at the clock. It was after one. Betty had said it was brunch, and she'd met Eleanor at ten. Surely they had to be done by now.

Mary was unloading the dishwasher when Betty strolled in looking especially lovely in a pale-pink silk suit that complemented her skin and blue eyes. She set her purse on the table and looked around the kitchen. "It smells good in here. Have you been baking?"

Mary smiled and pulled out a chair. "Sit. I have a surprise for you."

Betty stared at her. "What did you do?" She perched in the chair.

"Close your eyes."

Betty smiled. "You're not going to stick a sea slug or frog in my hand or anything like that, are you?"

Mary laughed. "No, I didn't think of that. But then, you made me promise that last time to never, ever do that to you again. I'd like to think I'm more mature now than I was at ten."

"If you say so. I'll cooperate, then." Betty folded her hands on the table and closed her eyes.

Mary got out her creation and set it on the table. "You can open them. Happy birthday!"

"A pie?" Betty blinked several times. "*You* baked a pie?"

"Yes! It's blueberry, if you can't tell."

"I don't know what to say."

"I wanted to do something special in memory of those summers we spent here together. You and Gram made the most wonderful pies. Every time I see one, it reminds me of how happy and carefree we were. And how lucky I am to have a sister like you."

Betty placed her hand over her heart. "I'm so touched. Thank you." Her voice gently cracked.

"Okay, we have to taste it." Mary hurried over to the counter where she'd placed two plates and forks. "I can't find a pie server."

"I'm not sure what happened to it."

"I'll just use the knife, then. Oh, I have another surprise for you."

"Another one?"

Mary almost danced to the freezer. "My newest concoction. Betty's Triple Berry ice cream."

Betty smiled. "This is overwhelming."

"I just hope you like it." Mary cut into the pie and placed the slices on the plates, then scooped up balls of ice cream. She added a sprig of mint from the garden on top of the ice cream and served it to Betty.

"So pretty," Betty said, picking up her fork. She took a dainty bite and looked up. "Tastes just like Gram's."

"That's the best compliment you could give." Relief washed over Mary. She sat at the table and tasted her slice. The sweetness of berries with the nutmeg and cinnamon balanced well with the hints of lemon in the ice cream. She felt herself relax for the first time all day. "So how is Eleanor? Did you have a good time?"

"It was very nice. She reserved a special room and invited the book club. It was fun having everyone there." She took another bite of ice cream. "And we had a meeting. Eleanor said we might as well save valuable time since we were all there."

"Hmm." Mary stuffed in a large bite of pie, squelching her negative response. Why would Eleanor not think that the valuable time spent was actually in celebrating Betty's birthday?

Betty finished off the ice cream, and Mary noted she still had half the pie slice left. "I didn't even think to ask if you'd had dessert already. You don't have to finish that, if you don't want."

"Oh no, it's delicious," Betty insisted, taking another dainty forkful. "I'm just eating slowly, enjoying it."

Something in Betty's voice didn't sound quite right, although her sister was being as gracious as always. She finished the pie and took her plate to the sink. "Well, I'd better get ready. Evan will be here in forty minutes."

"I'm going to change too." Mary hurried upstairs to her bedroom to survey her closet. She decided to forgo her usual khakis in honor of Betty's birthday. She picked out a sunny pale-yellow pantsuit with white trim. The inner blouse was sleeveless and the outer shell had long sleeves to protect her from the sun, while still being light and airy. She brushed her hair and added a light touch of mascara. A straw hat with a wide brim would complete the ensemble.

She still had twenty minutes, so she checked her e-mail. To her delight, there was an e-mail from her granddaughter Emma.

Dear Grandma,

We finished softball today, and my team came in second place for the whole season. I wish we were first, but Mom says we must be good sports. I hope you are doing good and I will get to see you before school starts. Mom says we have to get organized. I don't want summer to end.

Love,

Emma.

Mary dashed off an e-mail back, congratulating Emma on her team's accomplishment and that she hoped to see her soon too. If only she could get this business about John's baseball finished and be able to relax. If she wasn't any closer by tomorrow in solving the mystery, maybe she should concede the ball was gone and send a donation to Loving Hearts.

O ye of little faith, a voice whispered in her mind. She sighed. Didn't the Lord say that if someone had the faith of a mustard seed, he could move mountains? Until the Lord made it clear she should give up, she needed to keep trying.

She pulled her computer onto her lap. What else could she find out about Brent? She brought up the Cape League. She noted the team schedule and that they had been at Hyannis the previous Thursday. She thought about the wrapper she had assumed was Charles's, when in fact, the entire Blue Jays team had been in Hyannis. But at least now, she knew that Brent had been in the vicinity.

She read Brent's and Tyler's biographies, noted again that Tyler was a business major, and wondered if Tyler really meant it when he said he would leave school if he got a contract to play ball.

She clicked the link in his bio for Douglas University. A small photo of Tyler's smiling face popped onto the screen with another biography noting that he had an athletic scholarship, was finishing his junior year, and was majoring in business with an architectural minor. Team information flashed onto the screen, and she explored the site a bit further. There was a photo of last year's team and several action shots of Tyler in a stadium lined with sponsor banners. One banner grabbed her attention: Manning Enterprises. She still hadn't found out much about that company, other than it owned Baxter Construction.

Gus jumped up on the bed and rubbed against the computer screen. His tail swiped Mary's hand, and then he flopped down.

The university team roster was listed for the coming year, although it was noted as still tentative. She scrolled through the names, looking for Tyler, but he wasn't listed on the starting team.

Her cell phone rang. She tugged it out from under Gus.

"Mom. Hi!" her daughter Lizzie said. "I'm so, so sorry for not getting back to you sooner. It's just been crazy busy around here."

"It's all right, sweetheart," Mary said, thinking how wonderful it was to hear her daughter's voice. "I'm just glad to hear from you now. And I just got an e-mail from Emma. She said her team came in second."

"It was very close. The other girls only won by two runs, but, yes, it was disappointing. But she still loves the game and wants to play again next year."

"I'm glad. How are Luke and Chad?"

"Doing fine. Luke finished swimming lessons. Chad has been so busy with work that we haven't had a chance for a vacation, which is why I'm calling."

"Are you going on a trip?" Mary asked with a wave of disappointment that she probably wouldn't get to see them for the rest of the summer.

"No. Chad canceled that. He doesn't want to be gone that long. We were wondering if you'd mind a visit over Labor Day weekend."

"Mind? I'm thrilled! I was going to ask you if you could come down or if I should make a trip up there."

"That's terrific. Will it be okay with Aunt Betty?"

"I'll check with her, but I'm sure it's fine. As you know, we have all these extra rooms just waiting to be filled."

"I can hardly wait. One last hurrah before school starts," Lizzie said. "Is Aunt Betty around? I want to wish her a happy birthday."

"She'll like that. I'm upstairs. Just give me a minute to go find her." Mary hurried downstairs and went back to Betty's room and knocked. "Phone for you. It's Lizzie."

The door opened. Betty was dressed in a pretty peach pantsuit. Mary handed her the phone and returned to the kitchen. The pies still rested on the counter. She wrapped them with plastic wrap and stuck them in the refrigerator.

She remembered she'd left her computer on upstairs and went back up to shut it down. Gus was sitting in front of the keyboard staring at the screen. Mary reached around him and pushed the Off button.

"Silly kitty." She gave him an affectionate hug as he continued to stare.

She grabbed her hat and purse and was heading for the door when the doorbell rang heralding Betty's family.

"Let the games begin," she joked, but Gus didn't even look up.

The seats that Evan had reserved for the game were down on the second row, next to the batting cage—close enough to see the sweat on the players' faces as they each took their place at bat. Allison and Betsy sat on either side of their grandmother. Allison had dressed in her Little League uniform, and Betsy wore shorts and a sports jersey with a Red Sox cap.

Brent Bailey was pitching his heart out, hardly letting the opposing team have a chance at the bases. Tyler Matthews was in top form, snagging a couple of ground balls.

Bill Halliday sat on the front row, along with some other men who were taking notes. Mary assumed the other men were major-league scouts from the way everyone seemed to be treating them like royalty.

Mary caught sight of Bea down the row and waved. Stephanie sat beside her, looking slightly bored. Her gaze rarely left Brent.

"Aunt Mary?" Allison leaned over on Mary's arm. "Guess what I made my grandma for her birthday?"

"Did you color her a picture?"

"No."

"Make her something out of clay?"

Allison shook her head and swung her legs back and forth under the seat, looking very excited.

"Did you use paints?"

"Nope."

"What is it? You can whisper it in my ear," Mary said with a glance at Betty who was talking to Mindy over Betsy's head.

Allison leaned close, her breath warm on Mary's ear. "I can't tell you. It's a secret."

"Oh, you tease." Mary laughed and tickled her.

Allison squealed, although it was swallowed in the roar of the crowd as Brent struck out another player. Allison jumped up and down, clapping, and kicked over her cup. Soda went everywhere.

"Oh dear," Betty said, reaching for napkins and wiping down Betsy's legs.

Allison pouted, clearly upset. "I'm thirsty."

"We can get you another drink, but you have to be more careful, dear," Betty said.

"Sorry, Grandma."

"It's okay; you were just excited. I'm excited too, being here with you on my birthday."

"I can get her another," Mary said. "I want to stretch my legs." They'd been sitting on the hard benches for over an hour in the hot sun. Betty leaned closer to Mindy and indicated Mary was taking Allison to the concession stand.

The teams were changing sides as Mary and Allison sidled past fans to the aisle. They walked up the concrete steps and then down the hall to another set of stairs leading to the multitude of concession stands.

Mary breathed in the wonderful smells of hot dogs, pretzels, peanuts, and popcorn combined into one gigantic scent that always reminded her of baseball games and happy times. How Gramps and Gram would have enjoyed today. Gram always brought a transistor radio and earpiece to listen to the game, and if that wasn't available, someone, usually Mary, would narrate what was going on.

"There's the frozen lemonade." Allison pointed to a pink-striped wagon with a canopy over it. The icy drink appeared to be popular on such a hot day because the line held at least ten people. Mary sighed and took her place. They were in the shade so she wasn't in a hurry to get back to their seats.

Allison twirled in circles, showing Mary some of the ballet moves she'd learned from one of her friends.

"That's good," Mary said repeatedly and spied Bea and Stephanie perusing the vendor selections. She waved, but they didn't see her. Mary was glad Bea had taken time for some fun and convinced Stephanie to try a baseball game as well.

"Our turn." Allison tugged on Mary's arm. Mary paid for two lemonades, and after they got the frozen concoctions, Mary suggested they take the long way back to their seats. She turned in the direction Bea and Stephanie had gone.

Allison seemed happy with the idea. She ambled along, sucking on the big straw that came with the lemonade. A large man with an armload of peanuts and a drink carrier was heading toward them, and Mary almost didn't recognize him without his uniform.

"Hi, Chief," Mary said.

He glanced down at Allison who was back to spinning little ballet moves. "I see you have your hands full."

"I'm not complaining." Mary grinned. "Anything new on the investigation?"

He shifted the bags in his arms. "We put out a description of the missing merchandise, and I've had an officer calling stores. So far, no one claims to have seen Dom DiMaggio's cap or your baseball. We're expanding the radius. If I were the culprit, I'd sell them underground or someplace far away."

"Or keep it for myself."

The bleakness of the situation must've shown in her face because the chief said, "Don't worry, we have feelers out everywhere. Chances are good they will turn up eventually."

"Thanks, Chief," Mary said, knowing he was trying to be encouraging.

Allison had spun down the short hall that led to the stadium office and locker room. Mary hurried after her. "Allison, we shouldn't be back here."

Mary took Allison's hand and noticed a large bulletin board on the wall covered with flyers, obviously set up for the players, which contained tourist information about Ivy Bay, practice schedules, and a section of Who's Who in the Cape League. A table under the bulletin board held a phone book, restaurant menus, several Cape League programs, and a sports-agent directory.

Mary flipped through the pages until she found the page on Bill Halliday. He was listed as a certified MLB sports agent, and a corner of the page had a photo of a younger, smiling Bill. She quickly scanned the article.

After a short but notable stint as an outfielder in the minor leagues, Bill Halliday went on to become one of the most successful sports scouts for the Atlanta Braves from the late 1970s to 1998 when he opened his own sports agency.

Interesting. She hadn't known he was a ballplayer. The articles she'd found on the Internet had focused on the players he'd signed, with just a small description of him as an agent.

The rest of the article detailed contracts he'd made, and again she noted that he had seemed to slow down over the last five years.

Her gaze went back to the photo of the younger Bill. His smile seemed more genuine than it was now. His face was just a bit fuller, more youthful. A tiny dimple creased his cheek.

Allison tugged on Mary's hand. "Can we go watch the game?"

"Sure, honey. Sorry, I got distracted."

They walked back to the stands, and Mary spotted Stephanie leaning on the railing, talking with Brent. From his seat behind the dugout, Bill Halliday kept glancing over at them.

"Hey, you two. Having fun?" Bea came up behind Mary, holding an iced soda.

Allison nodded. "Yep."

Mary stepped closer to Bea. "Can I ask you something?"

"Ask away."

"If this is something you aren't privileged to answer, I'll understand. But can you tell me what Bill Halliday was looking for when he was in your office?"

Bea's forehead wrinkled. "I'm not sure who you mean. I've had quite a few people come through the office this week."

"It's the man down there behind the dugout, wearing the Red Sox cap."

"Oh, him. Yes, I remember. He was doing some research on the county. He needed records of births. Nothing confidential about it."

"How long ago was he looking for?"

"I think it was twenty years or so ago. Why?"

"Just curious what he's been doing. I saw him at the library doing research too, and he asked Stephanie for some statistics."

"Bea! Over here." Stephanie waved and flashed her big smile. Mary's heart skipped a beat. That smile. She'd seen it before.

Her mind rapidly connected the dots. She was pretty sure she knew now why Bill Halliday had been investigating obituaries and birth records. And why he was visiting the town hall so much. He wasn't looking for artifacts or demographics. He was looking for his daughter.

TWENTY-TWO

⬩◆◆⬩

Mary let Allison go ahead of her back to their seats, her mind still scrambled from her discovery. She gave herself a little mental shake. She needed to focus on Betty's birthday.

Evan was in Mindy's seat reading a business magazine while keeping one eye on the game.

"That took a while," Betty said as Mary sat down.

"There was a long line. Then I ran into Chief McArthur."

"I saw him earlier. I assume he's off duty since he's out of uniform," Betty said.

"Officially, yes, but I doubt he's ever really off duty much."

"Where did Mindy go?" Mary asked. She had an idea but didn't want to share it with Betty. Yet.

"She got a phone call and couldn't hear, so she went out," Evan said.

Allison held up her lemonade. "Grandma, do you want a taste?"

"Not right now, dear," Betty said.

Mary glanced at the score. Still 1–0 at the bottom of the sixth, and the Blue Jays were up to bat.

"We're still winning," Betty said to Allison.

"I want the Marlins to win."

"No way." Betsy glared at her younger sister. "The Blue Jays are our team."

"I don't care," Allison said. "I can change my mind."

"You can cheer for them, if you want to," Evan told Allison. "It's a free country. But I don't think that Bailey boy is going to provide much opportunity for you to cheer. He's hot tonight."

Brent came up to bat. He shifted his feet on the base and waited for the pitch. It was a curveball, and Brent swung. The ball arched toward them.

Allison jumped up holding her glove high, but the ball went past them to the upper rows.

"Great try," Evan said. Brent smashed the next pitch and advanced to first. Betsy cheered, but Allison just crossed her arms over her chest, her lips pressed shut.

Betty exchanged an amused look with Mary. A rosy glow kissed her cheeks.

"You're turning pink," Mary said to Betty. She pulled a tube of sunscreen from her purse. "Better safe than sorry."

"True. At least we know better now than when we were kids. Then we tried to get tan at every opportunity."

"You even used baby oil," Mary remembered. Luckily, both she and Betty had escaped burning too badly despite being fair-skinned.

"*Ew.* You're kidding, right?" Betsy asked.

"I never understood the baby-oil obsession," Evan said. "Girls still did it when I was in school. Why would anyone want to fry like that? I used baby oil to soften my baseball glove, not smear it on my body."

"I used it on you when you were a baby," Betty pointed out and laughed at her son's grimace.

The rest of the game passed quickly until the eighth inning when the Marlins tied the Blue Jays.

Mindy came back, sliding past them. "Sorry about that. My sister. She was having a minimeltdown about the baby." She glanced up at the 1–1 score. "What happened?"

"My team is winning," Betsy said.

"It is not," Allison said. "We're tied."

Mindy raised her eyebrows. "Seems I missed more than just the change in score."

Intense tension hung over the next inning. Evan even put away his magazine and leaned forward, his arms on his knees. The Blue Jays pulled ahead by one run before switching sides, and then Brent Bailey struck out the other team's first batter. Tyler dove for a line drive to third. He hit the ground hard and rolled, but the catch was good. Two down. Brent walked the next batter and then struck out the last.

The fans went wild. The Blue Jays were in the final round of the play-offs.

"We won! We won!" Betsy jumped up and down. She turned to Betty. "Can I get Brent's autograph?"

"If it's okay with your mom and dad," Betty said. She leaned toward Mindy. "I told her about what Mary and I used to do as kids. We'd wait downstairs between the locker room and the parking lot for the players to come out."

Evan looked at his watch. "That was a quick game. We have plenty of time until dinner." He glanced at his wife. "Okay with you?"

"Sure," Mindy said with a smile. "It's Betty's birthday, and we'll do whatever she wants to do."

A crowd had gathered by the hallway to the locker room, and people were congratulating the players as they came out. Two policemen were there holding the crowd back, but Tess Bailey waved them over inside the hallway.

"Isn't this exciting?" Tess said. "We're so proud of our boy." Blake wrapped his arm around her shoulders and gave her a squeeze.

Tyler walked out of the locker room with a slight limp. His uniform pants were torn at the knee. Several people clapped. Tyler looked startled for a second and then smiled.

Paige ran up to him. "We're going to celebrate. Are you ready to go?"

"I have a couple of meetings with some scouts in a few minutes," Tyler said. "Maybe after. Okay?"

"That's so awesome. Don't worry. The party won't be over anytime soon." Jamie giggled.

Tess rolled her eyes but still sounded giddy. "It's going to be a long, *long* night. You are all welcome to come over. We're going to start with supper at my house and then head over to the beach for a bonfire."

"We'd love to, but we're going to celebrate Betty's birthday. Maybe we can stop by after, if it's not too late." Mary looked at Betty, who nodded.

"There he is!" Allison said, pointing at Brent coming down the hall with Stephanie hanging on his arm and Bill Halliday at his side. Jamie and Paige rushed forward and threw their arms around him.

"Congratulations, Brent," Mary called out.

"Thanks, Mrs. Fisher."

"Great game," Evan said, pumping Brent's hand.

"Can I get your autograph?" Betsy asked. She held up a program turned to the page with Brent's profile.

"Sure," he said. "Do you have a pen?"

"Hey, Brent," the young blonde woman named Jessica called to him. "Wanna ride? You can drive."

Brent looked back at Stephanie and smiled. "No, thanks," he called.

"Well, if you change your mind, you know my number." Jessica gave him a coy smile and flounced away to her convertible.

A crowd swarmed around Brent and lifted him up on their shoulders, cheering as they made their way to the parking lot.

"Hey, he didn't give me my autograph," Betsy said.

"Come on, let's follow him," Evan said, hanging on tight to the girls' hands.

As the crowd jostled Brent, the duffel bag on his shoulder shifted, and papers fell to the ground.

Allison bent to pick them up. "What are these?"

"Baseball trading cards," Evan said.

"May I see them?" Mary asked. Allison handed them to her, and Mary gasped.

Among the half dozen cards she held were Red Sox players Rick Burleson and Pedro Martinez. She'd seen these before. In Mr. Rigsby's collection at the town hall.

TWENTY-THREE

---◆◆◆---

Mary clutched the baseball cards, not sure what to do next. These could be Brent's, her emotional side told her, but the logical side of her brain pointed out that the chances that he'd be carrying the same cards were almost nil.

The crowd set a laughing Brent on his feet, and he was basking in the glow of being a local hero. His dad slapped him on the back a couple of times, and Tess wiped her eyes with her sleeves.

"What's wrong?" Betty nudged Mary gently and looked at the baseball cards in her hand. "Are those what I think they are?"

Mary nodded. "I'm afraid so."

"Oh my." Betty's hand covered her heart. "The poor Bailey family. This is going to be terrible."

Terrible was right. Brent had risen to number one on Mary's suspect list, but now that it seemed she'd solved the case, she felt awful.

"I have to talk to Chief McArthur. I wonder if he's still here." Mary bypassed the happy throng.

The chief was leaning back on a car, talking to a uniformed officer as he watched the crowd. He glanced her way and said to the officer, "That's all, Stan. Just make sure the parking lot is clear before you leave."

"Yes, sir."

"Hey, Mary. What is it?" the chief asked.

She held out the cards. "These fell out of Brent's duffel bag when they were carrying him out here. I think they are Charles Rigsby's."

He took the cards in his big hands and looked through them. "You say you saw these fall out of Brent Bailey's duffel bag? You're sure?"

"Yes, it was just a few minutes ago. The rest of my family was there too."

His attention narrowed on Brent again. "Good work, Mary. Go on home. I'll take care of this."

Mary nodded, not really wanting to leave, but there was nothing she could do to help right now. She went back to where Betty and her family stood.

"Everything taken care of? Are we ready to go?" Evan asked, looking at his watch.

"I am." Mary looked over her shoulder. Chief McArthur stood with his arms crossed over his chest, watching Brent. Mary was glad he hadn't barged in and questioned Brent while everyone was still around.

"Look, Aunt Mary, I got the autograph," Betsy said, hopping up and down, waving her program.

"Me too," Allison said, obviously having changed her loyalty again. "Go, Blue Jays."

Mindy smiled and placed a hand on Betsy's shoulder. "Be careful. Watch for cars."

They crossed the parking lot, got in Mindy's minivan, and headed back to town.

"This has been a great birthday. Thanks, everyone," Betty said as Evan pulled up to the curb in front of the house.

"And it's not over yet," Mindy said. "Dinner tonight at the Harbor View."

"What are we wearing tonight? Casual or dressy?" Mary asked. She knew Betty always looked just right, and she wanted to make sure she didn't underdress for the Emerson family.

"Let's go dressy, but not too formal," Mindy said.

"You mean, I don't have to break out my tux?" Evan asked with a grin.

"I think you'd look very handsome if you wore it," Mindy winked at Betty.

Betty smiled. "Oh yes, a tux with tails. Perfect. Thanks, sweetheart."

"Now wait a minute," Evan said, and the ladies erupted into laughter.

"You can wear whatever you'd like, Evan," Betty said. "I'm just glad to spend time with you."

"I'll hold you to that," Evan said, relief in his voice.

As Mary and Betty walked up to the front door, Betty asked, "Are you okay?"

"Yes," Mary answered quickly, but then couldn't lie to her sister. "No. It's your birthday, and I'm feeling a little conflicted. I should be glad that the mystery surrounding the display may be over. I might even have a chance of getting John's ball back. But this just seemed too easy. Brent was still on my suspect list, but now..."

Brent had seemed to have motive because he needed money. He was knowledgeable about baseball, and he had shown interest in John's ball. But despite all that, Mary still had questions, like how did he steal the items and replace them without being seen?

Betty gave her an understanding smile and unlocked the door. "Mar, if you think there might be a chance Brent isn't guilty, then you need to find out. Don't worry about me. I've already had a wonderful birthday."

"Thanks, Bets. I'll still be on time for dinner," Mary said, giving Betty a quick hug.

Mary walked to Main Street. She passed Bailey's Ice Cream Shop, and instead of the normal long line, there was a sign on the door: "Gone to the Ball Game. Reopening Tomorrow." Someone else has written in colored pencil under the lettering, "Go, Brent!"

Mary opened the door to her shop.

"Hi! I didn't expect to see you at all today," Rebecca said.

"I didn't expect to be back. I just had some time before dinner and thought I'd drop by." Mary waved at Ashley in the rocker but then noticed the little girl was asleep. "Everything going okay?"

"Yes, we made several sales around noon. Then everything slowed way down. I figured people must've gone to the ball game. How was it?"

"We won. Brent Bailey almost pitched a no-hitter. I'm sorry you missed it."

"Oh, it's no problem. I'm not a huge baseball fan even though Ashley and Russell are. I'll go to a game sometimes, but mostly I enjoy the snacks."

Mary smiled, grateful that she had such an easygoing employee. "Next time, if there is a next time, I'll bring back whatever you want."

Rebecca grinned. "You may be sorry."

"Never," Mary teased, and they both laughed. Mary picked up her purse. "I'm going to head over to the town hall. If you need anything, just call."

Mary went up the street and into the town hall. The construction equipment stood idle, the crew gone. Inside, the building seemed too quiet and lonely with the display closed. Stephanie sat at her desk, staring blankly at the computer screen.

"Mrs. Fisher, did you hear? Brent Bailey is in trouble. He's at the police station now. Is he going to go to jail?"

"I don't know. It all depends if they can prove he stole the stuff from the display. The cap and baseball were worth thousands of dollars."

"Doesn't look good." Stephanie sighed. "This is going to ruin his life. He was so happy today too."

Mary nodded with agreement. Suppose Brent was the thief, he would have had to choose whatever he was going to copy, forge a copy, and then replace it. How could he do that without being noticed? That would take time and multiple visits. And he'd still need access to the original for more than just a few minutes. And he wouldn't steal an object during the day in case someone noticed it was missing. Maybe he could've taken it home in the evening and brought it back the next morning, but again, that would involve frequent visits.

"Are you sure Brent was never in here alone?" Mary asked.

"As far as I know, he wasn't," Stephanie said, looking worried.

So how was he able to switch memorabilia with fake ones? It was possible that no one noticed if one item was missing, unless it was something prominent. He'd have to take it, copy it, and replace it with the fake the next morning. Unless Brent had access to the building during off-hours, she couldn't see him having the opportunity to switch the originals. Not without help anyway. But how did he know about the security camera?

"Could Brent have gotten access to a key to the town hall?"

Stephanie shook her head. "I think Mrs. Leary said all the keys were accounted for, but she's having the locks changed tomorrow."

Mary walked over to the display. If Brent wasn't guilty, then who was? She was almost positive she knew why Halliday had frequented the display, and it had nothing to do with baseball memorabilia.

Stephanie followed her. "I still haven't been able to get in touch with a couple of people to pick up their items. I've left messages."

Mary went around the rope partition, examined what was left, and decided to consolidate the remaining items onto one table. She moved over the photos, two pennant flags, five baseballs, a couple of signed programs, and three mitts.

She moved the items over one by one and arranged them into an attractive display. She picked up the mitts last, and something rubbed off on her fingers. Oil? There was definitely a slight sheen on one. She ran her fingers over the pocket. The leather felt greasy, as if someone had recently tried to condition it.

"Stephanie, did the police look at this glove?"

"Sure, they went over everything. Why?"

The oil indicated that someone had recently worked with the glove. Mary stuck her hand inside the glove. The mitt still felt a little stiff, which was odd since it was an old glove. Or was it? The oil on her fingers was dark. Mary rubbed her finger over a scuff mark, and it faded away.

She remembered what Evan had said at the game about using baby oil on his baseball glove. But...she'd also seen a bottle of glove oil recently. The bottle had fallen out of the duffel bag Brent carried, but Tyler claimed the duffel was his, that Brent had mistakenly taken it. She hadn't thought much about it because Tyler was a baseball player. He seemed like such a nice young man. His family had money. He dressed nicely and drove an expensive car. Her mind flashed back to Tyler's receipt at the ATM that indicated insufficient funds. Maybe it wasn't an oversight. Maybe...

"Stephanie, can I use your computer for a few minutes?" Mary asked.

"Sure. Help yourself."

Mary's fingers flew over the keys and found the Douglas University baseball team page and scrolled down through the players. Again, she noted Tyler wasn't listed for third-base starting position. Why? He seemed to be playing very well here on the Cape. He'd even made a fantastic catch today, although he'd hit the ground pretty hard and was limping afterward. Had Tyler been limping before? Could he have a more serious injury? Was that why he wasn't listed as playing? If Tyler was benched for the next season, could he lose his scholarship? But why would that matter if his family was well-to-do?

She could find nothing else about him on the university site. She clicked through the other pages and came to the list of sponsors. Manning Enterprises was on it.

It seemed too much of a coincidence that Manning Enterprises would be the same company in charge of the town hall renovation *and* be a sponsor at the same university Tyler attended. Tyler had been friendly with one of the construction workers. How did they know each other?

"Is Mrs. Leary in?"

"She's always in," Stephanie said, continuing to look depressed.

Mary walked down the long hall, looking in the semifurnished rooms until she came to the back office. Stacked file boxes lined the walls surrounding a desk. Mrs. Leary's gray curls were bent over a stack of files. Mary knocked on the door. "Hi, Mrs. Leary. Sorry to disturb you, but I had a question."

"Come on in. I need a break anyway." Mrs. Leary pushed her glasses up on her nose and arched her shoulders back in a stretch. "What's your question?"

"I was wondering why the town hall committee chose Baxter Construction to fix the siding," Mary said. "They're not local. The parent company is Manning Enterprises from Boston."

Mrs. Leary tapped her pen on the page she'd been reading. "I don't really know. I was hired after the decision was made. Perhaps it's in the minutes from their meetings."

"Would it be okay if I took a look at them?" Mary asked. "It may be related to the burglary of our display."

Mrs. Leary frowned. "But I thought they caught the guy."

"They think they did, but I have a hunch Brent Bailey may be innocent and someone else might be involved. I'd hate for Brent to be blamed for something he didn't do."

"In that case, I suppose we should take a look, although I can't imagine how Baxter Construction is involved in all this." Curiosity brightened her tone as she glanced around the cluttered room. "It may take me a few minutes to find them. They're buried somewhere in this mess."

It took Mrs. Leary ten minutes to find the minutes concerning the repair work and another ten for Mary to find the name she was looking for.

Excitement tickled her spine as she asked, "Can I use the computer?"

"Be my guest." Mrs. Leary vacated her chair and looked over Mary's shoulder as she typed the name into the computer. An article popped up. After a quick read, she thought she had found the connection she needed.

She took out her cell phone and rang the police station. "Chief McArthur, please. This is Mary Fisher."

"I'm sorry, Mrs. Fisher," a nasally male voice said. "The chief is not available right now."

Mary stemmed the impatience that threatened to raise her voice. "I realize he's busy, but can you give him a message?" She rattled off what she suspected, thanked Mrs. Leary, and then rushed out the door to get her car before it was too late.

———

Mary drove into the stadium parking lot. The stadium lights were off, and dusk would be settling in soon. Chief McArthur had called her back on his way, and she told him in detail what she suspected.

Mary had hung up on him before he could tell her to stay away. She liked Tyler. He'd always had a smile for her and had nice manners. She hoped she was wrong about what he'd done, even though the evidence she'd built up in her mind told her she wasn't.

She glanced at the clock on the dash. She only had fifteen minutes until Betty's birthday dinner. She should be on her way now, but she felt a sense of urgency that if they didn't catch Tyler red-handed, they might never be able to prove anything. As soon as Tyler heard about Brent, he'd dump whatever stash he had left. She just hoped he'd been so busy that the rumor mill hadn't reached him yet.

She parked beside a trash bin and turned off the engine. No police cars were in sight. Several people were moving around inside the stadium gate. A half dozen cars were still in the parking lot. One of them looked like Tyler's BMW. Correction: his father's BMW.

Time ticked by. Where was the chief?

She called Betty on her cell phone and explained where she was.

"Take your time," Betty said. "That's more important than any old dinner."

"I'm going to be there, but I may have to meet you at the restaurant. Don't wait."

"I won't. Don't worry about it," Betty said. "And, Mary..."

"Yes?"

"I know Tyler seems like a nice kid, but be careful."

"I will." Mary clicked the phone shut and realized someone was walking across the parking lot. It was Tyler. He was carrying the team duffel bag identical to Brent's. He limped slightly as he approached the car. He put the duffel bag and a baseball bat on top of the car hood and opened the bag. He reached inside and then spread the flaps wider, searching even deeper. His movements became more frantic, and he pulled out clothes and dumped them on the ground.

The chief's car rolled in the gate, then backed up, blocking the exit.

Mary got out and approached Tyler, moving to where the chief could see her. Tyler was so preoccupied he didn't even notice.

"Can't find the mitt?" Mary asked.

Tyler jumped, grabbed the bat, and turned toward her. "What do you want?"

"Just to talk," Mary said.

He blinked and his stance relaxed. His eyes were bloodshot as if he hadn't slept for a while, and his face was coated with a fine sheen of sweat. "Oh, it's you, Mrs. Fisher. What did you say?"

"I was watching you search through the bag. I figured you couldn't find the baseball glove or the trading cards you switched at the town hall last night."

"I-I don't know what you mean." He moved toward the driver's door. "I'm late for the party. I gotta go."

"That's not your duffel bag, is it? The police have yours. You and Brent have identical bags, so it's easy to get them switched. You've done it before. This time, Brent picked up the wrong bag. They found the baseball cards and the mitt.

The ones from the display. They thought Brent stole all those things. He's in the police station right now."

"You're crazy. Brent is fine. He's celebrating. I need to go." Tyler reached for the door handle.

"Son, I think you should drop the bat and come with me." Chief McArthur stood behind Tyler.

Tyler looked from the chief to Mary and then back again.

"You must be under a lot of pressure with your father wanting you to follow in his footsteps and take over the business," Mary said in a gentle voice. "That's why you're majoring in business and minoring in architecture."

"I just want to play ball. I'm good at it, even if…"

"I assume your parents were forcing you to make a choice? You needed money to hang on until you got a contract or at least got back to school on a scholarship."

Chief McArthur moved closer. "Son, put down the baseball bat."

Tyler tensed as if he were preparing to run. Then he dropped the bat. It bounced on the pavement, the sound startlingly loud in the mostly empty parking lot. His gaze met Mary's, and tears welled up in his eyes.

"Tyler, why didn't you tell anyone you were in trouble?" Mary asked gently.

"I didn't think anyone would care."

TWENTY-FOUR

———◆◆◆———

W hat did he mean that nobody would care?" Betty asked as they lingered over lunch. Mary had decided to shut the shop down for the afternoon since it appeared just about everyone in town was going to the celebration at Albert Paddington Park.

"He figured he'd never get sympathy coming from a well-to-do family," Mary said. "Who would feel sorry for him? His family owns Manning Enterprises, a successful business. Manning is his mother's maiden name, which is why I didn't make the connection at first. They used to have a summer place here, and Tyler's father, Mike Matthews, still has connections here.

"Baxter Construction is a subsidiary of theirs. I found an article where it stated that Mike Matthews' son was being groomed to take over the business someday. That's why Tyler was majoring in business and architecture. But he really just wanted to play pro baseball."

"They must've put a lot of pressure on Tyler," Betty said with a sigh.

Mary took another bite of the Cobb salad Betty had prepared. "His family wasn't worried about it until he started getting noticed by scouts. They wanted him to quit, and when he refused, they cut off his funds."

"Why didn't he just wait until he graduated and was out on his own to pursue baseball?"

"Because he has a weak ankle and actually was supposed to be resting it this summer. There was a possibility he wouldn't play the next season, which is why he wasn't on the first-string roster at Douglas University. He was worried his years playing ball would be limited. Then he was cut off. When he found out how much sports memorabilia went for, he got an idea. He could draw well and make copies and sell the originals. And he might've gotten away with it. People might not have noticed the forgeries until summer was over and he was long gone."

"Poor kid, but that's no excuse to steal." Betty refilled their glasses with iced tea. "How did he get in the building without anyone noticing?"

"He had a friend on the construction crew that he knows from spending his summers here. The crew knew who he was, and he could come and go without much notice. He managed to get the building key and make a copy so he could get in there at night. He also knew about the security camera since Mrs. Leary borrowed one from the construction crew.

"Remember that Ivan's Bakery wrapper I found? It fell out of his pocket while he was in there. I thought Charles Rigsby had dropped it, but Tyler must have gone into the bakery when they were playing in Hyannis."

"Will Charles get his merchandise back?"

"Maybe some of it. Tyler didn't exactly sell the stuff to reputable dealers. The police will follow up and see what they can trace."

"I hate to ask, but did he sell your baseball?"

"Actually, no," Mary said. "Tyler lost it."

Betty raised her eyebrows. "Lost it?"

"Brent and he had lockers next to each other, and they kept accidentally switching bags. The ball was in his duffel bag, which Brent accidentally brought that night at the beach party. Tyler got nervous because I was there and stashed the ball in one of the flower planters at the beach. But when he went back the next day it was gone."

"Then someone must've picked it up. The ball should still be around town somewhere."

"I hope so."

Betty took her last bite of salad and wiped her mouth with a napkin. "I was just thinking that if Tyler was so good at forging things, then why didn't he put Sparky Lyle's finger smudge on the ball?"

"I asked him that. He says he did, but it hadn't dried totally and came off when Brent handled it."

Betty sighed. "I'm sorry you had to go through all this. I still have faith that you'll get your ball back. Remember, with God, all things are possible."

"You're right." Mary wanted to give her sister a hug for the comfort she provided. Her love for her sister reminded her that her surprise was in the cupboard. She retrieved the small wrapped box and placed it in front of Betty.

"What's this?"

"A birthday gift."

"But you already gave me a gift," Betty protested.

"The pie was just part of it. Go ahead and open it."

"You're so sweet." Betty daintily loosened the paper from the box and slid out the box. She opened the lid and gasped. "How? When?"

Mary placed her hand on her sister's shoulders and looked down at the photo frame she held. It was a double frame with two photos side by side. On the left side, Mary had placed a copy of the photo, which had been in the baseball display, of Betty and Mary as youngsters enjoying the baseball game. On the right was a gorgeous candid black-and-white of Mary and Betty side by side that had been taken just the previous day at the game.

"Stephanie did me a favor and got permission to copy the photo of us when we were kids, and I asked Mindy if she could take a photo of us at the ball game. Remember when Mindy went to take a phone call? She took it then."

Betty reached up and grasped Mary's hand. "This is perfect. Thank you so much."

"You're welcome. Now let's celebrate with blueberry pie."

Betty leaned back in her chair. "Actually, I'm feeling quite full. I'd love to have some later."

Mary sat down opposite her sister. "Since when do you turn down sweets?"

"I do ... sometimes."

"*Hmm,*" Mary said, picking up the same vibe she'd gotten yesterday. "Well, of course we can save it." She felt a little awkward, which she almost never felt with her sister, so she made some conversation to fill the silence. "I really enjoyed learning how to bake pies. I want to try some cream pies next. Remember Gram's coconut-cream? I didn't really like coconut until I tried that pie, and then there was the banana-cream too. Which was your favorite?"

"Well, they were both good." Betty stared at her plate.

"You must be a treasure trove of information with your experience working with Gram," Mary continued. "Maybe you could teach me some of Gram's techniques. We'll have so much fun baking together."

"I was never as good as Gram." Betty toyed with her napkin and then looked up. "I'm not sure I remember everything."

Mary narrowed her eyes. "You know what? Now that I think about it, I don't remember you ever baking a pie in all those Christmases and Thanksgivings we've had together over the years."

"Well, no, but—"

Mary was starting to understand. "In fact, you don't have any pie recipes in your recipe box, and Gram's pie recipes were all in the attic. I just assumed that you had memorized the recipes, but you don't even have a pie server down here."

"There used to be. I'm not sure where it went."

"Betty Nelson Emerson. You don't like pie, do you?"

Betty's face pinkened. "Actually...no. I'm sorry."

Mary's mouth fell open. "Don't be sorry. I'm just shocked. You baked all those pies with Gram. I thought you loved baking."

"I went along with the marathon baking sessions because it seemed to make Gram happy, and it turned out I had a knack for it."

"And I didn't have that knack, which was obvious the few times I got stuck in the kitchen during pie-baking time. I envied you and your relationship with Gram. Now I wish I had stuck around the kitchen instead of being outdoors."

"But...I envied you. I really wanted to be outside playing on the beach and to read Gram's mysteries for her."

Mary met Betty's gaze, and they both burst into laughter until Betty wiped tears from her eyes.

"I really don't regret the time with Gram," Betty said. "I learned a lot, and I still make her cookie recipes every Christmas. We just made so many pies that I decided that I wasn't going to make one ever again, if I could help it. If Edward wanted pie, I bought it."

"But you really were good at it," Mary said. "I love your cookies and cakes."

"Tell you what? The next time the baking urge strikes, we can take cake-decorating lessons together."

Mary laughed again. "Deal." She stood. "How about some Betty's Triple Berry ice cream? Or have you been hiding an aversion to ice cream all these years too?" Mary joked.

Betty smiled. "You know that's not possible. I'd love some ice cream."

Mary had a slice of pie with her ice cream and then went upstairs to change. She was looking forward to the celebration and hoping for a chance to hear how Tyler was doing. She wasn't ready to give up on the ball yet either. It had to be out there somewhere.

She nibbled on her lower lip, which still tasted of blueberry. She smiled at the photo of John. "You would've enjoyed the pie fiasco."

Gus lifted his head from the patch of sunlight he was snoozing in on the floor, gazed at her for a moment, and then lay down and put his paw over his nose.

"Sleepyhead." Mary smiled and changed into her khakis and a white top with flowery eyelets around the wide boat collar. She sat on the bed to put on her shoes and spied Gram's devotional book on the nightstand. She cradled it in her hands and wondered what Gram would think about Betty's pie revelation and Mary's attempt to master them. She'd probably have a good laugh.

Gram would probably also tell her to make every feasible effort to recover John's ball and place her problem in God's hands and accept the outcome.

She turned to the page where Gram had starred the verses Matthew 6:19–20: *Do not store up for yourselves treasures on earth, where moths and vermin destroy, and where thieves break in and steal. But store up for yourselves treasures in heaven...*

She bowed her head. "Lord, I'm grateful for the years I had with John. I still miss him so much. I forgive Tyler. I would love to get John's baseball back and donate it to Loving Hearts, but if I never see it again, please let whoever possesses it experience even just a little of the happiness in the life that ball represented to me. Thank You. Amen."

She opened her eyes, and Gus leaped into her lap. She held his little face between her hands. "You be a good kitty while I'm gone. Keep your claws off the furniture."

Her laptop was resting on the bed, and Mary closed the lid. Earlier, she'd written Lincoln King a letter explaining what had happened and thanked him again for his assistance.

She headed downstairs, humming the opening hymn from last Sunday's service, "Blessed Assurance," and found Betty dressed in a pretty pastel-blue pantsuit and ready to go.

Mary set the second blueberry pie she'd made in a basket, in case she saw Henry. She also put in some paper plates, plastic forks, and a knife to cut the pie with. She was prepared for a picnic should the need arise.

They decided to walk to Albert Paddington Park because it wasn't far from their home. A string quartet was set up in the gazebo. People were milling around the grounds by the gazebo, which were crisscrossed with stone paths lined with wooden benches set among trees, flowers, and bushes. Food booths lined one side of the park. The smell of barbecue filled the area. Mary spied a booth with the sign Bailey's Ice Cream.

"Mary!" someone called, and Mary turned to see Bea waving at her. "I'm glad I found you. I have wonderful news."

"Is your sister better?" Mary asked.

"My sister?" Bea asked with a puzzled tone.

"Yes, she was in the hospital, and you said you were worried," Mary said. "The prayer group prayed for her."

"But why?" she asked, still looking confused, and then she pealed with laughter. "That was so kind of you. Did I give the impression she was at death's door? I'm sorry. I was worried about her hospital bill because we weren't sure if the insurance covered it. She got a nose job, of all things. Decided after seventy-three years she hated the one she had. Turned out, she actually did have a deviated septum, so it got paid for."

"I misunderstood. What a relief she is okay." Mary giggled.

Bea grinned. "She's a little nuts, but what can you do? She's family, and I love her."

Betty raised her eyebrows at Mary in a silent tease that she had that in common with Bea. Mary resisted sticking out her tongue like she would have when she was seven.

"Anyway, I wanted to share a surprise with you. Despite the bad experience Charles had with us, he has decided after some persuasion to donate a permanent display to our town hall. Three glass cabinets that can be locked. He'll provide more baseball artifacts."

So that was the business Bea had referred to. "That's wonderful," Mary said.

"Charles may seem a bit formal and stuffy, but he's really a sweet guy."

"That's very generous of him," Betty said.

"He'll be here for the unveiling next month." Bea looked beyond Mary and waved. "Oh, there's Stephanie. Over here!"

Stephanie didn't look up. She seemed in deep conversation with the tall man walking beside her.

Bea squinted. "Who's she with? They look so serious."

"Bill Halliday," Mary said. "And I have a feeling it's very serious."

Betty grabbed Mary's arm. "What do you mean, serious?"

"Serious in a good way." Mary smiled and shared what she had confirmed with Stephanie earlier. "I had been wondering why Bill was over at the town hall frequently, visiting the display or having Stephanie gather information for him on Ivy Bay. I also saw him researching obituaries in the library, no doubt trying to find a connection between Stephanie and the late aunt who left Stephanie's mother a cottage around here. He was trying to confirm that he'd found his long-lost daughter."

"You mean . . . ?" Betty's smile grew. "Stephanie?"

Mary nodded. "A while back, Stephanie mentioned that her biological father was a ballplayer and she never knew him. Halliday was a ballplayer for a brief time in the minor leagues before becoming an agent. Stephanie was adopted by her stepfather and has a different name. When I found a photo of a younger Bill at the stadium, it all came together. Stephanie and he have the same smile and the same little dimple."

"Oh, look, you can really see the resemblance." Betty nodded toward the father and daughter, who were smiling at each other now.

Bea clasped her hands together as she watched. "I hope and pray they'll have a good relationship. I've come to care for the girl."

"I think they will. It's wonderful they can be with each other after all these years," Mary said and exchanged smiles with Betty.

Bea looked at her watch and gave a little gasp. "Got to run. I'm supposed to be helping Dorothy by being one of the judges in the drawing contest. Catch up with you later."

"Oh dear, I forgot," Betty said. "Dorothy recruited me to judge too. I'd better head over there."

"Have fun," Mary called.

She wondered if Henry was at the park yet as she walked past the Bailey booth, which was decorated with pink-and-white-striped fabric. Paige and Joe were behind the table in front of a portable stainless-steel freezer, selling baseball-shaped ice-cream scoops. Tess came out from the back, carrying a box of ice-cream cones. She was setting them down on the table when she spied Mary.

She rushed out of the booth and threw her arms around Mary, in a hug. "Bless you for clearing things up for Brent. Thank you, thank you, thank you. I don't know what we'd have done if he had gotten in trouble and lost his chance at a professional contract. He's been spending money like crazy, thinking his life was all set." She gave Mary another hug. "I can't say it was wise of him, but dealing with a high credit card balance is one thing. A criminal record is quite another."

Mary smiled and was about to express her agreement with Tess when the band stopped playing, and Dorothy moved to the gazebo, waving people over.

"I want to thank everyone who came out to celebrate our baseball team," Dorothy said. "We have a fun afternoon planned. First of all, let's thank our musical group who came over from Sandwich to play for us."

There was a round of applause, and Dorothy continued. "The drawing-contest results will be announced shortly. At two o'clock, relays and an egg toss will be held in the clearing on my left. We're also having a pie-eating contest, which you can sign up for over there at the first booth."

Mary caught Betty's eye and grinned. Betty grimaced and shook her head.

"There are lots of booths from our local merchants," Dorothy continued. "Please visit them. Partial proceeds from the profits go to support our local team, the Ivy Bay Blue Jays. The players are here, willing to be photographed with you and give autographs." People clapped and whistled.

Mary noticed Chief McArthur edging toward the microphone. Dorothy glanced at him. "And now we have a word from our chief of police, Benjamin McArthur."

The chief said a few words about parking and keeping kids off the road for their safety and then had a request. "One of our citizens lost a special baseball signed by the Red Sox team. We believe someone may have found it down near the Little Neck Beach. It has great sentimental meaning to its owner, so if you have it or have seen it, please contact me or go to the information booth. There is a reward being offered."

Dorothy took over the microphone again and directed people over to the trees where the drawings hung.

"Who offered a reward?" Mary asked the chief when he approached her.

"Tyler. He also put an ad in the newspaper's lost-and-found section."

"I'm touched. Thank you, Chief, and tell Tyler thanks too," Mary said, a warm feeling spreading through her. It was so good to be part of a small town where people cared enough to help one another, even a busy police chief. And it sounded like Tyler was indeed trying to make things right.

"I just hope the announcement does some good. Have a fun afternoon," the chief said and strode away.

Mary saw that Susan was setting up a bakery booth. "Mary, I love the Cupcake Bakery Mystery book. I'm already a third of the way through it."

"You're really moving through it. I just dropped it off yesterday morning," Mary said with a laugh. "I'm glad you like it."

She browsed the booths some more, lingering over some lovely homemade crocheted scarves that might make Betty a great Christmas present and then spotted Henry coming toward her across the grass. He wore a light-blue shirt that accented the sea-green color of his eyes.

"Mary, I was hoping you were going to be here. I heard about what happened. Congrats on another mystery solved."

"Thanks." Mary held up the basket. "I brought you a blueberry pie."

"Oh, now I'm really glad I came." He grinned, lifting the towel and looking in the basket. "I think I'll have pie for lunch."

"Don't you want to get something else first?" Mary said, gesturing to the food booths.

"As my grandson Brody has taken to saying lately, 'Eat dessert first, so if the world ends in the next few minutes, at least you had the best part of the meal.'"

"Does that work with his mother?"

"Nope." He grinned.

Mary smiled. "Oh well, there are advantages to being a grown-up. Let's find a bench and have dessert first."

The time passed quickly as Mary and Henry ate pie and talked. Mary related the story of Betty's reaction to the pie, and Henry laughed.

"I never would've guessed Betty hated pie."

"I was shocked." Mary smiled. "I thought I knew everything about my sister. I guess it's great that one can discover new things about people you care about."

"But, hey, a side benefit is that you learned to make great pie." He pointed his fork at his slice. "This tastes as good as your grandmother's."

Mary's cheeks warmed. "My pie-baking skills were pitiful before Susan helped me."

They talked for a while about fall plans for their businesses, and then Betty joined them. She declined pie with a twinkle in her eyes.

"Evan just got here with his family," Betty said. "They went to get something to eat."

"Happy birthday, Betty, a day late," Henry said. "I hope it was fun."

"I got to spend it with family, so, yes, it was perfectly wonderful," Betty said with a big smile as Evan and Mindy joined them.

Mindy spread a blanket on the ground. "Any word about Uncle John's baseball?"

"Nope, but I'm not giving up hope," Mary said with a sigh.

"It's a shame," Evan said. "Someone from out of town could've picked it up and left with it."

"Evan," Mindy scolded gently, "that's not helping."

"It's okay." Mary smiled. "If that's true, I hope whoever has it will enjoy it." She would just send in a check to Loving Hearts regardless, she decided. It wouldn't be as much money as the ball might've fetched, but it would at least be something.

Henry bumped his shoulder against hers and gave her a smile.

Isabella Hiller ran up. "Allison, do you want to play catch?"

"Wish I could, but I didn't bring my glove," Allison said to her teammate.

"That's okay," Isabella said. "I brought two."

Allison got up and ran across the grass to where Bob Hiller and his family sat under an oak tree.

Evan had engaged Henry in conversation, and Mindy went off with Betsy for ice cream. Mary turned to Betty, "How did the judging of the drawings go?"

"I'm not sure I knew what I was doing," Betty said, sounding slightly distressed. "I had a terrible time deciding how to score. They were all good."

Mary patted Betty on the arm. "I'm sure you did wonderfully. You have excellent taste." Mary looked over to the art area. "So who won? Anyone we know?"

"I can't remember who got first in the two younger divisions, but Paige Bailey won in the oldest division. She was ecstatic."

"I'm so happy for her," Mary said with delight. Paige had been so worried over her drawing. It looked like Tyler's drawing skills had at least helped someone after all.

Mary leaned back on the bench feeling content and thinking of how grateful she was for the life God had given her.

"Watch out!" Isabella called as Allison missed a catch and the ball bounced toward Mary. She stopped it with her foot and picked it up.

Just as she had wound back to throw it, she did a double take. The ball was dusty, but there were scratches or . . . could it be?

She rubbed off the dirt and turned the ball over. There, under Sparky Lyle's signature, was a smudge.

ABOUT THE AUTHOR

From her first introduction to the beginner readers with Dick and Jane, award-winning author Kelly Ann Riley has wanted to be a writer. She started penning tales at an early age and received special recognition for her short stories. Later, she became a reporter and the editor for her high school newspaper.

Now Kelly Ann enjoys writing romantic suspense and cozy mysteries. She lives in Alabama with her family and numerous pets. She loves visiting the East Coast and has wonderful memories of Cape Cod. Kelly Ann is an avid reader and, like Mary, enjoys spending leisurely hours with a good mystery. You can contact her through her Web site at KellyAnnRiley.com.

A CONVERSATION WITH KELLY ANN RILEY

❧

Q: *What's your favorite vacation spot?*

A: My favorite vacation spot is the ocean. It doesn't really matter which ocean or beach, I just love exploring coastlines, sinking my toes in the sand, searching for shells and driftwood, breathing in the briny air and watching the waves break.

Q: *What was something interesting or important that you learned while researching and writing this novel?*

A: It was great fun learning about baseball memorabilia. In some ways it's like treasure hunting. You never know what that baseball card or signed baseball might be worth someday. I also found the history of the Red Sox fascinating. I'd heard about the "Curse of the Bambino" but never really understood what it meant. Who would've thought that with the sale of Babe Ruth to the Yankees it would be eighty-six years between World Series wins for the Red Sox? I don't believe in curses, but it does make for interesting baseball lore.

Q: *If you could go to Ivy Bay, which place/shop would you visit first?*

A: Mary's Mystery Bookshop would be my first stop in Ivy Bay. I love bookstores and I look for them wherever

I'm visiting. I can spend hours browsing the shelves. I'd chat with Mary and Rebecca and ask Ashley what she'd recommend for my young nephews. I'd tell Gus how handsome he is and see if he'd let me pet him. Then after selecting some mystery novels, I'd pop by the Tea Shoppe to grab some iced tea and head for the beach for a leisurely afternoon of reading by the bay.

Q: *Do you have any pets? Have they ever helped you solve a mystery like Gus helps Mary?*

A: Our menagerie consists of sixteen pets, including horses, cats, dogs, parakeets, a yellow-napped Amazon parrot, turtle, and Betta fish. As far as solving mysteries, they do sometimes tattle on each other. When my Pomeranian mysteriously escapes the fenced backyard, the other dogs are quick to point out the direction he's gone. However, in other cases, such as when a houseplant mysteriously ends up spilled on the carpet, four cats can be sitting around it, all expressing profound innocence of the crime as I clean up the mess.

Q: *Mary often goes to the library when sleuthing out a mystery. What's the library like in your hometown?*

A: I love the library system in Huntsville, Alabama. The library was founded in 1818 and now consists of a large main library downtown and numerous smaller branches all over the county. If I were trying to solve a mystery like Mary and needed historical data, I'd probably start at the main library where they house a Heritage Room that contains one of the finest genealogy collections in the region. They also have computer-based resources as well as print and microform collections—lots of information that Mary or a mystery writer could find very useful.

Q: *What's your favorite type of book to read?*

A: I love mysteries and suspense. If a fun romance can be tossed into the mix, even better.

Q: *Mary loves to snuggle up with a cup of tea or a quilt and read at the end of the day. How do you like to spend the quiet hours of an evening at home?*

A: When I was a child, I'd usually end my days reading a book, even if it meant that I had to pull the covers over my head and use a flashlight, hoping I wouldn't get caught staying up past my bedtime. Nowadays I still love to crawl into my cozy bed with my Amish quilt and read myself to sleep every night. Sometimes on those evenings when my husband needs to get to bed early, I still pull out my trusty flashlight to finish an exciting chapter or two. I'm just grateful I don't have to resort to hiding under the covers anymore.

GRAM'S BLUEBERRY PIE

Easy Butter Piecrust

>*2 cups all-purpose flour*
>*¼ teaspoon salt*
>*⅔ cup cold butter*
>*4–5 tablespoons cold water*

Combine flour and salt in a large bowl. Cut in butter with a fork or pastry blender until the mixture resembles coarse crumbs. Stir in just enough cold water until flour mixture is moistened. Divide the dough in two and make slightly flattened balls. Wrap each dough ball with plastic wrap and refrigerate for at least thirty minutes. Roll one dough ball out into a twelve-inch circle and place in a nine-inch pie pan. Roll out other dough ball when ready to place on top of filling.

Pie Filling

>*4 cups of blueberries*
>*1 cup of sugar*
>*3 tablespoons flour*
>*½ teaspoon grated lemon peel*
>*½ teaspoon cinnamon*
>*½ teaspoon nutmeg*
>*¼ teaspoon salt*
>*1 tablespoon butter, cut in small pieces*
>*1 tablespoon lemon juice*

Preheat oven to 425 degrees. In a large bowl, gently mix berries and sugar. Set aside. Combine flour, lemon peel, spices, and salt in another bowl and then gently mix into the berries. If the mixture seems too watery, you can add a little more flour. Dot pie filling with butter flakes and sprinkle with lemon juice. Pour mixture into piecrust.

Roll out top crust and cover berry mixture. Crimp dough edges. Make small slits in top crust to vent. Place on cookie sheet (to catch spills) and bake for thirty-five to forty minutes or until crust is golden brown. If edges brown too quickly, cover crust edges with foil.

FROM THE GUIDEPOSTS ARCHIVES

---◆◆◆---

The heart of the prudent getteth knowledge; and the ear of the wise seeketh knowledge. —Proverbs 18:15 (KJV)

When I was a boy, my dream was to be an outstanding baseball player. I enjoyed attending twilight league games at our school field. To me, the travel, the competition and the adoring fans seemed like great fun. Besides, this was the Depression and the ballplayers were being paid.

During the summer, our fourteen-room home was a haven for African Americans seeking to vacation. When the guests arrived, I carried their bags to their rooms. Then at dinnertime, I donned a white coat and waited on tables. The guests were always received with warmth and hospitality, yet Mother and Father demanded I keep my distance from them. Being overfriendly was forbidden.

One day the barnstorming Philadelphia Black Giants came to town to play our hometown team. The Giants were superb, and my dream glowed brighter. Near the end of the game, I noticed the town officials huddled in the stands, their faces a mass of worry. The Giants needed accommodations for two nights, but the town's inns and guesthouses wouldn't accept them. Father was contacted, and the baseball players came to stay at our home. I was thrilled!

Early on the second morning, one player wandered into the backyard and shook my hand. I threw caution to the wind and questioned him, confessing my desire to be a baseball player. He listened, his eyes glistening, and said, "Go to school, young man, and get an education. I didn't."

My dream of baseball eventually faded, but those words stayed with me.

Knowing Father, my dreams were for the moment while Your direction was for a lifetime. —Oscar Greene

A NOTE FROM THE EDITORS

We hope you enjoy Secrets of Mary's Bookshop, created by the Books and Inspirational Media Division of Guideposts, a nonprofit organization. In all of our books, magazines and outreach efforts, we aim to deliver inspiration and encouragement, help you grow in your faith, and celebrate God's love in every aspect of your daily life.

Thank you for making a difference with your purchase of this book, which helps fund our many outreach programs to the military, prisons, hospitals, nursing homes and schools. To learn more, visit GuidepostsFoundation.org.

We also maintain many useful and uplifting online resources. Visit Guideposts.org to read true stories of hope and inspiration, access OurPrayer network, sign up for free newsletters, download free e-books, join our Facebook community, and follow our stimulating blogs.

To learn about other Guideposts publications, including the best-selling devotional *Daily Guideposts*, go to ShopGuideposts.org, call (800) 932-2145 or write to Guideposts, PO Box 5815, Harlan, Iowa 51593.